IMPOSTER

BY ANTONY JOHN

Dial Books

an imprint of Penguin Group (USA) LLC

DIAL BOOKS
Published by the Penguin Group
Penguin Group (USA) LLC
375 Hudson Street
New York, New York 10014

USA/Canada/UK/Ireland/Australia/New Zealand/India/South Africa/China
penguin.com
A Penguin Random House Company

Library of Congress Cataloging-in-Publication Data
John, Antony, date.
Imposter / by Antony John.
pages   cm
Summary: "Seth Crane can't believe his luck when he lands his first big movie role, but when secrets
only Seth knows—things his costars told him in confidence—start showing up in tabloids, it quickly
becomes clear that nothing in Hollywood is as it seems"—Provided by publisher.
ISBN 978-0-8037-4124-9 (hardback)
[1. Actors and actresses—Fiction. 2. Motion pictures—Production and direction—Fiction.
3. Fame—Fiction. 4. Love—Fiction. 5. Impersonation—Fiction. 6. Hollywood (Los Angeles,
Calif.)—Fiction. 7. Mystery and detective stories.] I. Title.
PZ7.J6216Im 2015
[Fic]—dc23   2015006691

Printed in the United States of America

1 3 5 7 9 10 8 6 4 2

Designed by Jasmin Rubero
Text set in Sabon MT Std

For Nick Green

IMPOSTER

1

"I WAS AFRAID YOU WERE NEVER going to drink the poison." Ellen adjusts the straps of her sleeveless dress. The front curtain is still drawn, and she wants to look perfect for the audience. "Were you watching me the whole time?"

She sounds suspicious. Maybe even a little freaked out. The honest answer is *Yes, I was watching you*, because in character, that's what felt right.

But I'm not Romeo anymore, and she's not Juliet. I'm back to being Seth, who went out with Ellen once after rehearsal and thought it might mean something. I also thought I was a shoo-in for a new series of Chevy commercials, but I guess I was wrong about that too.

The curtain parts. We lock arms and step forward with the rest of the cast. The standing ovation is spontaneous, the camera flashes persistent. Energy hums through us like a current.

I ought to smile. It's closing night of the first fully sold-out production in Valley Youth Theater Company history. We've had excellent write-ups in the local newspaper. The rest of the cast are practically cheering themselves, but I can't join them. The spotlights feel too bright, too hot.

"Bow!" Ellen stage-whispers.

I follow her lead, and when she retreats, I do as well. As the curtain closes, she tilts her head and clicks her tongue like a mother chastening her child. "Focus, Mr. Crane," she teases.

Our cast mates exchange celebratory hugs. Ellen hugs me too. "See you at the party," she whispers.

As she saunters past the front row of props, her friends fall in line beside her. She doesn't look back.

"Would've been nice if you could've smiled, Seth." My brother's voice drags me around. Gant Crane, future paparazzo, stands stage left, examining photos on a ridiculously expensive camera. "I mean, I've got some awesome shots of the play, but the curtain call . . ." He shakes his head to underline how bad I must appear on the camera's small screen.

"You can just delete those ones, right?" I say.

"Uh-uh. Your director wants the full album."

"I'll give you ten bucks."

"She's giving me a hundred."

"A *hundred?* For one evening?"

He raises an eyebrow. "It's only the stars of the show who get paid nothing. I told you not to get into acting."

It's true—he told me that. He's annoyingly smart for a sophomore.

"You going to the party?" he asks, flicking his head toward the back of the stage.

"Later."

He knows the word *later* is significant. "Is this about the Chevy commercial?"

"No," I say. But I can tell he sees right through that lie too.

I did two low-budget TV commercials back in middle school, but the Chevy gig would've been huge. National exposure. Good money. They'd pretty much told me the part was mine. Instead, this afternoon I got a one-line email saying they were moving in a new direction.

"I just want to stay out here a minute," I tell him. "Try to feel normal again."

This time he raises both eyebrows. "News flash, Seth. You're wearing pointy shoes and five coats of makeup. Nothing normal about that."

Gant snaps another photo and leaves. Brow furrowed, I probably look more like Hamlet than Romeo.

I slide around the front curtain and survey row after row of empty velvet seats. With the audience gone and the spotlights off, the place no longer seems magical at all. The wooden planks beneath my feet creak slightly. The air is tinged with the still-there smell of paint from the props that were only finished four days ago. I know because I helped to paint them.

"Little odd for the star of the show to be out here alone, isn't it?" someone calls out.

A guy ambles toward me. He looks about thirty. Goatee. Untucked white shirt and dark blue jeans.

I look around, but I'm the only other person here. "Costar," I say.

"Uh-uh. Not all Romeos and Juliets are created equal. You know it. I know it. Everyone in the audience knows it." He flutters a program. "Says here that in addition to his work with the

Valley Youth Theater Company, eighteen-year-old Seth Crane has appeared in the short movie *Taken Out,* as well as commercials."

He places his hands on the stage and pulls himself up. Sits on the edge, feet dangling. "I'm Ryder. Ryder Whatley." He extends his hand. I step forward and shake it. "So what's the issue, Seth?"

"Issue?"

"Show's over. You ought to be celebrating. But you're still here."

"Yeah, well . . . I lost out on a commercial today."

"That's too bad. Did your agent say why?"

"I don't have an agent."

"Hmm." He pulls out a card. Below his name is written: WRITER—PRODUCER—DIRECTOR. He has a Los Angeles address.

My heartbeat quickens. "What are you doing in the Valley?"

"Glad you asked." He takes out his cell phone and touches the screen. Pulls up a movie website that shows production status on a film called *Whirlwind.* "You heard of this?"

I sit beside him. My legs dangle farther than his. "Yeah. Sabrina Layton's in it."

"*Was* in it. Kris Ellis too. But then they split up in real life and everything went into limbo. Now we have a script and shooting schedule, but no leads."

"Didn't anyone else audition?"

"Sure. Hundreds. But once the biggest teen actors in Hollywood signed on, I had better things to do than wade through hours of audition tape." He chuckles. "Which is ironic, 'cause now I'm doing it anyway. Well, except for this evening."

Ryder pinches the bridge of his nose. "Look, Seth, community

4

theater isn't my thing. But someone I trust told me to check you out. After I read that write-up in the newspaper, I figured, why not? And you know what? Watching you onstage, it was like I was seeing the character in my movie: the face, the movements, the voice. . . . What I'm saying is, I want you to audition."

My feet bounce lightly against the side of the stage like I have no control over them. "When?"

"Tomorrow morning." He turns his business card over and points to an address handwritten on the back. "There's a conference room at this place. Ten o' clock work for you?"

Before I can answer, a cheer erupts from backstage. When it's quiet again, the whole situation feels surreal—losing out on a commercial one moment, and auditioning for a movie role the next.

"I don't get it," I say. "There must be hundreds of guys who want this part."

"Sure there are. But sometimes we're looking for exactly the kind of person who's not looking for us."

He watches me, waiting for yes. He must know how much I want this. *Need* it. It's written all over me.

With the audience gone, the noise from the lobby has all but died away. Nearby, the party is in full swing, but I won't go. I have other, bigger goals.

"Ten o' clock," I say. "I'll be there."

2

BY THE TIME I GET UP, Dad's already in the kitchen in his creased pants and white T-shirt, fighting a losing battle with the steam iron.

"Do you have another interview?" I ask.

He nods.

"Can I help?"

He grips the iron tighter, his right hand so reliable. But his left still won't cooperate and the shirt shifts on the tiny ironing board. Now there's a sharp crease diagonally across the front. His stroke isn't just evident in every word and gesture, but even in the clothes he wears.

Three years ago, Dad suffered a transient ischemic attack—a kind of mini stroke. Thankfully it was minor, and at fifty-two, he was relatively young. Unfortunately, Mom was sick too, and he played it down so no one would panic. He should've gone to the ER. Should've had a CT scan or an MRI of the brain, and an echocardiogram of the heart. He should've taken blood thinners. But he wanted us to focus on Mom. So we did. Right up to the day, five weeks later, that he suffered a major stroke. Now only the right side of his face works—same for the rest of his body—

and he has trouble speaking. He gets angry easily. He wants every-thing to go back to the way it was three years ago.

He's not the only one.

"Seriously, Dad," I say. "I can do it."

He sets the iron on the board and backs away. Five minutes later, I've pressed his shirt and even worked out the crease.

"Th-thanks," he says.

"No problem." Then I realize that's not true—it's a major problem for him. "I mean, anytime."

As Dad slopes off to his bedroom to dress, I join Gant in the cramped living room. He's sprawled across the sofa, admiring his latest crop of downloaded photographs on my laptop computer. At least, that's what I figure he's doing, but this picture is grainy and out of focus.

"What are you doing?" I ask.

He taps the screen. "Trying to find out who downloaded foot-age of last night's performance. There was an announcement before the play: no photography. But someone filmed it anyway, and now your cast mates will be checking themselves out on You-Tube instead of waiting for the official photos."

"Who cares?"

"*I* care. It's bad for business. What's the chance that director uses me again if no one orders photos, huh? This is my job."

"You're sixteen, Gant. Not sixty."

"So? I'm making as much as Dad, aren't I?"

Right on cue, our father emerges from his bedroom. I hope he didn't hear what Gant said.

For years, Dad worked in university finance, doing accounts

and audits and payroll. He could do the job just as well now as he used to, but he doesn't come across the same in interviews anymore. Today's meeting isn't for a finance job anyway—those are always Monday through Friday. He promised us he'd cast the net wider, but realistically, that means settling for a job he doesn't really want and for which he's overqualified.

He stands in the doorway, awaiting my appraisal. The shirt is fine, but the tie knot is a mess. I want to fix that too.

"Looking good," Gant says.

Dad produces a defiant smile and heads out.

Gant waits for the door to close. "It won't be his tie that stops him from getting a job. So don't pretend like it matters."

I want to tell him he's wrong. That sooner or later Dad'll get a job and things will change for us. But Dad hasn't had steady work in almost a year.

Then again, what if he didn't need to work?

Last night, I could hardly sleep for thinking about the audition. At three a.m., I was just about ready to forget the whole idea, rather than risk another disappointment. But the world looks different at eight a.m.

If my father can walk through that door, so can I.

3

RYDER OPENS THE DOOR WIDE LIKE a deferential servant and, with a sweep of his arm, invites me to enter the airy, uniformly beige conference room.

"I was afraid you might not come," he says.

I try to stay calm. "I think, maybe I'm meant to do this."

"So you're a fatalist."

"More like an aspiring optimist."

He gives an abrupt laugh, like a dog barking. "Nice."

Across the room, a woman in a black business suit stands beside a video camera mounted on a tripod. "I'm Tracie," she says. "I'm an attorney for the production company. I'm here to make sure everyone plays nicely together."

Ryder *tsk*s. "I always play nicely. It's our producer, Brian, you need to worry about."

She raises an eyebrow. "Speak of the devil, he's on standby on a video conference link, if you want." She adjusts the camera so that it points straight at me. "So Seth, I hear you missed out on a commercial. Why'd you want to do commercials anyway?"

I wish Ryder hadn't told her about our conversation. Who misses out on a commercial one day and lands a movie role the next?

"I want to be an actor," I say. "Do real work."

"Earn real money, you mean."

"That too. My dad's not doing so well."

Tracie gives a sympathetic nod, but her expression doesn't change. Even her bobbed brown hair remains perfectly in place.

Ryder pulls out two chairs and we sit side by side. A laptop computer rests on the table beside a small stack of pages.

"The top sheet is a nondisclosure agreement," announces Tracie. "I need you to sign that before you read for us."

"What's said in this room, stays in this room," Ryder explains. "You'll understand why, soon enough."

It's just one page. Barely fifty words. A promise that I won't repeat anything that's said today. I sign it with Ryder's pen, my hand shaking so hard the signature looks fake. Tracie walks the length of the table and takes it from me.

"Okay, then," says Ryder, tapping what looks like pages of a script. "This movie is about star-crossed lovers—a boy and a girl pushed to the limit by circumstances they can't control. They're a team, but when everything around them is collapsing, even a perfect couple can be collateral damage. For this scene, you take the part of Andrew. I'll be Lana."

I scan the lines of text: the words of a boy and a girl nearing the end of the road together. I nod once and begin to read, though my voice hardly rises above a whisper: *"So what happens now?"*

Ryder doesn't try to speak in a girl's voice, thank goodness. In fact, he doesn't act at all. *"We spend some time apart."*

"And what is that supposed to mean? If we're breaking up, then call it what it is."

"Would that make you happier?"

I pause. *"Happier? No. But I gave up on that a long time ago. Now I'd settle for honesty. Just a sign that any of it was real."*

"That would be nice, wouldn't it?"

An ambivalent end—under different circumstances, I might appreciate that. But right now I'm fixated on the camera at the end of the table, and the realization that the screenwriter is sitting beside me.

We turn to the next scene—*Ext. A park.* I'm still Andrew, but Ryder is playing my father now. We argue, and finally he asks me why I've changed. Why I'm not the boy I used to be. The scene ends without an answer, but in my mind, I'm thinking that change isn't necessarily bad. How much easier would things be for my real father and me if I got this job?

As we work through page after page, I begin to realize why Ryder might've seen me in this role. I *am* Andrew. The biggest difference between us is that I don't have a girlfriend, let alone one as committed as Lana.

Finally Ryder opens up the laptop. He cocks his head to the side. "Well?"

A voice comes through the computer, deep and brusque: "Good. Real good. Let me talk to him."

Ryder turns the laptop around. The guy on-screen is older, maybe late thirties, square-jawed and serious. "Seth, I'm Brian Halsey. I'm out of town at the moment, running auditions for the part of Lana. Now, you're probably wondering why we made you sign a nondisclosure agreement."

"Kind of. Yeah."

"Until recently, this was a Sabrina Layton and Kris Ellis movie. They came as a package deal, and that suited us just fine. Well, until they stopped being a *package*. No one's saying what happened, but it was pretty clear they wouldn't be able to work together. Not on a movie as intimate as this."

"It's easy for a smaller movie to get lost in the shuffle," says Ryder, taking over, "but with Sabrina and Kris involved, everyone was talking about *Whirlwind*. People started posting spoilers before I'd finished the script. It's crazy, but that's the way it is these days. You with me?"

"Sure." I glance at the nondisclosure agreement. I can see why they don't want me discussing any of this stuff outside the room.

Ryder follows my eyes. "Our job is to keep everyone talking about *Whirlwind*, even without Sabrina and Kris. The only way to do that is to keep up this veil of secrecy about the whole production—script, casting, locations . . . *everything*. Once we've recast the lead roles, we can be open again."

He sounds apologetic, as though I'll be appalled at the trickery. But actually, I respect him more for telling me straight up what's going on. Why shouldn't he use Sabrina and Kris's notoriety to keep everyone interested in the picture?

Brian's been watching me the whole time. "Be honest, Seth. You just did a reading. What do you think of Ryder's script?"

"It's good," I say.

"Glad you think so. But I don't think it's the script that hooked Sabrina and Kris."

Ryder is practically bouncing beside me. "We sold them on the vision of a new kind of movie. Instead of sets and a film crew, they were going to film each other."

"Film each other *how*?" I ask.

"However they wanted. Prearranged camera setups. Head-cams." Ryder clasps his hands together. "Look, you've been onstage, so you know how real it feels. The way I see it, the only way to make a new kind of star-crossed lovers movie is to put viewers in the heart of the action. Forget lavish sets and pretty cinematography . . . we want it raw and cramped and sweaty and messy. We want you to dig deep, live this role until you can't tell where Seth ends and Andrew begins. Once all the actors are ready, we wind you up and set you free. See what the hell comes out of it. Understand?"

I understand that he just switched from *they* to *you,* and even though it might have been a mistake, I feel like I'm closing in on something. "So, it's like a movie version of reality TV?"

"No. This is more like Method acting. *Scripted reality,* we call it. As director, I'll make the final cut, but I'm more like an editor really, shaping raw material. You control the camera. You can tweak dialogue, add material, establish relationships *your* way. Hell, even film scenes without me knowing, or when your costars beg you not to. Sometimes you'll be so stressed out, you'll say stuff you shouldn't and so will they, and it's all good, because it'll be *real*. It'll redefine what a movie can be."

"It's also going to require a new approach to publicity," says Brian. "Sabrina and Kris could sell this project by themselves, but we need you in the public eye. Forget doing press junkets after filming wraps, we want everyone to know who you are *now*. We need them to see how gutsy you are for tackling something like this. We want people talking, Seth. Can you make people talk?"

I can't tell if they're still auditioning me, or if I'm auditioning them. There's so much energy in every word, like they're anxious for me to climb aboard. "Yeah," I say. "I can do that."

"I think so too," agrees Brian. "So I'm going to ask you just once: How much do you want this role?"

"I'd do anything for a chance like this," I say without hesitation.

He gives a sharp nod. "Good. I think you'll be perfect."

I can't believe I've heard him right. I knew this was no ordinary audition—I saw it in Ryder's eyes from the moment I entered the room—but still . . . no matter how well you perform, there's always that moment of eerie silence at the end of the play when you wonder: Will the audience clap? Will they stand? Will they just walk out?

"This wasn't just a reading, Seth," Brian explains, filling the silence. "It was a screen test. Tracie and I have been watching you ever since you entered the room. How you carry yourself. Your professionalism, focus, engagement. We're looking for someone who's smart enough to recognize that these are uncharted seas, and who's willing to dive in anyway."

Ryder rests his elbows on the table. "You've probably got questions."

My mind is spinning, but I have to ask *something*. "Who's playing Lana?"

"I'm casting right now," says Brian. "We've got three excellent options. None of them are Sabrina Layton, but maybe that's a good thing."

I nod, like I actually care who they cast. Truth is, they could put me opposite an animated Martian and I'd still sign on.

Tracie sidles up to me. "Welcome aboard, Seth. You'll be wanting this." She places a document on the table. My name is typed on the front of the contract, like they knew all along how this would go. "I'll fax a copy to your agent."

"I don't have one," I say.

"But you've done commercials."

"My mom used to handle everything." Tracie looks like she's expecting a fuller explanation, so I add, "Before we moved to California."

She taps the pages. "Hmm. Well, we need to be moving forward, so you've got a couple options: You can hold off signing and try to find an agent ASAP, or you can sign now and parlay this role into representation down the line."

The way she says it makes it seem like a simple decision. But what if I can't find the right agent in one week? What if Ryder or Brian changes his mind?

"I could read it right now, yeah?"

"Sure." Tracie points to a box at the bottom of the page. "I'll need you to initial each page here, and sign the last. Take your time. If you have questions, just ask. My job is to protect the interests of the film, and as of now, that includes you."

It's got to be fifty pages, at least. I read and initial each one. I'm feeling impatient and elated, but also cautious. I'm eighteen, old enough to know that putting a signature to a page, *any* page, carries weight.

"Can I get a copy of this?" I ask.

"Absolutely. I'll run one off when you're done."

I keep reading. Tracie bustles around me, and though my heartbeat is racing, I feel sluggish, like a million tiny needles are pricking my skin but the signals are reaching my brain on tape delay. I need to show them that I'm a professional, but really I just want to run home and celebrate.

Once I've signed the final page, Tracie gathers the sheets together. For a few moments, I just sit there, trying to make sense of what has happened. Then I start chuckling to myself like a crazy person.

"How did you know?" I ask Ryder. "That you wanted me, I mean."

Ryder leans back in his chair. He's smiling, but doesn't laugh. "When I saw you onstage yesterday, I knew right away you're the one we've been looking for."

Brian, still present on the laptop screen, nods emphatically. "You'll be perfect, Seth. Trust me. This role was practically made for you."

4

SAME CRACKED CONCRETE PATH. SAME ALUMINUM
porch with drooping gutter. Same off-white door, unlocked. Gant
and I have picked up a lot of skills trying to keep the house liv-
able—carpentry, plasterwork, even a little painting. Dad has the
knowledge but not the strength and coordination.

We don't even own the place, but the landlord gives us a break
on the rent in return for repairs. For months I've wondered how
Dad will manage once we both leave home.

Now I have my answer.

"Dad?" I shout.

Gant emerges from the bathroom. "He's still out."

"But the car's gone."

"He can drive fine."

"The doctor said—"

"Seth!" Gant stifles a laugh. "Come on. Dad's going to do stuff
like this. That's the whole trouble with parents. They grow up so
damn fast."

For once, I feel like I can laugh about it too.

I slip into the kitchen and pour a glass of water. There are
smudges along the rim.

Gant follows me and takes a seat beside my open laptop. I bought it with money from my last commercial, almost four years ago, but Gant uses it more than I do. He's downloaded so many photos, it doesn't run as fast as it used to.

"You were badass," he says, pointing at the screen.

It's a photo from last night's performance. Tybalt and me, swords crossed, moments before I slay him. My features are twisted into a furious scowl.

The front door opens and Dad appears in the kitchen doorway, car keys clenched tightly in his hand.

"How did the interview go?" I ask.

"They . . . they . . ." He clamps his mouth shut and shakes his head.

He doesn't need to explain. They could've used any one of a hundred reasons to reject him. Potential employers know how to discriminate without getting into trouble.

We fall into an all-too-familiar silence. Five minutes ago, I wanted to shout my good news like the hero of a Broadway musical, but now I'm not so sure. Does my good fortune make up for Dad's disappointment, or just rub salt in the wounds?

Then again, what choice do I have? Preproduction starts next week.

"I've been offered a role," I say.

All smiles, Gant raises his hand so that we can bump fists. "The Chevy people came to their senses, then?"

"Not a commercial. A movie."

"A *movie*?"

"It's called *Whirlwind*. I auditioned this morning." Everything comes out sounding like a question. "The director was at the play last night. He's offered me the lead role."

18

Dad's left eye blinks rapidly.

"We'll rehearse for a week or two and be filming by New Year. They're putting me up in the Beverly Wilshire."

"Seriously?" Gant whistles. "You could drive to Beverly Hills in forty-five minutes."

"They want me close. There's going to be a lot of promotional stuff. In January, I'll have a tutor too, so we don't have to worry about me missing school."

Dad grunts. I can't tell if it's deliberate or if it just slipped out.

"I know it sounds incredible, but it's how a lot of actors get discovered. I've got a contract and everything." I pull it from my backpack and place it on the kitchen table.

"You signed a contract without checking with Dad?" Gant sounds incredulous.

"I'm eighteen. They're paying me a hundred thousand dollars."

It's my trump card, and it has the desired effect. They stare at me, waiting for the punch line, not daring to believe it's true.

"Two installments. First installment on January first." I don't want to sound so excited about the money, but they have to realize how this changes everything.

Gant pretends to read the contract. "How many other people auditioned?"

"Hundreds. But after they finished casting, the leads pulled out. Now they're kind of scrambling."

Gant begins to type. Research is his answer to everything. It doesn't seem to occur to him what that means—how he's lost the ability to trust good news.

For once, I'm happy to let him do it. I know what he'll find.

19

He scrolls down the page. "It's true. *Whirlwind. Preproduc—* Whoa!" He leans back suddenly. "You're not seriously replacing Kris Ellis."

"Someone has to."

He and Dad exchange glances. Even Dad has heard of Kris Ellis.

"Come on," I groan. "I'm going to be in a freaking movie. It's—" I'm about to say *a hundred thousand dollars,* but stop myself. "It's two months." I turn to Dad. "The director's going to call you. Wants you to be okay with everything."

Dad leans against the counter. He looks tired and confused. I think he has a million questions, but doesn't know where to begin.

"Mom would've liked it," I say.

We mull the words over together. After my first play in elementary school, Mom started taking Gant and me to Sunday afternoon children's shows. Then matinees, as we got older: Arthur Miller, Tennessee Williams, and a bunch of other playwrights whose work I didn't really understand. Summers were for Shakespeare in the Park, which I liked more because we always took a picnic. Dad used to stay behind, though; theater wasn't part of his world.

From the way Dad's looking right through me, I get the feeling he's thinking of Mom now. How she booked my first paid acting gigs. Of course she'd be happy for me.

Dad's cell phone rings, startling us.

"That's probably Ryder," I say. "I gave him your number."

He tugs at his shirt collar and leaves.

Gant pushes his chair back. Paces around the room and finally settles, leaning against the door frame. Arms folded, he looks like one of those moody, rebellious guys from 1950s movies. James Dean, or someone like that.

"This is really sudden," he says.

"Has to be. Filming starts soon."

"Sure, but . . ." He glances at the laptop, and his frown shifts to a grin. "Are you seriously starring with Sabrina Layton?"

"No. She dropped out too, same as Kris Ellis."

"Bummer. Probably not worth taking the role, then."

Dad's pacing along the hallway, his uneven footsteps loud on the laminate floor. He's hardly speaking.

Gant returns to the table. "I'm going to miss you," he says.

"It's less than an hour away."

"Yeah, but . . . you're probably taking the laptop too, right?"

I roll my eyes. "Nice, Gant. Real nice."

"Well, Dad's computer is even older and crappier than yours, and I can't run my photo editing software. Actually, it's kind of selfish of you to take this role."

I pretend to punch him on the arm.

"Y-yes," says Dad, breaking his silence. "Hmm-hmm."

I wait for the questions to commence—*How long is the shooting schedule? How many hours of tutoring per day? Will Seth be home for Christmas?*—but Dad hangs up.

I join him in the hallway. "Y-you can d-d-do it," he says.

Even with the contract signed, I was bracing for an inquisition. Instead Dad is smiling. We hug, and he laughs, and in this instant, our whole world seems to shift.

Two-thirds of it, anyway. I wait for the remaining third.

Gant is two years younger than me, but has the jaded attitude of an older brother. Perhaps that's why things don't feel completely right until he joins us—almost like he's the one giving me permission to go.

5

MY ROOM AT THE BEVERLY WILSHIRE Hotel is spectacular. Gant opens the patio doors and stands on the balcony. Dad runs a hand across the designer jackets and pants and shirts in my closet. When I emailed Ryder my sizes, I figured it was for movie costumes, not a new wardrobe.

Dad removes a dark blue suit and white shirt and hangs it from the top of the closet door. Ryder has left a note on the jacket: *WEAR THIS.*

Ten minutes later, I emerge from the en suite bathroom in my new outfit. Gant and Dad exchange critical glances, like judges grading a contestant. "N-nice," says Dad.

"If you're into suits," adds Gant.

"Which I'm not," I remind them.

Dad points to the closet and laughs. "Th-th-think again."

We drive to a house in the Hills, where a large guy with a shaved head and a Bluetooth earpiece stands by the door, eyes scanning the horizon suspiciously. I say good-bye to Dad and Gant in the car, but they continue to watch as I approach the guy. He seems to look right through me.

I raise a hand—the kind of lame greeting that ought to get me kicked off the grounds. "Hi."

He flicks his head in response.

"Can I come in?"

The corner of his mouth twists into a smile. "Hell, yeah. You're the star of the show now, Mr. Crane." He nods to himself. "The *star*."

I can't tell if he's serious.

He pulls open the door and ushers me inside the largest home I've ever seen. Everything but the bedrooms and bathrooms is open-plan. The kitchen, dining room, living room, media room, and library all flow together. Recessed spotlights in the ceiling cast rings of light around the cavernous room like daubs of color on a monochrome painting. People avoid them, preferring the view from the shadows.

There must be a hundred guests here. A few of them languish on leather furniture, while more spill onto the outdoor patio, where women in stylish dresses sip cocktails in the glow from the swimming pool's underwater light. Guys laugh too loudly, wanting to be heard having fun.

I'm a half-hour car ride from the Valley, but I've landed in a different galaxy.

Eyes turn at my arrival. I hug the perimeter and head for an unpopulated corner. There's a bathroom, so I slip inside and lock the door.

Marble countertops and sinks. A mirror that covers an entire wall. Soothing music piped in through hidden speakers. A row of scented candles on a shelf. The only thing missing is a personal masseur.

I take in my reflection. Hair, artfully disheveled. Dark blue slim-fit suit, courtesy of Ryder. I look less like me than ever before, but hey—it might be fun to impersonate a movie star.

When I unlock the bathroom door, Ryder's waiting for me.

"Constipated?" He pauses a moment and erupts in laughter. "I'm just messing with you, Seth. You need a moment to calm the nerves. I get it. Everyone'll get it. It's natural."

He wraps an arm around me and leads me to the center of the room. "How's the hotel?"

"Amazing."

"Good. Brian complained that there's a perfectly good, cheap motel on the interstate, but at the Beverly Wilshire they appreciate their guests' privacy. You're going to be grateful for that, soon enough. Talking of money"—he taps the shoulder of an older guy with wild hair and horn-rimmed glasses—"Seth, this is Curt Barrett. He's our financier."

"Our leading man!" Curt takes my hand and pumps it up and down mechanically. "Talk about culture shock, eh?"

"You could say that."

He gives an understanding nod. "Well, between you and me, I think you're going to fit right in. Just be yourself. Have fun. If you can't let your hair down, then what's the point, you know?"

I can't tell if he expects an answer. "Is this your house?"

"Yes. Funny things, these houses. All this glass for maximum transparency. But then we hire security teams, and put up ten-foot fences and trees so no one can see us. I think that's Hollywood in a nutshell. Appear to show everything, but always control the view." Ryder clears his throat, and Curt laughs. "Listen to me!

One cocktail and I think I can nail an entire city with a single sentence. If I were you, I wouldn't stick around to hear what I say after my second drink."

Curt takes a handful of nuts from a bowl on the table beside him—cashews and pistachios, by the look of them; no cheap peanuts here, thank you—but pauses before eating. "No," he continues in a lower voice. "If I were you, I'd go talk to the redhead on the patio. The one who's been eyeing you ever since you arrived."

I fight the urge to look straightaway. Channeling the new me, I shake his hand and give a casual salute as he raises his empty glass and moves on to the bar.

I see her as soon as I turn around. She's taller than the women around her. Her green dress shimmers in the light from the pool. Her dark red hair is pulled high in a sleek ponytail.

As our eyes meet I freeze. She's too beautiful to approach, like a painting secured behind several panes of glass. But what will she think of me if I don't talk to her?

In all my years of acting, I've never been so conscious of how I look when I move. My arms and legs feel awkward and stiff. She watches me the whole time, waiting, a faint smile teasing the corner of her mouth.

"I'm Sabrina." She offers her hand. In heels, she's only a few inches shorter than me.

We shake. "I've seen your movies," I tell her.

"All of them?"

"Some. Saw *Swan Song* last week."

"Ugh." She rolls her dark eyes. Manages to make even that look sexy.

"You don't like it? You won an award."

"That movie was only made to win awards. I thought it was self-indulgent and melodramatic."

"No sequel, then, huh?"

She smiles fully at last. "Well, as my agent reminded me: Never say never." She narrows her eyes and leans a little closer. "But seeing as how my character died at the end, it'd be kind of difficult, don't you think?"

My face flushes red. I wonder how bad it would look for me to run straight out of the party.

"Hmm," she murmurs, running her thumb across her lips. "You didn't watch all of it, huh?"

"No. I-I kind of thought it was, well . . . self-indulgent and melodramatic, I guess." She seems surprised that I actually say this out loud. She's not the only one. "Sorry."

"No," she says quickly. "This is good. I like honesty. Which means we're compatible, doesn't it, Seth?"

Sabrina Layton knows my name!

"I didn't think you'd know who I am," I say.

"Oh, I know you, all right." Her voice is silky smooth, every word delivered with teasing certainty. It's impossible not to be nervous beside her. Impossible not to want to impress her.

"So tell me something about me," I say with a confidence I don't feel.

"Okay. Let's see . . . you're out of your element here, and you wish it felt better than it does. You hate not knowing who most of these people are. You haven't got a drink even though everyone else has one. And my guess is, you won't take a cocktail because you're worried what people will think of you for it." She tilts her head to the side. Her ponytail swings languidly in amber silhouette.

"Anything else?"

"Yeah. You didn't choose those clothes."

Somehow, my heart beats even faster. "How do you know that?"

"You're too buttoned up."

She places her glass on the wall and draws closer to me. I hold my breath as she reaches up and undoes a second shirt button. As she adjusts the cloth, her finger slides underneath and brushes against my bare skin. Such a fleeting movement, but it's electrifying.

"Better?" I croak.

"Better," she agrees. "Sends a different message."

"Really?"

"Yeah. Two buttons undone says that although I get the lead role in local stage productions, I'm still just your normal laid-back high school senior."

"Undoing one extra button says all that?"

"All depends which button." She picks up her glass and downs most of the contents. "Tell me something, Seth Crane. Do you always go red so easily?"

"Yes." I take the glass from her and finish it off. "Now you tell me something, Sabrina Layton. Do you always drink water from a martini glass?"

She cocks an eyebrow. "Yes."

"Very clever."

"Aren't I? Why don't you get us two more?"

Fighting the urge to run, I head back inside. One of the servers pours springwater into two clean martini glasses for me. He watches me closely, but doesn't say a word. I think he might be jealous.

And why wouldn't he be? Sabrina Layton is talking to me, and wants to talk more. Everyone nearby seems to be watching me, as if breathing the same air as her makes me a celebrity too.

I keep the glasses high as I weave through the guests. Air runs across my chest where Sabrina has unbuttoned my shirt. Suddenly it's as though no one else at the party exists. Deep down I know it's all an act, but it's my fiction as much as hers. We're writing this scene together.

I stop before the patio doors.

There's another guy standing beside her. Tall, with muscular arms and shoulder-length hair that drapes across part of his face. It's Kris Ellis, one-half of Hollywood's favorite former teen couple. As Sabrina looks up and catches my eye, he wraps his arm around her.

"Is that one spare?" A girl points at the glass in my left hand. She looks about sixteen. Black hair styled short in a pixie cut. Cute instead of beautiful.

"I guess so," I say, handing it to her.

She clinks our glasses and we stare at the patio together. "Well, it looks like their separation didn't last long."

"No."

She turns to face me. "I'm Annaleigh, by the way. Your star-crossed lover."

That gets my attention. I don't know who I thought she was,

but costar didn't occur to me. Or maybe I'm not thinking at all. One conversation with Sabrina Layton and I'm starstruck.

"I'm Seth," I say.

"Yeah, I know."

"Last time I checked, I didn't have a lover." I frown, realizing how weird that sounds. "In the movie," I add, backpedaling. "Because, you know, she hadn't been cast."

Annaleigh's fighting a grin. "I'm a late addition."

I look at her properly. Notice her large blue eyes accented with a thin band of black eyeliner. The blush on her cheeks. Her small hands. I wonder if Ryder picked out her yellow dress the way he selected my clothes, and if she's as freaked out about being here as I am.

She raises a finger to her mouth, but stops herself before she bites the nail. "You're tall," she says, as if she's just noticed the ten or so inches between us. "You must be, what . . . six-three?"

"Six-two."

"Hmm. Guess I'm shrinking, then." She tilts her head toward Sabrina and Kris. "You realize, if this carries on, ours could be the shortest careers in Hollywood history."

"Why?"

"Because everyone knows they were first choice for the leads. If they get back together . . ." She chuckles. "Well, then I'd have cool stories about flying first class, and this crazy party in a ridiculous house. Yeah," she says, like she's trying to convince herself, "that'd be an okay consolation prize, I guess."

We're not the only people watching them. The eyes that followed me just moments ago are focused on Sabrina and Kris now.

"That's not why they're here, though, is it?" I ask. "To get their roles back?"

"I don't know."

Kris runs his hand over Sabrina possessively. She doesn't look pleased about it.

"Sabrina's beautiful," says Annaleigh.

The way she says it makes me feel guilty for looking outside when she's standing right beside me. "So is Kris."

"Uh-uh. He's attractive, not beautiful."

"There's a difference?"

"Attraction is superficial. And something tells me Kris Ellis is the most superficial person here." She takes a sip from her glass, and grimaces. "This is water."

"Yeah. I'm only eighteen."

"So? I'm only seventeen."

"You want me to get you a cocktail?"

"No, it's probably best if I don't get buzzed, cut from the movie, and arrested all in one night. Water's fine. But I wouldn't mind sitting down."

I follow her to an empty couch. Even though we're attracting glances, no one approaches us to chat. People circulate in a constant wave of motion. Sitting on a couch must be too much of a risk, I guess—no one wants to be stuck talking to the same person for too long.

Me, I'm happy to sit. Annaleigh is the least intimidating person here by far.

She puffs out her cheeks and exhales slowly. "I've got to say, prom is going to be really anticlimactic after this."

"You don't have waiters handing out cocktails at your prom, huh?"

"Shocking, I know." She raises her glass.

"Unthinkable." We clink again. "So where are you from?"

"Arkansas."

"You don't sound like it."

"Good. I'm trying to blend in."

I hesitate. "My mother was from Arkansas. I liked her accent."

"I'm sorry. I wasn't trying to . . ." She makes eye contact and snorts. "What am I saying? Of course I was being rude about Southern accents. I guess I'm self-conscious about it here." With every word, a little more Arkansas creeps back in.

"You sound more comfortable already."

"Hmm. Just don't let me talk like this in front of that financier guy. If his first choice was Sabrina Layton, I can't imagine he'll be happy with my drawl."

"We'll keep it between us, then."

She bumps my arm playfully. "Deal."

As people walk by, I catch glimpses of the patio. Kris still has his arm on Sabrina, but she's leaning away from him like something's wrong.

"Have you seen Ryder?" I ask.

"No. Why?"

"Hold this." I hand Annaleigh my glass and stand. I can't see Ryder anywhere. "What about Curt?"

Annaleigh stands too. Follows my eyes to the drama unfolding between Sabrina and Kris. "They're not in the movie anymore. What are Ryder and Curt supposed to do?"

I don't have an answer for that. I just know there's about to be a scene. Sure enough, Sabrina bats Kris's hand away, and he grabs her arm, roughly this time.

I slip through the patio doors. Sabrina's expression has changed again—no longer indifferent or uncomfortable, but frightened. I can see it in the way she tries to pull away from Kris, desperate for space.

"Everything okay?" I ask. I'm shooting for light and friendly, but it comes out loud and anxious.

Kris spins around. Glares at me like I've just asked the stupidest question in the history of the world—which, in a way, I guess I have.

"This has nothing to do with you," he says.

"Sure. I know. It's just . . . Curt Barrett wants to speak to Sabrina, is all."

Kris narrows his eyes. He smells BS, but my face is frozen in a vacant nothing-to-see-here smile, and he can't be sure. If he's wrong, he might have to answer to that huge bald guy by the front door.

One of Sabrina's dress straps hangs off her shoulder. She pulls it back up like she feels naked. As she walks away, a tear runs down her cheek.

Kris watches her go. "Do you think you're my replacement, Seth? Is that what you think?"

I don't know if he's talking about my role in the movie, or if this has something to do with Sabrina. I don't want to pick a fight with him, but I'm not sure how to make peace either. Before I can speak, his eyes shift to something over my shoulder.

He steps toward me so quickly I flinch. "Oh, you're gonna take photos, are you?" he snaps.

Behind me, the guy who served the drinks earlier is leaning against the patio doors, cell phone pointed toward us.

An arm falls across my shoulders. A moment before, I thought Kris was going to punch the guy. Now his hand locks us together instead. He's the same height as me. Similar build, too. So why do I feel small beside him?

"Smile, Mr. Crane," he mutters. "Cameras are a-poppin'."

I peer at Kris. Take in those famous deep-set eyes and the thin layer of stubble. It's easy to imagine he's spent his whole life being told he's hot. And whatever was going on inside of him just a moment ago has already been locked away so deep there isn't a trace of it on that pretty face.

His isn't just a winning smile. It's victorious.

The server continues to take pictures. I have no idea how many he's taking, or why. All I know is that I couldn't smile if my life depended on it.

Kris raises his hand, bringing the impromptu session to an end. As the server shuffles away, Kris leans in close. He squeezes my shoulder, fingers digging into the flesh. "Welcome to Hollywood, Seth. I'll be keeping my eye on you."

6

THE HOTEL BED IS QUEEN-SIZED. IT'D probably be the most comfortable bed I've ever slept on, if only I could sleep. Instead my mind replays Kris's thinly disguised threat like a movie trapped on an endless loop. I can still feel his arm clamped against me, recall the lightning-quick switch from seething hatred to open smile. Onstage, I try to be ready for anything, but no one told me a cocktail party is a stage too.

It's still dark outside when I get up. I pull out my laptop and check for messages. There's only one, from Gant, reminding me that celebrity autographs go for a premium on eBay. Trust my brother to plan for my retirement before I've done a day of work.

I fire back an email—Dad's preferred mode of communication ever since the stroke—but I don't send it. Detective Gant will notice if it arrives at four o' clock in the morning, and Dad will have questions about why I'm up so early.

I type Curt Barrett's name into a search window. Turns out, he's Executive Director of Project Development at Machinus Media Enterprises, specializing in everything from reality TV shows to cutting-edge investigative documentaries. Judging by his extensive credits, he's definitely earned that fancy house.

I type Sabrina's name next. I tell myself it's just a way of passing the time, but it draws me back to the world of the party and makes my heartbeat race like it did just a few hours ago.

There are literally thousands of hits. Photographs, too, like a one-girl fashion parade. Hard to believe an eighteen-year-old's life can be so exhaustively documented. I read her biography, even though I already know most of it: She was born in East L.A., and raised there until her parents used her income to buy a condo in Westwood. After their messy divorce and a tumultuous custody battle, she appealed for and was granted legal emancipation at the age of sixteen. She began dating Kris Ellis a month later, and the media assault, already in full swing, became an around-the-clock issue for her. She hasn't spoken to either parent in two years.

I return to the photographs. I've looked at pictures of celebrities before, on websites and in magazines, but this feels different. I've seen that teasing smile up close, heard that voice and watched those lips, and every word she spoke is branded on my memory. Being with her was like appearing on a Broadway stage and playing myself—confusing, sure, but exhilarating too. I wish it wasn't a one-time-only performance.

Impossible not to wonder what might have happened if Kris had stayed home. And why anyone would've invited him and Sabrina to the same party in the first place.

7

ANNALEIGH AND I SHARE A TAXI to our first rehearsal. Beverly Hills bustles with pre-Christmas energy, and I gawk at the impeccably dressed pedestrians and parade of expensive foreign cars.

"This place is so pretty," Annaleigh murmurs, staring out the window. "I feel like I've landed in a dream."

"No kidding."

In less than a quarter hour, we pull up at the production company's offices—a one-story building with few windows and a bunker-like concrete exterior. A stocky twenty-something woman with long, bleach-blond hair ushers us inside.

"I'm Maggie," she says. "I'm just an intern."

"Not *just* an intern," Ryder corrects her. "Maggie's in film school at USC."

He leads us along a short corridor to an empty room with a spotless oval table and smart black office chairs. Sun streams through a window, so he closes the blind. "Can I get you something to drink? Juice? Water? Coffee?"

"Water," says Annaleigh.

"Me too," I say. "And maybe coffee." It's only two o'clock, but feels later.

Maggie leaves with our order. Seated at the table, Annaleigh raises her hand to her neck, and then upward until she touches her short hair. It's an awkward motion, as if she used to have long hair and forgets that it's gone.

Neither of us is exuding confidence today.

"So," Ryder begins, "did you have time to look over the script this morning?"

Only for about ten hours.

"Yes," we answer in unison.

"Okay, then. What do you think of your character, Seth?"

I'm not sure why, but I look at Annaleigh before answering. "I like how Andrew takes charge of his family because his dad's not around. But, I don't know . . . I guess I don't see how someone that responsible goes all in with Lana the first time he sees her."

"Because I'm awesome, that's why," says Annaleigh.

"Glad you like your character," Ryder says.

She hesitates. "Yeah. Although actually, I think audiences are going to get pissed if she doesn't stand up for herself some more."

"Her family is a nightmare," I point out.

"Lots of people have crappy families," she replies. "I don't think Lana should be shooting for the sympathy vote."

Ryder purses his lips. "Well, I suppose I asked for your opinion. Look, if you want to tweak the character, even change the backstory, then go ahead. I mean it when I say that I want you to *own* these characters."

"Then why have a script at all?" I ask.

"Good point. I like to think of it as a road map for the story. This movie is about star-crossed lovers—doesn't matter how perfect they are together, external forces are going to pull them apart. So if you feel like you're getting away from that, use the script to keep things on track."

"Wouldn't you tell us if we're getting off track?" asks Annaleigh.

"If I'm there, sure." He sees Annaleigh's puzzled expression, and holds up one finger. "As director, I'll take over some scenes completely. Like when you're out in public—crowds don't always behave how you want them to. But the smaller, intimate scenes will feel more authentic if you're in complete control. Just the two of you. Alone."

Annaleigh tilts her head. "Like the opening scene?"

"When Lana and Andrew meet, you mean." Ryder gives a knowing smile. "Look, we're not going for some deep, intellectual love, okay? We're going for infatuation—love at first sight."

"I get that, but . . . I'm with Seth on this one. I'm having a hard time buying it."

Ryder doesn't seem offended at all. "Does *Romeo and Juliet* feel realistic?"

"Not exactly."

"Do you like it anyway?"

"Sure."

"Exactly. Seth does too. Right?"

I nod.

"Look, you're both fifteen in this movie. Everything is new to you. All that matters is, we feel a spark, a connection. Without it, the entire movie falls apart."

Annaleigh snorts. "No pressure, then."

Ryder laughs too, flashing perfectly white teeth. "We've got a few rehearsals for you two to get acquainted. Before long you'll be as comfortable acting here as you were back in Arkansas."

"Except Seth'll be filming me," she reminds him.

He *tsks*. "One guy with a headcam has to be a lot easier than a live audience."

"What makes you think our plays had an audience?" she dead-pans.

I smile. I've seen my fair share of half-empty theaters.

"Listen, hundreds of people auditioned for these roles, but you're the ones here," says Ryder, knocking on the table for emphasis. "I've seen each of you carry a stage play, so I know you can act. What I want now is something real. Something edgy. I want you to pour yourselves into these characters and create a world together. As long as you trust each other, good things will happen." He slides a few sheets of paper over to us. "All right, pep talk over. Here's the alley scene. Feel free to improvise."

I take a deep breath, and read the first line word for word: *"Where's your brother now?"*

"I don't know," replies Annaleigh, her voice a little higher than usual, less assured. *"He doesn't normally leave me."*

"Does he know I'm here?"

"If he knew that, I don't think he would've gone. Now it's my turn to ask a question. Did you follow me tonight?"

"Yes. Is that okay?"

"No. And yes. I'm glad you— Shhh. What was that?"

"I don't know."

"*I have to go.*"

Next is a direction: *Lana kisses Andrew.*

Annaleigh looks at me, eyes flitting everywhere and nowhere.

Maggie saves us, bustling into the room carrying four paper cups on a cardboard tray. "You two okay?" she asks. "You look flushed."

"It's a powerful scene," says Annaleigh.

Maggie gives us our drinks and places an extra cup beside an empty seat. She retreats to the corridor just as Brian strolls in.

I didn't see him at the party last night, but I recognize him from the computer screen during my audition. He's intimidating in person—tall and powerful, with chiseled features and a military buzz cut. Even his light gray business suit, tie loose and top button undone, can't soften the hard edges. There are two small cases in his left hand and a newspaper tucked under his arm. He shakes our hands with a firm, businesslike grip.

"Good to see you both," he says. "Everything going okay?"

"So far," says Ryder.

"Pleased to hear it."

Brian hands the cases to Annaleigh and me. Inside each one is a small but expensive-looking video camera.

"It's a top-of-the-line portable camera," he says. "Lightweight, anti-shake, auto-focus, very hi-def. Water resistant, but not waterproof, so don't push it. There's a head strap in the bag too. Obviously, only one of you at a time will be wearing a camera during filming—it'd look pretty stupid if you appear onscreen with a camera strapped to your head—but it's important to get used to it now."

"What's with the new cell phone?" Annaleigh asks, holding up the other item from the case.

"Think of it as a precaution. I've given each of you a new phone number, and programmed in some others you ought to have. If you add more contacts, keep it to close family, okay?"

I can't believe my luck. The minutes are about to expire on my old phone, and I've been meaning to upgrade. But I never would've bought one as expensive as this.

"I've already got a phone," says Annaleigh, reaching into her bag. She places the old one beside the new. It looks even more decrepit than mine.

"No offense," says Brian, "but if they haven't done it already, your friends'll be publishing your number on Twitter soon. You can guess what'll happen after that." He turns to me. "Especially now that you're front-page news."

I stop gazing at the phone as Brian unfolds the newspaper and slides it across the table. "Recognize anyone, Seth?"

There's a photograph of Kris and me—black-and-white, but unmistakably us. Kris is smiling, a happy camper at a happy party. In contrast, I look psychotic.

Below the photo is a caption: *Changing of the guard.* There's a story too: three columns dedicated to Seth Crane, my extracurricular interests, and an account of the "miraculous" stage performance that landed me my first movie role.

"How do they know this stuff?" I ask.

"There are these people called *reporters,*" says Brian. "They do *research.* Now, any particular reason you look like you want to beat the crap out of Kris Ellis?"

I struggle to catch up with what's happening—what this *means*. Annaleigh fiddles with her new phone and sips her water robotically, giving every appearance of someone who has no stake in the outcome. But everything I do will reflect on her.

"He was . . ." I swallow hard. Annaleigh stops sipping. "He and Sabrina were fighting."

"Stop the presses," says Brian. "Boyfriend and girlfriend have fight."

"*Ex*-boyfriend and girlfriend," interjects Ryder.

"Fine. Ex. Look, Seth, something like this happens, you've got to let us know."

"He tried," says Annaleigh. She turns to Ryder. "He was looking for you at the party, but you weren't there."

"When was that?" asks Ryder.

"About ten minutes after I met Curt Barrett," I say.

Ryder points his finger at Brian. "I was outside on the phone. Talking to you."

Brian places both hands flat on the table. "Point is: You've got to be careful. This kind of thing can take on a life of its own."

I feel stupid. Defensive too. "Got it," I say. "Don't pick a fight with major Hollywood stars."

Ryder snorts. Brian's expression doesn't change at all. "Do you know who took this photo?" he asks.

"One of the servers. A guy."

"Well, we won't be seeing him again. Not now that he's sold these pictures."

"Why were Kris and Sabrina at the party anyway? I thought they dropped out."

"They did. Kris wasn't meant to be there."

Annaleigh holds up her new phone. "Uh, talking of Sabrina, why is her number on here?"

Someone knocks on the door before Brian can answer. He opens it at once.

"Sorry I'm late," says the new arrival in an unmistakable husky voice.

Annaleigh turns to face me, but I can't tear my eyes away from the doorway and the girl standing there. Her hair is down and frames her face. Her tiny jean shorts and gauzy white tunic look simple, yet effortlessly perfect.

Sabrina gives a gentle wave, and takes her place at the table.

"WHAT'S THAT?" SABRINA ASKS, POINTING AT the newspaper on the table. She turns it toward her and sees the photo of Kris and me. "Oh."

The photo is humiliating enough. Watching Sabrina take it in is even weirder, like it barely makes sense to her—something she has already consigned to the distant past.

Ryder hands out new sheets of paper. "Here's your schedule," he says. "I'll be producing dailies in a couple weeks, so get practicing with the cameras. As soon as you're ready to begin shooting, go for it. You can see there are some promotional obligations too. We need to get the word out about this movie. Any questions?" He slides more pages to us. "Okay, then. Let's give this a try."

It's an entirely new scene. There's even a new character, and it's pretty obvious that she's supposed to be my sister. Before I can laugh at the craziness of having Sabrina Layton for a sister, Annaleigh starts reading. Two pages later we're pledging our love to each other.

Everything is moving too quickly, in life and on the page. A few minutes ago, my character didn't have a sister. Meanwhile, Sabrina's ex-boyfriend has declared war against me. By now, Gant will definitely know I'm front-page news, which means that Dad will probably be second-guessing himself for letting me do this film at all.

Fictional Andrew may not know what's in store, but real-life Seth feels blindsided by the present. It's a miracle I can recite my lines at all.

Ryder brings things to a close a couple hours later. As he and Brian leave I stay glued to my chair, pretending to sort the pages of our quickly evolving script.

Annaleigh stands. "So you're back," she says to Sabrina.

Sabrina nods. "I want to be a part of this."

"Me too," I say. "But after today's performance, don't be surprised if Ryder finds a new Andrew Mayhew."

"No one wins an Oscar in the rehearsal room," says Annaleigh helpfully.

Sabrina waves her hand through the air like she's cutting between scenes. "Enough about the movie. Let's go someplace."

"Thanks, but I'll pass." Annaleigh pats her camera case. "I've got some new toys to play with."

Once she's gone, it's just Sabrina and me. Last night, we were inches apart and I was nervous. Now we're several feet apart and I'm petrified.

"Just us, then," she says.

"Yeah."

She tilts her head so that her hair falls across one eye. She looks mysterious and alluring. "Good."

I follow Sabrina outside. A couple minutes later, I'm sitting in her Prius and we're pulling into traffic, heading north. It's strange to see her driving—it's something an ordinary person would do, and I can't place her in that role. I want to text Gant a play-by-play: *Sabrina signaled! Sabrina checked her rearview mirror! Sabrina CHANGED LANES!!!*

"So I hear you make a kick-ass Romeo," she says.

"Huh?" I'm still composing imaginary text messages. "Oh. Yeah, well, I guess I do better when Shakespeare writes my lines."

"You must have some weird conversations, then. Seriously, though, it's impressive that you pulled off a convincing Romeo."

As impressive as having made fifteen movies?

"Thanks. I was just playing myself really. Method acting, you know?"

"But Romeo's kind of a dork."

"Exactly." I don't know what the heck I'm saying, but I guess I'm hitting my lines, because Sabrina rewards me with a rich, throaty laugh. "So you're back in *Whirlwind,* huh?"

"Yeah," she says. "And this time I'm all in."

"What do you mean?"

"My agent didn't want me to do this movie the first time around. Didn't like the small budget and *really* didn't like the concept of actors filming each other. Said it would rob us of creative control. What he really meant was that he wouldn't be able to bully the director into using flattering camera angles if the director wasn't the one with the camera. But the way I see it, we'll have more control than ever."

We stop at a red light. Cross-traffic shunts by, a never-ending stream of vehicles.

"What did your agent say to that?" I ask.

47

"He said I was making a career-changing mistake."

"Ouch. What did you say?"

"I said it was an even bigger mistake to have an agent who doesn't get me. Then I fired him."

"*What?*"

She smiles, like this is all a big game. "It's okay. There are other agents. Trust me, I get calls every day."

The light turns green. Ahead of us, the road climbs steadily upward.

"Anyway," she continues, "the new contract's pretty much the same as the last one, and my agent already looked over that. It's not like I need someone to tell me how to sign my name."

I glance at Sabrina's slender fingers, and the wide silver bracelet perched halfway along her tanned arm, and the soft cotton of her tunic. The curve of her breasts. Her face is so famous, she'd be recognized on all seven continents.

In my mind, I text Gant an update: *In case you weren't sure, I can confirm that Sabrina Layton is HOT.*

She looks at me. "What are you thinking?"

"Uh, that's it's kind of crazy I'm driving with you."

"Why? It's just a car."

"Sure. And you're just a girl."

She frowns. "I *am*. And you're just a boy. We have more in common than you realize."

"We do?"

"Sure. We're willing to risk everything for a chance to make a new kind of movie. Most actors wouldn't do it. But you and me, we want to feel the rush of trying something different. I'm tired of sleepwalking through the same old roles."

"I've never thought you were sleepwalking."

"Yeah, you have. I saw it in your face when we were talking about *Swan Song* last night. I want to know what it's like to get nervous again, because that's being *honest,* you know? That's what this is all about—making the first really honest movie, where everyone is equal because anyone can film at any time. We can even shoot a scene without the director knowing. Just think about it, Seth—having that control, that . . . intimacy."

She looks at me, and for a moment I think she might be talking about being intimate with *me*. Then I remember that she's cast as my sister, and start laughing instead.

"What?" she asks, smiling.

"I just had a funny thought."

"Siblings making out is funny?"

I definitely need to text Gant.

Sabrina pulls over at a roadside cafe. "You hungry?"

"Yeah."

"Me too." She takes a twenty-dollar bill from her purse and hands it to me. "Can you get us sandwiches to go? There's someplace I want to take you."

We get out of the car. I'm about to head inside when I realize that she's not following. "What kind do you want?" I shout.

Sabrina peers over her shoulder, hair fluttering across her face. The sun illuminates her left side, leaving her right in mysterious shadow, and for a moment I'm right back at the party, watching her from afar, wondering if something so beautiful can possibly be real.

"I trust you, Seth," she says. "I think you know what I want."

Ten minutes later, we're back in the car. Sabrina leans over to click her seat belt and our heads almost bump. She breaks the silence with another round of laughter, her breaths laced with the odor of cigarette smoke.

It bothers me, that. Scuffs the sheen of perfection.

"Did you choose wisely?" she asks.

"I hope so, yeah. Where are we going?"

"Somewhere quiet, so I can tell you stuff that matters."

"Like what?"

"Like how sorry I am that Kris was at the party last night. If I'd known you were going to be there . . ." She starts the engine. "Some things end naturally, I guess. Others, not so much. Guess it serves me right. I've never been good at keeping friends."

We head west on Sunset Boulevard. I've driven the street before, several times, but never in my wildest dreams did I imagine making the journey with a movie star. "What about Genevieve Barron? There are thousands of photos of you two."

She raises her eyebrows. "Thousands?"

"Uh, that sounds kind of stalkerish, huh?"

"No. Knowing that Gen and I were friends doesn't qualify you for that. You'd need to know really detailed stuff. Like, how Seth Crane missed out on a Chevy commercial."

A part of me feels embarrassed; another part feels flattered that she's been checking up on me as well. "So you're a stalker too."

"No. I just like to research my costars."

"All of them?"

She covers her mouth to hide the smile. "Well, half of them."

I think we're back to flirting again.

She reaches across me and flips open the glove compartment. Removes a pair of shades and slides them on. I have to make do with squinting as we face the sun head-on.

"So you and Genevieve," I say. "Did something happen?"

She grips the wheel a little tighter. "You paparazzi now?"

"No," I say quickly. "Just finding it hard to believe anyone wouldn't want to be your friend."

"Ah. Well, there's not much to say. We did three movies together, but she wanted out. She's in college now. Doesn't make it back much." Her eyes linger on the rearview mirror. "I guess she's pretty into her studies. Or maybe she needed to get away from here."

"Why?"

Sabrina tilts her head from left to right, like she's weighing up how much to tell me. "So she can find out what real life feels like."

We continue to the end of Sunset, where the road follows the hills like switchbacks on a mountain trail. Sabrina turns right onto Pacific Coast Highway, attention split between the road and her mirror.

I turn around in my seat. "Is something back there?"

"Forest-green Mazda. It's been following us since we left the rehearsal."

The car is about fifty yards back. I can't see the driver's face behind the sun visor.

"Why would someone follow us?"

"Are you serious?" She accelerates gradually, holding the outside lane. "Your Hollywood education's about to begin, Seth Crane. And it won't be pretty."

We nudge over the speed limit. I glance at the side mirror. The car is still tailing us. "We should just pull over."

It's like she doesn't hear me.

"Seriously, Sabrina. There's no point in—"

She jerks the steering wheel to the right. We knife across two lanes and skid to a halt just off the highway. Behind a cloud of dust, the Mazda passes right by. I get a split-second view of the driver's profile—a youngish male—but not his face.

"Are you all right?" I gasp.

Sabrina's eyes are fixed on the vehicles flashing past us. "I don't like being followed."

I want to tell her it was a crazy thing to do and maybe he wasn't following us at all. But Sabrina's hands are shaking. Maybe I'd be paranoid too, if I were her.

She breathes in and out slowly. "Let's go eat."

It's reassuring to feel solid ground again. I fill my lungs with brisk, salty air, and roll up the sleeves of my shirt. Sabrina locks arms with me like it's the most natural thing in the world, and leads me to a tunnel under the highway.

We emerge onto Topanga Beach. The sun is setting over the ocean, casting long shadows of a lone couple and their dog. To the left, the lights of Santa Monica pier blink on, and beyond that, Venice. If Sabrina had planned this trip to the minute, she couldn't have picked a more beautiful time to arrive.

We stop a few yards from the water's edge and sit on the cool, hard sand. "Keep your eyes peeled," she says. "You might see dolphins."

I'm not optimistic about that. It's already twilight, nothing but the glow of the December sun as it's swallowed by the ocean.

"Do you come here a lot?" I ask.

"Used to." She coils her hair around her right hand and drapes it over her shoulder. "I don't go out much anymore."

I hand her a sandwich and she pretends to weigh it in the palm of her hand. "Vegetarian special."

"How do you know?"

"I don't. I just hoped, is all. It would mean you've read about me, and bothered to remember stuff. It would show you care." Her features, twisted and tense, relax suddenly. "Do you think we're going to be friends?"

A few minutes ago, we were laughing and flirting. Now, as we unwrap our sandwiches and eat, things feel different.

"I think that anybody who buys me food and doesn't ask for the change is my kind of person," I say.

She holds her hand out, palm open, and I give her the money. "Good. Because anyone who can be bought for twenty bucks is my kind of date."

She raises her eyebrows and takes a bite of sandwich. Then she turns to the ocean, and for several silent minutes, it's like she's forgotten I'm even here.

When we're done, I fold the wrappers and slide them into my pants pocket.

"Why did you think that Mazda was following us?" I ask.

"Because every time I looked in the mirror, it was there," she says.

"Could've been a coincidence."

"That's why I drove off the road. It happened right in front of him, but he didn't even slow down. Could you ignore something like that?"

I shake my head.

"Exactly. They never stop watching, see."

"What about now?"

"Even now." She begins to open her purse, but stops herself. Tilts her head to the left instead. "There's a guy a hundred yards away. Has a camera. Long lens. I don't imagine he's shooting the gulls at twilight."

I glance across the beach. "The camera isn't pointed at us."

She cups my elbow and pulls me to a stand. "You're sweet, Seth. I like seeing the world through your eyes."

We walk along the beach to an outcrop of rocks. Sabrina perches on one, while I take a seat on the sand beside her. She opens her clutch purse and removes cigarette papers and a pouch of tobacco.

I've never seen anyone roll a cigarette before. It's unnerving how smoothly she does it, like an actor delivering memorized lines in monotone. She licks the gummy edge of the paper and seals it, places it between her lips. "You don't approve," she says without looking at me.

I shrug. "Why do you do it?"

She removes the cigarette and stares at me. There seems to be a lot going on behind that stare. "Because it's not illegal."

"That's a pretty weird reason."

She gives a wan smile. "Point is, they don't follow me with cameras in case I do something they can write about. They do it because they have to write something. When there's no story, they make one up." She lights the cigarette with a lighter—not a disposable one either—and exhales smoke in a steady stream. "This is the closest I come to keeping control of the story."

"Okay."

"You don't believe me. That's fine—you'll learn. It doesn't end with one guy in a Mazda. Just do a little research tomorrow and you'll see this moment captured for posterity as well." With each hand gesture, the glowing tip of her cigarette slices the air. "Anyway, I don't smoke much."

"Liar." I mean it to sound kind of funny, but her eyes grow wide. "I mean, you smoked at the cafe today. You roll your own. And you have a silver lighter. There's probably an engraving on it too."

"Impressive. You sure you're not paparazzi?" She holds out the lighter and I take it. I figure it's a gift from Kris, but the engraving reads: *Love, Mom.*

"Your mom gave you a lighter?"

"Still wonder why I wanted legal emancipation?" She stares at the ocean. "That's how my parents were back then. Each trying to outdo the other—give me anything I wanted just as long as I promised to go live with them. Then they'd go to court and say all the terrible things the other was doing." She takes the lighter back. "Dad found this in my stuff along with cigarettes. Used them as evidence that Mom wasn't fit to have custody."

"How is that evidence?"

"I was fifteen."

"*Fifteen?* Your mom . . ." I swallow the comment. No need to state the obvious. "How do you have it now, if they took it as evidence?"

"Dad gave it all back to me the moment we left court. Responsible parenting one-oh-one, huh?"

I try to imagine how it must have felt to be in the middle of her parents' war. To be viewed as a winnable commodity, even as they let her hurt herself. Who could behave like that and still maintain they loved her?

"I was earning over a million dollars a year when I was fourteen," she continues. "I'd like to tell you it was a surprise to see how much my parents wanted a piece of that pie, but everyone knows that's bull. Fact is they put me in front of a camera when I was three months old. I was in four major advertising campaigns before my fifth birthday. I was almost seven before anyone realized that Mom's homeschool curriculum was nonexistent. The year I turned eight, I earned more than my parents combined. And they were responsible for all of it. They just never asked me if it's what I wanted."

"Was it what you wanted?"

"That's not relevant anymore. I was a child. I did as I was told." She bows her head, and her hair falls across her face. She doesn't sweep it away.

Sabrina says she wants us to be friends, but I still don't understand why she's telling me these things. In fact, I don't recognize this version of her at all—not from her movies, or her interviews, or her photos, and definitely not from last night.

"Can I give you some advice?" she says finally.

"Sure."

"You ever heard that Rita Hayworth saying? 'They go to bed with Gilda. They wake up with me.'"

I shake my head.

"Gilda was her most famous role. But it was just a *role*."

"I get it. You want me to separate the real you from the characters you've played."

She hesitates. "Actually, I'm not talking about me. I'm talking about you."

I press my palms against the beach. I'm focused on her every word, but I have no idea where this conversation is going. Sabrina's unpredictable, but not random. There's a point to all this.

The cigarette has gone out. She relights it, perhaps for the benefit of the camera she's certain is clicking away in the shadows. "Do you know what Rita Hayworth did wrong?" she asks.

"Became a movie star, I guess."

"No." She stares at the smoke wisping away. "She saw herself as two distinct people—the real Rita, and the one made up by screenwriters. Only, the fictional one was better. Sexier. None of the imperfections."

"And you know the solution?"

"Yeah. Go one step further. Divide yourself in three. The characters you play on-screen, the public persona, and the real you. Every time you step outside, you switch to the public persona. It's another role, true, but it's one you can keep forever. Don't let them use you, Seth. Assume you're being watched at all times. Judged. Photographed."

"Like we are now, you mean?"

"Exactly."

"Ah." I scan the horizon. The man with the camera has moved on. We're alone. "So who am I talking to at the moment? Real Sabrina? Or your public persona?"

Sabrina continues to watch her cigarette, but she doesn't smoke. Hasn't taken a single drag since she first lit it, in fact. And when her eyes drift down and lock in on mine, I know why—because I don't approve. Public persona Sabrina wouldn't care. She's showing me that I'm getting the real her. She's letting me in.

She slides off the rock and nestles against me. We stare into the blackness together. Our arms and legs and feet touch.

At last, she stubs out the cigarette. "Like I'd tell you."

9

IT'S ALMOST TEN O'CLOCK WHEN I get back to my room.
I call home so Dad will have my new phone number and know I'm
okay, but Gant says he's already asleep. "Nice photo of you in the
newspaper," he adds. "You look badass."

"Uh-huh. What did Dad say?"

"You're front-page news, bro. Dad's probably framed the picture already. Seriously, though, you want to tell me what went
down?"

"Not really."

"It's pretty weird they stuck you at a party with Kris Ellis,
right?"

Answering will only encourage him. "Not as weird as spending
this afternoon alone with Sabrina."

He's momentarily silent, and I love it. "Whoa. Back up. Sabrina
Layton?"

"Yeah."

"Why the hell would she talk to you?"

"Gee, thanks. Way to kill the vibe."

"No, it's just . . . *Sabrina Layton*." He murmurs her name like
it's a prayer. "She's so . . ."

"Cool?"

"Hot." He busts out laughing. "She *is*, though, right? It's a fact. And she's hanging out with you. Which doesn't make any sense."

"Gant!"

"No, no, no," he says. "I just mean, she quit the movie, remember?"

"And now she's back in. Says she likes the project. I think she's having some kind of crisis."

"She *told* you that?"

"Yeah. And a whole bunch of other stuff too."

"Wow." He clicks his tongue. "Last week, you were killing yourself for Juliet. Now you're Sabrina Layton's arm candy."

"We're not dating or anything."

"Whatever. It's a step up."

I like hearing Gant say this, but still . . .

"You won't mention this to anyone, right?" I say.

"Are you kidding? You just hung out with Sabrina Layton and you're afraid it'll be *me* spilling the beans?" He tsks. "It'd be a miracle if someone didn't get a photo of you together. Heck, if you'd told me you were going one-on-one, I would've come down and taken the photos myself—made some quick money."

"Ha-ha. Good night, Gant."

"Good night, Romeo."

I hang up, and scroll through the numbers on my cell. Sabrina's is there, but I don't call her. It would feel kind of stalkerish. So instead I open my laptop and pull up images: Sabrina, Sabrina and Kris, Sabrina and Genevieve.

I do a search for *Genevieve Barron*. Turns out, she's a student at California Institute of the Arts, but the only link is to a story about her transition from actor to artist. There's a quote about her needing to leave Hollywood to rediscover her "center." She thanks her parents and God for helping her on her journey.

I look up the institute's website. The campus is in Santa Clarita, only thirty miles from Los Angeles. So nearby, yet there aren't any photos of Sabrina and Genevieve together that date from the past month. Friends grow apart, I get that, but few have their separation illustrated so starkly.

It seems crazy to feel sorry for one of the most desired girls in America, but looking at all these photos, I think I finally understand why Sabrina wants to be friends with me. Together, they chronicle the people she's lost: her parents, her boyfriend, her best friend, and even her agent. Costars, love interest, and even stock characters have exited stage left. And when I scan the photos for their replacements, the ones who've won recurring cameos in her life, there's no one onstage at all.

10

I NEED TO CLEAR MY MIND, so I put on swim shorts and head for the hotel pool. It's dark outside, but the bright lights from the fitness center cast a warm glow over one end. Behind the large plate-glass windows, Annaleigh maintains a rapid pace on a treadmill. She has the metronomic, flowing gait of a seasoned runner. She also has a video camera strapped to her head.

I slip into the pool and begin swimming: four short lengths of each stroke. When I turn onto my back, the hotel looms above me, festooned in Christmas lights. My life, previously so mundane, has become a fairy tale.

When I switch to breaststroke again I realize that I'm not alone. Annaleigh sits on the edge of the pool, legs swishing through the water. She's changed into a two-piece swimsuit. The underwater lights give her an ethereal appearance. Well, except for the head-cam.

"I don't think treadmill footage is going to win many Oscars," I say.

"Hmm. What about footage of a naked Seth Crane?"

"I'm not naked."

"That's hard to tell from where I'm sitting."

A man emerges from the hotel, sees us, and stops. "Is that a, uh, camera?" he asks, staring at Annaleigh.

"Sure is," she says. "We're movie stars, see."

"I can't believe you don't recognize us," I add.

In the moment before he turns around and leaves, I'd say the guy looks a little freaked out.

Annaleigh grins. "Can't believe he didn't recognize us, huh?"

"You're the one who said we're movie stars," I point out.

"'Cause we are. Could be a while before anyone knows it, though."

"Hmm. We need to make headlines."

"You could try starting a fight with Kris Ellis. Oh no, wait—you already did!"

"Kris is small-fry. I need a bigger target." I smack the water. "I'm going to take down Hollywood!"

Annaleigh whistles. "Wow. You do think big." She removes the headcam and offers it to me. "Remind me not to get in your way."

While I adjust the strap, she pushes off from the edge and slides into the pool. She ducks down, and swims a length underwater. Beams of light dance around her like flames. When she reaches the end, she does a tuck-turn and continues back toward me without stopping to breathe.

She surfaces beside me. I expect her to gasp for air, but she doesn't. "Penny for your thoughts," she says. She sweeps her short hair back. It's spiky, but cute.

"I was just thinking: How can any of this be real? Why *me*, you know?"

"Yeah, I know."

"I've lived near here all of high school, but everyone knows there's two Hollywoods. There's the place where Muggles walk around on sidewalks and cars drive bumper to bumper, and there's the magical Hollywood, where people's faces are on billboards a hundred feet tall, and anything can happen."

She thinks about this for a moment. "Did you really just go all Harry Potter on me?"

"I think so, yes."

"Hmm." She puts her hand over her mouth to cover the grin. "I see your point, though. It's hard to believe this is real."

"So what about you?" I ask. "What are *you* thinking about?"

She points toward the top of the hotel. "I'm thinking that penthouse up there is where Richard Gere and Julia Roberts got cozy in *Pretty Woman*."

I follow her finger. "No way. My dad loves that movie."

"All dads love that movie. Or maybe it's just Julia Roberts they love."

"Do you blame them?"

She rolls her eyes. "Don't get me started." She smiles again, but her expression is serious. "Do you believe in that whole Pygmalion, ugly-duckling-turns-beautiful-swan thing?"

"I don't know. I mean, *Pretty Woman* is hardly trying to be real, right? But yeah, I do think people become more beautiful the longer you know them."

"Really? The way I see it, most people can hide their flaws for a while, but eventually the truth comes out."

If she's talking about Sabrina, she's wrong. I know now that

Sabrina's not perfect, but she's more fascinating than ever.

"Here," says Annaleigh, swimming close. "My turn again." She eases the camera over my head, her fingers running through my hair. A few seconds later, the lens is pointed at me. "So did you and Sabrina hook up today?"

"What?"

She wields an imaginary microphone. "It's what all our viewers want to know."

I splash her. Then I remember Brian telling us not to test the waterproof capabilities of the camera.

"I would've hooked up with her, if I were you," continues Annaleigh.

"And if you weren't me?"

"I would've hooked up with Kris instead."

"After what he did at the party?"

"We're talking about hooking up, not getting married. Anyway, since we're at Hogwarts, I'd just use a memory charm on him afterward to make him forget. Wouldn't want him to go all stalker on me."

"Is that a problem for you normally?"

"Absolutely. Ex-boyfriends trail me around like puppy dogs."

"Maybe you smell like bacon."

She busts out laughing. "That is the weirdest thing I've heard in years. I'm so glad I'm filming. This is going straight on YouTube."

"What?"

"Kidding! What happens at Hogwarts, stays at Hogwarts."

She climbs out of the pool. Grabs a couple towels and tosses one to me as I join her. Lays the camera gently on a deck chair.

"I'm sorry I didn't come with you and Sabrina this afternoon," she says. "To be honest, she kind of intimidates me."

"She's cool."

"Yeah. She and Kris were the coolest, most beautiful couple in all of Hollywood. Makes you wonder what went wrong between them."

I wrap the towel around me. Annaleigh does the same. The air is chilly, but neither of us moves.

"Hey, we're going to look out for each other, right?" she says finally.

"Yeah. Definitely."

"Promise?" She holds out her closed fist.

I bump it. "Promise."

11

WE SPEND THE MORNING REHEARSING, AND the improvement is dramatic. Ryder sits at the head of the conference table, nodding like a bobblehead doll as we nail scripted lines and improvise others. The only downside is that Sabrina isn't around to see it. Or maybe that's the reason things go so well.

After three hours, two bottles of water, and a cup of coffee, Ryder wraps things up.

"Is Sabrina all right?" I ask.

"Sure," he says. "We just felt there was no need for her to be here today. There's only so much she can do until things change."

Annaleigh and I glance at each other. I don't know what Sabrina thinks needs to *change*, and I'm not sure I want to.

Ryder drops us at the hotel at one p.m. Five minutes later, he texts me instructions to pair the white shirt with the gray sports coat, and the blue jeans with the white Converse sneakers.

This afternoon's theme is preppy.

He arrives at my room at two fifteen p.m., a full forty-five minutes before the press junket is due to start. Casting a critical eye over my appearance, he awards me two thumbs-up. Since he told me exactly what to wear, I don't know whether to be flattered or relieved.

"And you'll change into black for the party later," he says.

I point to the suit already hanging beside the closet.

"Great. It's going be at the headquarters of Machinus Media Enterprises. Curt's a big deal there, so this is our chance to draw some attention to the movie. Get people noticing you, and talking about you. Kind of like this press junket." He furrows his brow. "You okay?"

"Just nervous."

"Yeah. Look, I need you to remember something, Seth: Every actor, actress, director, producer, composer, cinematographer . . . hell, every single crew member had to start somewhere, right? Literally, there was a project where they went from being new to being professional. I bet a lot of them had doubts the whole time they were filming, but the ones who make it are the ones who keep going, no matter what."

He joins me on the sofa and leans forward, elbows on knees. "Everyone at this junket believes you were cast for a reason. Your job is to show them, *Hell yeah, there's a reason I was cast.* So for the next couple hours, I want you to put your true self aside and create an alter ego—good-looking, talented actor who's about to take the world by storm. Okay?"

"Okay," I tell him, because that's what he wants to hear. Behind his pep talk is a message, though: He needs me to create an alter ego because real Seth isn't cutting it. "Actually, Sabrina said something like that—about dividing yourself into different people."

"Well, if anyone would know, it's her." He makes eye contact, but breaks it quickly. "When did she tell you that?"

"Yesterday. We went for a drive."

"Interesting."

"What is?"

He produces a closed-mouth smile. "We never wanted Sabrina to pull out of the movie. I asked her to come to Curt's house so I could sell her on rejoining. But after our conversation she was still totally on the fence. Then she meets you. Next morning, she's ready to sign on the dotted line." He pats me on the shoulder. "So tell me, is that a coincidence? Or does Sabrina Layton see the same promise in you that I do?"

The press junket is in the aptly named Champagne Room. Chandeliers hang from the ceiling and crystal sconces adorn the walls. Annaleigh's eyes are as wide as mine. I wonder if she's thinking of that movie *Pretty Woman* again. I can totally empathize with a rags-to-riches story right about now.

Ryder leads us to a narrow table on a stage. Annaleigh sits to my right, Sabrina to my left. Mine is the only seat without a microphone.

In an ideal world, I'd create an alter ego who savors the improbability of being sandwiched between two hot girls. But as Ryder introduces the movie and us with a prepared statement, real Seth just feels freaked out. It doesn't help that Brian is standing sentry at the back of the room, looking like a disgruntled bouncer.

There must be fifty people here. Most of them are reporters, I guess, but some are photographers. Sabrina exchanges a nod with half of the front row as if they're longtime friends. One of the front-row attendees raises her hand. "Kind of strange to have the junket before you've started filming, isn't it?" she asks Sabrina.

Sabrina turns to me, eager to share the limelight. But her hand rests on the base of the microphone, and so it's Annaleigh's mic I drag toward me. "It's, uh . . . well, it's a different kind of movie," I say, my voice booming around the room.

The reporter never takes her eyes off Sabrina. "Different, how?"

"We're being given unprecedented control," Sabrina explains. "Not just over character development and dialogue, but even the filming itself. Being here today, talking to you, it's like we're going on record. This movie is a process, see? Today's plan for the movie could change tomorrow. We want witnesses to that evolution."

"You want *witnesses*?" The woman snorts. She's clearly not a card-carrying member of the Sabrina Layton fan club.

But I'm beginning to understand what drew Sabrina back to this movie. "I think what Sabrina's saying is that everything's going to affect a movie that's as real as this," I explain. "If we're behind the cameras, deciding when and where and how to film, the real world is going to matter." I picture the photo of me and Kris. "People getting in the way of what we're doing is going to matter."

A new reporter raises her hand. "So you're asking people to stay away?"

"No," says Sabrina quickly. She smiles at me like we're explain-ing a problem to a bunch of particularly dense kids. "We're saying the audience will own this movie like never before, because they'll literally have played a role in what it is." She's excited now, all bristling energy and unshakable confidence, the polar opposite of the melancholy, introspective girl on the beach. "Look, Seth and I can't just block off a street when we want to film each other. People'll be able to get on frame, say stuff, screw around with us. And yeah, it might piss us off," she admits, chuckling, "but you've got to admit, it doesn't get any more real that that."

Our audience looks just as confused as before, but their eyes flit between Sabrina and me now. She has identified us as a team. Perhaps that's why the next reporter points his pen at Annaleigh.

"So you're the love interest, then, Anna," he says flatly.

"Annaleigh," she says. But the microphone is still facing me, so her voice is lost. After a long moment, she slides it closer. "Annaleigh," she tries again. "And yeah, I'm one-half of the couple."

"What can you tell us about your character?"

"Well, my name's Lana. I guess you'd say I'm from the wrong side of the tracks. I've been kind of beaten down, but then I meet Seth . . . I mean, Andrew. He's the good guy. Brings me out of my shell." She shakes her head, disappointed by her answer. "The movie's so much more than that, though. It's about trying to do the right thing and still getting it wrong. The way we're trapped by things we can't control—events, family . . . love. Seth's right," she adds. "Audiences are going to connect with it because it's going to feel scarily real."

Actually, Sabrina was first to say it, but I think Annaleigh knows that.

"Scarily real," the guy repeats. "Are you speaking personally? Because it must be intimidating to be playing this particular role, right?"

"When it's your first movie, everything's intimidating."

"But to be playing opposite Sabrina . . ."

Annaleigh shrugs. "Sabrina's a great actress. We're thrilled to have her on board."

"But this was her role, right?"

"*Was*, yes."

"And that doesn't freak you out? To be playing against someone like that?"

She almost bites her thumbnail, but stops herself. "Okay, yeah, sure . . . it's intimidating."

"We went over some material yesterday," interjects Sabrina, "and Annaleigh's great for this role."

"Better than you would've been?" asks a woman at the back.

Sabrina raises her hands like she's surrendering, but she doesn't answer.

"So what *is* your role, Sabrina?"

"I'm Andrew's best friend. His very *possessive* best friend." Sabrina links arms with me, and raises one perfectly arched eyebrow. "It won't require much acting, let me tell you."

Everyone in the audience laughs. Cameras flash. Flirting is good for business.

"You mean *sister*." I whisper the words, but I'm leaning toward her, so the microphone picks them up.

"Best friend," Sabrina insists. She turns to the audience. "I met with the director first thing this morning and told him that a best friend would add layers of complexity that a sister doesn't. This is exactly why I want to be in the movie. To feel like I'm creating a character instead of *re*-creating her, if that makes sense."

Sabrina's on a roll again, volleying questions with a dash of self-deprecating humor and a million-dollar smile. Our arms are still linked, which means that I'm a part of every photograph. She looks at me constantly, as if she's speaking for both of us. And I almost give in to it, the fantasy that I'm no longer Seth Crane. That I'm Andrew Mayhew, and I'm destined to love and be loved. To be a hero.

But Annaleigh is beside me too. Out of frame and out of the discussion. She seems smaller than before, a bulb that grows dimmer as Sabrina's light shines brighter. Like the pivot of a teeter-totter, I watch one girl rise and one girl fall.

Ryder closes the junket on a high note. Leaves the reporters wanting more.

"Great job," he tells us, slapping the table. "You nailed it."

He's right. The press got value for money today. But ever since Sabrina dropped her *best friend* bombshell, Annaleigh hasn't said a word. Now Brian is glaring at Annaleigh from his place at the back of the room. Maybe Ryder should give her the same pep talk that he gave me.

Maybe he already did.

We step into an anteroom. It's quiet here. There are no cameras or questions. No one seems relaxed, though.

"Mind if we talk, Sabrina?" Ryder asks. He flicks his head toward another room. "In private."

"Sure." Sabrina turns to me and pulls me into a hug. "See you at the party tonight, okay?"

She leaves before I can answer.

Annaleigh's leaving too, but by a different door. "Hey, you okay?" I call after her.

She stops. "Yeah."

"Good." There's an awkward silence. "Do you want to . . . I don't know . . . talk?"

She tilts her head back and closes her eyes. "What's there to say? This morning, Sabrina's character was your sister. Now she's your *possessive* best friend." She makes air quotes for the last words. "I wonder what best girlfriends get to do to you that sisters don't."

"I guess Ryder's trying to add dramatic tension," I say, aiming for lighthearted.

"Then he'd better buckle up, 'cause there's going to be plenty of that." She gives an imitation of a triumphant smile, but I'm not fooled.

"Sabrina's not going to take your role, Annaleigh."

"Maybe she doesn't have to. Remember what Ryder said at the rehearsal this morning? About how Sabrina will be skipping rehearsals until things change. I don't think he was talking about our acting. I think he's rewriting the script for her."

"So what? We can change the script, remember? We can improvise our lines. We're the actors here, not Ryder."

"And he's the director. Which means he can leave every last scene on the cutting room floor." She points to the room next door, where Ryder and Sabrina are talking in private. "Come on, Seth. If that junket made one thing clear, it's that there's only one real star here. And it sure as hell isn't you or me."

12

ANNALEIGH IS LATE. SO IS RYDER. I stand in the lobby, shadow-like in a tailored black suit, watching people glide past as if I'm not even here.

There's only one real star here. And it sure as hell isn't you or me.

My phone rings.

It's Ryder. "Something's come up," he says, voice breathy. "I'm going to be late getting to the party. Brian and Tracie can't make it either."

"Is everything all right?"

"Yeah. It's good news, but I can't say anything yet. You'll be fine, right?"

The last time I attended a party, I ended up on the front page of a newspaper. I can't do any worse than that. "Sure," I say.

I hang up as Annaleigh draws alongside me, stylish in a moody, all-black ensemble: satin shirt, tailored pants, and pumps. Ryder wants us to match, I guess.

"Our chaperone just ditched us," I tell her.

"What happens now?"

"Well, since there's no one to watch out for you, I take advantage of your innocence by linking arms and making idle chitchat."

"Sounds scandalous. Don't tell me: Then you cast me aside."

"You'll be soiled goods."

"No one'll marry me."

"*Tsk*. Guys!"

"Yes," she says, linking arms anyway. "Guys."

We head out to the waiting limo. Safely inside, Annaleigh rests her head against the window. It's a wide backseat, and there's a lot of real estate between us.

"I was worried about you this afternoon," I say. "You seemed . . ."

"Depressed?" She reaches for her neck again, for the long hair I'm pretty sure she used to have. "I'm fine. That stuff about Sabrina being your friend instead of your sister caught me by surprise, is all."

"She said you're great in the lead role, though."

"Based on one read-through."

"Sometimes once is enough. I only saw you on the treadmill for a moment last night, but I can tell you run track."

"Uh-uh. I just run by myself. I do it to get out of the house mostly. That's why I started acting too—so I have something to do when the days are short." She lowers her voice. "When I'm in a play, I can go almost a full day without being at home."

She peers up at me, which is how I realize that I'm sitting very straight. I had her pegged as a classic overachiever—fit, smart, motivated—and now I realize that it isn't just her accent that she's been keeping under wraps.

"Is home so bad?"

She bites a fingernail. "It's complicated. My parents and me, we don't get along. The things my dad does . . ." She shakes her head, closes the book so soon after opening it. "What about you? Why do you act?"

I'm still clinging to her confession, wanting to know more, which is probably why my answer is unguarded. "It's the only time people really notice me. Most of the time I feel like my dad and brother and me, we're completely invisible. Like, nothing that happens to us can ever move the needle for anyone else."

"But it's different when you're acting."

"Yeah. When I'm onstage, everyone watches. They don't even see Seth Crane. They see whatever character I'm playing, and the character *matters* to them, you know? I want to feel like everything I do and say—every single moment—really matters."

The limo slows down. Cameras flash through the closed tinted windows.

"You're not in character now," she says, "and the cameras are waiting for you anyway."

I get out and wrap an arm around Annaleigh protectively. I try to carve a swath through the hustling photographers, but they're reluctant to move aside. Their flashes burn white spots at the center of my eyes.

No wonder Sabrina told me to divide myself in three. If this is what it feels like to *matter*, it's not what I expected. Onstage I'm in control no matter how bright and hot the spotlights, but here I'm a patient on a gurney as a team of surgeons examine every part of me. They're invasive and unapologetic. I belong to them now.

Annaleigh startles me by putting her hand in mine. "This way," she says, taking charge.

Machinus Media Enterprises is housed in a large open-space industrial building. A cacophony of modern art hangs over concrete walls. The music is loud and the mood lighting is low, as if everyone prefers to exist in a state of perpetual twilight. I recognize their faces anyway, though, because there are celebrities here—teens and adults, actors and musicians. They linger at the bar in the center of the room, and huddle in the nooks and crannies that fan out from the corners.

I remind myself what Ryder said about getting people to notice me, but I'm not about to introduce myself to strangers. Maybe I should follow Gant's advice instead: *Celebrity autographs sell great on eBay!*

"What are you smiling about?" asks Annaleigh.

"I was just thinking, I'm so out of my league."

"We," she corrects. "*We* are so out of our league."

My cell phone chimes. I hope it's Ryder, our personal choreographer, offering directions for how to behave, but the text message is anonymous: *Get a drink, imposter.*

I tense up. I don't like that word—*imposter*—and I especially don't like that it's anonymous. Only a few people know this number.

I look around the room, but the only person I recognize is Curt Barrett, our financier, and he's too busy schmoozing to send a text. As our eyes meet, he peels away from his entourage and joins us.

Like a busy maitre d' Curt introduces us to people whose names I instantly forget, and some whose names I've known for years—a reality TV host, an award-winning character actor, a former child star. An official-looking photographer records every introduction.

Curt steers us toward a tall guy with long hair. "You've already met Kris Ellis, haven't you?"

Kris tilts his head. "Don't I know you from somewhere?" he asks me.

He's flanked by at least half a dozen guys, all of them watching me. I recognize a few from TV shows, but not the others. They shadow him as closely as bodyguards.

As I gawk at the entourage, Annaleigh steps forward. "We haven't met," she says. "I'm Annaleigh."

"I know who you are." A smile pulls at the corner of Kris's mouth. "Interesting junket this afternoon. I kept thinking: I wish I could see more of the female lead."

Annaleigh blushes. "You would've seen plenty of her if you and Sabrina hadn't dropped out."

"I'm just saying, when it comes to junkets, people often say too much. Sometimes less is more."

"And more is less, yeah. Which one am I, by the way? More, or less."

Kris knows she's teasing him, but he laughs anyway. And once he laughs, his posse laughs too. Difference is, they're all still looking at me, not Annaleigh.

"So," says Annaleigh. "You got any career advice for us?"

Kris looks at Curt loitering a few yards away and lowers his voice. "Sure. Curt Barrett is a visionary. If he's putting up the money for this movie, he clearly believes in it. Don't do anything to change his mind."

"You mean, like dropping out without warning?" I ask.

Kris flexes his jaw muscles. "Exactly."

"He still invited you here tonight, though."

"You might say we made up." On cue, Kris's entourage laughs like well-trained dogs. "But you're not me. Not everyone deserves a second chance."

My phone chimes again, startling me. I glance at the screen: *Smile for the cameras.*

None of Kris's guys has a cell phone out, so they can't be sending the texts. Plenty of other people around the room have phones out, but I don't know any of them.

"Is everything okay?" Annaleigh whispers.

I don't want to freak her out. "Yeah . . . fine."

"Seth, Annaleigh," booms Curt, rejoining us. He's clearly anxious that we remain within his gravitational pull. "I don't think you've met Tamara."

Kris peels away as the new arrival steps up.

"Tamara Pelham," she says, shaking our hands. She has the angular face and dramatic makeup of a model. "You're the ones in *Whirlwind*." She runs a finger around the rim of her wineglass. "Tell me, what's it like working with Sabrina?"

"She's a talented actress," says Annaleigh, staying close to me.

"Actress, yes. Must be hard to know where you stand with her."

"That's kind of the point of semi-improvised drama, right?" I say.

Tamara smiles, but it doesn't reach her eyes. "You two are cute. Funny too," she adds like we're part of the evening's entertainment.

"Funny's good." I turn to Annaleigh. "Don't you think so?"

"Absolutely. Almost as good as a drink. Want one?"

"Sure."

As Annaleigh leaves, Tamara's eyes drift over my shoulder. "Time for me to go too, I think."

She steps away as Sabrina arrives, like a partner cutting in during a dance. Did Annaleigh see Sabrina coming? Is that why she left?

Annaleigh and I aren't the only ones who have had another wardrobe change. Sabrina's black cocktail dress ends well above her knees. She's wearing her game face too: teasing lipstick smile, eyes dark and smoky.

"Well, if it isn't my favorite costar." She kisses me on the cheek. "I trust you weren't taken in by the competition."

"Competition?"

She locks our arms and leads me away. Guests raise cell phones to capture the image of us together, hips touching, perfectly in stride.

"Did Tamara get what she was after?" Sabrina continues, ignoring my question.

"What was she after?"

"Oh . . . news. Information." She leans in close. "She's the model Kris has been seeing in secret since we broke up."

So that's what Sabrina means by "competition"—for *Kris.* "Why is it a secret?"

"Because he likes to keep his options open. Plus, she's engaged."

"*What?* Does anyone know she's seeing Kris?"

"Sure. But no one will say a word. In this business, the moment you start shooting your mouth off is the moment you put yourself next in the firing line."

Guests turn to face us, cell phones at the ready. They stand in a bunch, wearing identical alcoholic smiles. All except for a young curly-haired guy on the left. He keeps one phone aloft as he talks on another. He isn't even watching us, which makes me think he's filming us, not photographing.

Sabrina tugs my arm and we keep moving.

"What about the press?" I ask. "Do they know about Kris and Tamara?"

"Maybe. But you don't make money by revealing gossip on Twitter. You make it in an exposé—something with good sources, so you're safe if anyone sues for defamation or slander." Does she memorize this stuff, or is it the kind of thing you learn from a life spent in Hollywood? "Anyway, they're safe for now."

Safe seems an odd choice of word, but I don't ask her about it. We're almost to the back of the building, and the crowd has thinned out. Even the official photographer seems reluctant to follow. Presumably he likes to stay where the action is.

"I thought we'd be having our rehearsals here," says Sabrina.

"In this room?"

"No, in one of the rooms next door. It's where Kris and I had read-throughs. But Ryder wants a closed shop. Says it'll be easier to keep the dailies under wraps if we're in our own building."

We round a corner and are completely alone. The corridor is narrow and poorly lit. I think I prefer Ryder and Brian's office to this place.

"I wasn't sure you were coming tonight," I say.

"Think I'd miss a chance to see what outfit Ryder laid out for you?" She obviously means it to sound funny, and her smile flattens out when she sees my reaction. "I'm sorry. That came out wrong. Although," she adds, "you've looked pretty uncomfortable ever since you got here."

"So it was you who sent the texts, huh?"

"What texts?" The question sounds sincere. But of course it would—Sabrina's an actress.

She breaks eye contact. Famous or not, she looks shy, demure as she bites her lip. "Forget what I said just now. The clothes look fantastic on you. *You* look fantastic. That dimple on your left cheek, the way you smile with your eyes and try to tame that cowlick—it's all just so . . . *real*."

At the beach yesterday, she could hardly lift her eyes from the ground. Now they rove, taking in every part of me. In the whole crowded building, Sabrina has found the most private place to talk. It's impossible not to wonder why.

My body is rigid, but my thoughts race. Why does she like me when she hardly knows me? Am I a rebound? A way to get back at Kris? What if we're photographed? I don't ask any of these questions, though. As long as I'm face-to-face with Sabrina, I can live without answers.

She leans forward, lips almost touching my ear. "I need to use the ladies' room, but you'll wait for me." Her voice rises at the end, but I'm not fooled—it's a statement, not a question.

She's absolutely right too.

Sabrina rakes her fingers across my chest as she disappears around the corner.

I wait for several minutes, rooted to the spot. Servers pass me, carrying trays of empty glasses. They cast suspicious looks. Without Sabrina beside me, I feel conspicuously alone.

My phone chimes again: *She's playing you.*

The words jolt me. Sabrina would never send this text. But then, who did?

I turn the corner and survey the room.

Annaleigh rushes over. "Where have you been?"

"I was talking to Sabrina." I look past Annaleigh, but there are so many people, and so many phones.

"You needed some privacy, huh?" She doesn't sound amused.

"We were just talking. What's going on?"

"Maggie's here. Remember Maggie? From the office? We had an interesting chat. Ryder sent her because he's busy rewriting the script."

"For Sabrina?"

"No, Seth. Not Sabrina. Turns out we've got another new cast member. Brian and Tracie are working on the contract right now."

I try to stay cool, but I can see in her eyes that this is big. "Who is it?"

"Ryder seems to think I need a best friend too. Says it'll provide symmetry. You know, because Sabrina and you are BFFs." She sounds exasperated. "Speak of the devil . . ."

I force myself not to turn around. I'm playing catch-up here, and from the way Annaleigh is staring at me, I know there's more to come.

"Who's been cast, Annaleigh?"

She gives a rueful smile. "Kris Ellis."

13

"WHAT DID I MISS?" SABRINA ASKS.

She rests her fingers provocatively on my arm. I stare at her hand, the black polish carefully applied to each fingernail, and feel only the wrongness of everything: Kris's casting, the anonymous text messages.

I expect Annaleigh to say something, but she's already heading toward the bar and Kris. Is she about to argue with him, or is she hoping to make a good impression on her newest costar?

Sabrina slides her hand under my arm and pulls me around, her eyes dancing, cheeks flushed.

"Was it you who got Kris back into the movie?" I ask as she leads me back to our secluded nook.

"Yeah." She stands closer to me than before. Her impossibly dark eyes keep roaming, never fixing on me. "It's just a small part."

"Until you can get your original roles back, you mean."

"What?"

"If you and Kris are getting back together, you should just be honest about it."

The corner of her mouth twists upward in a smirk. "Wake

85

up, Seth. If I wanted Annaleigh's role, I'd ask for it." She nods at my shocked expression. "You heard what they were saying at the junket. You saw all those people photographing us just now too. How many people took photos of you and Annaleigh, huh?"

I hate her for saying that. It's true that Annaleigh and I hardly make a ripple in this sea of celebrities and socialites, but I never thought Sabrina would lord it over us. Will anyone even remember us when Ryder presents Sabrina and Kris as a package deal again?

"This is our big break, Sabrina."

"I know." She squeezes my arm. "Relax, okay? Everything will work out."

I can't shake the feeling that I'm a bit player in Sabrina's elaborate plot.

"You trust me, right?" she says. "I opened up to you. Told you everything."

She's wrong about that. The Sabrina who sat with me on the beach told me everything, but that vulnerable girl has gone now. This version of Sabrina seems distant and untouchable. I feel like I'm watching her cycle through her three personas.

She runs her hand behind my head and pulls me in for a kiss. Coils her leg around me, so that our hips touch. For a few moments, I silence the voices in my head. Shut out the doubts. Sabrina is so freaking beautiful, and we're kissing.

"See?" she says, biting her lip. "You've got to learn to trust me."

She makes it sound like a threat, as if there's a price for crossing her. I don't think it's a coincidence that this entire scene is playing out in a darkened corner where no one will see us.

A clattering sound to the right distracts me. A middle-aged woman apologizes as the curly-haired guy retrieves his phone from the floor. When he straightens, he glances over and sees me watching. He slides the phone away and leaves.

"I think he was filming us," I say.

"Let it go," Sabrina mutters. "These guys'll drive you crazy."

"Crazy enough to skid off the road? That guy in the car yesterday was just following us. This one's *filming* us."

"So what? Hundreds of people here have cameras."

Yesterday she was paranoid about a photographer one hundred yards away. Today someone films us kissing, and she blows it off. It doesn't seem to occur to her that I might have an opinion about this too. This isn't the same as sitting side by side on the beach. How much of our kiss did he get? What does he plan to do with the images?

I expect the guy to head toward the bar, where he can blend in. Instead he's making for the nearest exit. Who shows up to a party alone, and leaves by the side door?

"Send any texts recently?" I call out to him.

I'm not expecting him to react at all, let alone look anxiously over his shoulder. But as our eyes meet, he runs.

Instinctively I chase him.

He opens the emergency exit, which triggers an alarm. I remember Brian warning me to stay out of trouble, but I don't plan to stick around and explain to security that it wasn't me. I follow the guy into an alleyway. He's twenty yards ahead, his footsteps echoing against the sheer brick walls to either side. At the end, he turns left onto a street and I lose sight of him.

By the time I get there he's gone.

I place my hands on my knees and catch my breath. From the right, someone shouts my name. A camera flash blinds me. Like insects drawn to bright light, other photographers close in.

I'm about to run again when a car pulls out from a nearby parking spot. I probably wouldn't notice at all, except that the car lights aren't on.

I walk toward the vehicle. Maybe I'm crazy, but everything feels connected in this moment: Sabrina's behavior, the news about Kris, the mysterious texts, and the curly-haired guy who's been filming us. Just before I get there, the car pulls into traffic, tires squealing.

It's the forest-green Mazda.

"Seth!" A woman's voice this time, but I don't turn around. I'm too busy staring at the car's taillights.

Maggie stands beside me. "What are you doing out here? Did you open the emergency exit door?"

"No. It was someone else."

She shepherds me back to the entrance as photographers swarm around us. The bouncers wave us through.

"What's going on?" Maggie asks.

"Is it true about Kris?"

She sighs. "It's complicated."

"No kidding."

I just want to check that Annaleigh's okay and get the hell out. But Annaleigh's not at the bar with Kris. Sabrina is.

She's holding court, surrounded by celebrities. Kris stays close, his hand on her arm. It's like watching a replay of our first meeting: Sabrina, flirty and ravishing; Kris, overbearing and possessive. Only this time she doesn't look like she needs rescuing. Actually, they seem perfect together—relaxed and beautiful and back in the spotlight, as Tamara observes them from across the bar.

Earlier I felt uncomfortable, but this is worse—like walking into high school on the first day of freshman year, the new kid from Ohio intruding on cliques formed months or years ago. There's no room for me here.

I'm about to leave, when Kris's voice carries clear across the room. "Seth. Wait up!"

I turn away, but he jogs up behind me.

"Hey," he says, grabbing my arm. "Where are you going?" His fingers dig into the flesh as I wrench my arm away.

"To find Annaleigh," I say.

"She already left. Looked pissed too. What did you do to her?"

"Nothing. You know damn well why she left."

He smiles. "I think you're imagining things. Hollywood's a stressful place, I get it."

"You think you're untouchable."

"And I think you and your babysitter ought to get on home. It's got to be past curfew."

"She's not my babysitter."

"Well, I sure as shit hope she's not your date." He flicks his eyes toward her. "Nice dress, by the way. Takes guts to wear something like that."

Maggie peers down at her dress, shapeless and bright, a blinding contrast to the tailored darkness of the other women's attire. Even in the low light it's obvious that she's blushing.

I want to hit Kris so bad. I want to *hurt* him. But as I step forward Sabrina hustles over and wedges herself between us. She shoves a hand into our chests, looking at each of us in turn. Then, with an angry grunt, she continues toward the exit. Everyone falls silent as she leaves.

"Please, Seth," says Maggie. She seems close to tears. "Let's just go."

Kris's friends at the bar regard me with superior expressions. They know I can't win. Kris has the press on his side, as well as legions of fans and a personal entourage.

What do I have?

I lock arms with Maggie and escort her from the building. Only one photographer is there to capture us, his apologetic flash like the last dying ember of a fire. All the rest are pursuing Sabrina.

Who can blame them?

14

MAGGIE'S CAR IS PARKED A COUPLE blocks away. I
arrived in a limo, but I'll be leaving in a beat-up Chevy. If this is a
metaphor for the evening, it's not very subtle.

There's a child's car seat in the back. "Do you have a kid?" I ask.

She turns the keys and the car coughs to life. "Yeah."

We pull onto a busy street I don't recognize. Outside my window the L.A. lights blur together. There's an almost liquid quality
to everything.

"Are they going to get rid of me, Maggie?"

Her face creases like she's hurt. "No."

"I figured Ryder would be pissed at Sabrina and Kris for dropping out. Now he's doing anything to get them back in the movie."

"I'm sorry. I know it doesn't seem fair."

"I'm sorry too," I say. "The way they treated you tonight . . ."

She takes a deep breath. "I knew it'd suck."

"So why were you there?"

"Are you serious? After what happened between you and Kris
the other night? Brian wanted someone to keep an eye on you,
and he and Ryder and Tracie were all busy. Hell, I couldn't even
keep you out of trouble." She slams her palm against the steer-

ing wheel. "I told Brian I didn't want to go. He said it'd be fun, but that's what people always say when they don't know how bad things can get. There's a reason some of us want a life *behind* the camera. I don't belong at swanky Hollywood parties, especially not when I'm wearing the lamest dress in L.A."

"Kris was out of line."

"It wasn't just Kris. Even the bouncer wouldn't let me in until I put Ryder on the phone. When I got inside, no one spoke to me. Literally, people turned away."

I lean back in the seat. "I hated it too."

"Is that why you ran out?"

"No. I was chasing this guy who's been following Sabrina and me."

Maggie leans hard on the gas pedal, and the car jolts. "Someone's been following you?"

"Yeah. He tailed us yesterday. And then he was at the party tonight. I recognized his car."

She huffs. "This is so wrong."

"What is?"

"Everything. My whole life, I've been obsessed with movies. They're the ultimate escape from reality. But now I'm in the middle of the drama, watching assholes like Kris Ellis take over. Him and Sabrina Layton—some freaking team."

"They're not even supposed to be a team anymore," I say angrily. "He's seeing Tamara Pelham."

"What?" She puffs out her cheeks. "Tamara's engaged. An investment banker in New York, I think. Son of some European aristocratic family."

"She looks kind of young to be engaged."

"Nineteen. Same as Kris."

"I can't imagine . . ." *Getting engaged at nineteen,* I'm about to say. But maybe that's how this new world works: the impulse to forge bonds, followed immediately by the need to break them. No wonder everyone looks past me to the soap opera world of the Sabrina Laytons and the Kris Ellises. They're so much more compelling.

The valet at the Beverly Wilshire raises an eyebrow as Maggie pulls up. Not many rusty Chevys idling outside the hotel, I guess.

"Thanks for the ride," I say.

"You're welcome." Maggie flicks the keys dangling from the ignition. "You know, before Annaleigh left, she told me about you and Sabrina."

"Which Sabrina's that?"

She thinks I'm playing it cool, but I'm not. I don't have a clue who Sabrina is anymore, let alone what she's up to.

"Watch out for yourself, Seth."

As the old Chevy pulls away, filling the air with exhaust fumes, Maggie's words play over in my mind. I need to do more than watch out. I need to keep my distance. Sabrina is a star—get too close and I'll surely be burned.

15

THE REHEARSAL IS SCHEDULED FOR TEN a.m. At nine thirty, Ryder sends a text canceling it.

I go to the office anyway. I want to check that Maggie's okay. I also want to tell Ryder and Brian what Kris said to her last night.

Yes, I'm tattling. No, I don't feel bad about it.

Ryder answers the door. "You got my text?" he asks. I nod. "Yeah. Sorry for the late notice, but our cast is in flux."

My first thought is that Annaleigh has quit, but surely she wouldn't. And there's no way Ryder would kick her off the movie the day after the junket. Which leaves Sabrina. She was angry last night. Is she ditching the project again?

"I'm sorry," I say. "Are you going to replace her?"

"*Her?*"

"Sabrina."

"This is about Kris, not Sabrina. Seems he's been seeing Tamara Pelham, and the press got wind of it."

Across the room, Brian spins his chair around to face me. "She's engaged," he snaps. "Some rich guy who wants to make life real uncomfortable for Kris. So he's pulled out of the movie. Again!"

I feel like I did at the party, two steps behind. Did Sabrina leak this news to get back at Kris? No, she said it herself: Revenge is a dangerous game to play when you've got something to lose.

The main door opens and Maggie steps in. When she sees me, she freezes, like I'm the last person she wants to meet.

"Can we, uh, talk?" I ask her.

She looks at Brian before answering. "Sure."

"Something the matter, Seth?" he asks.

"No, it's all good."

I head to the rehearsal room so Maggie and I can speak in private. Before I close the door, Ryder and Brian join us. Maggie doesn't sit down.

"What's going on?" demands Brian, all business.

How to explain? "Last night," I begin, "Sabrina told me about Kris and Tamara."

"Uh-huh. You and everyone else, probably. What's that got to do with Maggie?"

"Seth passed it along to me," she says.

"It's juicy gossip, all right," says Ryder with a weary smile. "But now we should get back to the more pressing task of damage control."

Maggie doesn't move.

"Tell Seth you had nothing to do with that story getting out, Maggie," says Brian.

She shakes her head. "I'm not going to lie to him."

Ryder and Brian stare at each other. They're still on the same team, but Maggie's on the opposite side of the table now.

"You'd better not be saying what I think you're saying," Brian mutters.

"Seth deserves to know the truth."

"You'd really sell us out?" says Ryder.

She looks from one man to the other and shrugs.

Brian grits his teeth, jawbones visible beneath clean-shaven skin. "Enough of this crap. You're fired."

Maggie heads for the door while I struggle to keep pace with what's unfolding. She's basically admitting that she leaked the story. She has lost her job, and maybe even jeopardized her place at film school. And for what?

"Why did you do it, Maggie?" I ask.

She stops in the doorway. She's breathing fast. "You've seen how it works. Kris and Sabrina can say and do whatever the hell they want, and no one calls them on it. You're never going to shine as long as they're the ones in the spotlight. But now Kris is gone."

"You stupid woman," snarls Brian, fist pressed tight against his forehead. "You have no idea what you're talking about."

"Oh really? Then why was I at the party in the first place, huh? Because you two were busy selling your souls to get Kris freakin' Ellis to sign on, that's why." She turns to me, her expression different, pleading. "Do you really believe Kris was in this thing to play second string to you? You stood up for me, Seth. Now I'm standing up for you. Doesn't matter how much Kris wants to bring you down, he's *done*. And I'm glad I was the one who made it happen."

"What about Tamara?" I ask.

"What about her? Tamara lost the moral high ground when she cheated on her fiancé."

"And Sabrina?" adds Ryder. "What if we've lost her too?"

Maggie grips the door handle. "Then good riddance. She's no different from Kris. We all know why Annaleigh left the party early last night."

Brian glares at her. "Get the hell out!"

"Why shouldn't Seth know what she said about him?" she fires back.

"What *who* said about me?" I ask.

"Why, your dear friend Sabrina, of course. Said the first read-through wasn't a rehearsal, it was a humiliation. Called you a fucking mess. Said that if that's all you've got, the whole movie is screwed. Those are pretty much direct quotes, by the way. Just ask Annaleigh."

Maggie slams the door behind her and I'm alone with the two men who control my future. Do they feel the same way as Sabrina? Is that why they wanted Kris on board?

Maybe Sabrina's right—I *was* a mess at that first rehearsal. Still, I can't believe she said those things. Who does that to a fellow actor?

"Is it true, what Maggie just said?" I ask Ryder.

He looks at everything except me. "It's what Annaleigh told us."

"Look, I'm sorry," I say. "I was distracted during the read-through. I'd just seen the picture of me and Kris in the newspaper and—"

The door flies open and Tracie blusters in. "Did you just fire Maggie?"

"Yeah," says Brian. "And don't tell me I can't legally do that."

"You can't legally—"

"Bullshit! She leaked confidential information. Seth told her about Kris and Tamara, and she sold the story."

"I know what she did, Brian. I was listening at the door."

"I thought you made her sign a nondisclosure."

"I did, but it only covers the movie. Kris never signed a contract, so technically he's nothing to do with the movie. Neither's Tamara. And Maggie knows it."

Silence. A few words from Tracie and Brian's pent-up anger counts for nothing.

"We should sue her anyway," says Ryder.

Tracie purses her lips. "For what? Telling the truth? If we so much as threaten her, she'll name her sources. In other words, *Seth*." She turns to me. "So are you willing to go on oath and say she's lying, or would you admit that you told her everything she passed along?"

I lower my eyes. "I'd have to admit it."

"Uh-huh. And tell me, who gets thrown under the bus then— her, or you?" She puts her fingers under my chin and forces me to look her in the eye. It's the first time she has seemed remotely sympathetic. "Take it from me—Maggie didn't commit a crime. She sold information she never should've had. It may feel the same, but it's not."

Tracie perches on the edge of the table and crosses her legs. "Now, Maggie was saying Kris and Sabrina say and do whatever they like. I know what Sabrina said about you last night. What did Kris say?"

"He made a snide remark about Maggie's dress."

"Hmm. What a class act." She looks at Brian and Ryder. "And you wanted him back in the movie."

"Kris is guaranteed box office," says Brian. "A few minutes of screen time and he might've doubled our receipts."

"So this is all about money now?"

"That's pretty hypocritical, coming from someone who bills by the hour." Brian circles the table, fists twitching at his sides. "If I ever see that woman again . . ."

Tracie turns in a slow arc. "Leave the room, Brian."

"What? I'm not going any—"

"Get out! I'm not asking."

I figure there's no way he'll go, but he does. I'm glad too. Brian looks like he wants to make someone pay, and with Maggie gone, I'm the guiltiest person here.

Tracie doesn't continue until Brian is gone and the door is closed again. "Now then, Seth. Who told you about Kris and Tamara in the first place?"

"Sabrina. I never thought Maggie would tell anyone."

"It's not your fault." She presses her fingers together in a steeple and taps her lips. "Look, if you hear any other gossip or rumors, you come straight to us, okay? Not your father or brother. Not your friends. *Us*. I can only spin this stuff so much. Eventually someone's going to notice that the trail of breadcrumbs leads here."

"What about Sabrina? Kris is going to know the story came from her."

"Not necessarily. Anyway, this doesn't get any better for her if we drag it out. The best thing is to put it behind us. Give it one news cycle and the media will be on to another story."

Tracie wraps a tendril of hair around her ear like she's putting everything in order again. But the look on her face assures me that things aren't in order. There are still loose ends, things she'll have to deal with.

Ryder hasn't said much. He just stares at some sheets of paper on the table—his revised script, I guess. The top sheet is covered in red pencil markings. Do those markings return Kris and Sabrina to their starring roles? I'll probably never know, but it's possible that Maggie just saved Annaleigh and me from drifting into irrelevance.

"I'm sorry, Ryder," I say.

He looks up. "Tracie's right—it *will* blow over. We just need time to get things back on track."

"Can I go home?" I ask. "For Christmas Day."

"No," he says firmly. "We've got to get the focus back on you and Annaleigh, and you need to get used to each other."

"I know you probably feel guilty, letting Kris and Tamara's affair get out," adds Tracie, "but Kris is gone now. You're our star. Understand?"

I understand all right: They want me to cover up what happened, not just for the sake of the movie, but for my sake too. If Maggie's the leak, I'm the source.

Tracie pulls out her wallet and hands me a wad of twenties. "Here, take it. I'll get reimbursed."

"I can't."

"Sure you can. Go buy your dad and brother a present. Heck, buy yourself something too. Your first paycheck comes New

Year's Day, but you've earned an advance. Consider it our commitment to you."

She pats me on the shoulder—a gesture of support and strength. Also an acknowledgment that someone has screwed up, and it's not only me.

"You won't tell anyone about this, right?" she asks.

I feel the bills in my hand. Think about how it would feel to lose everything. "I won't tell anyone," I say. "I promise."

16

IT'S COOL AND CLOUDY OUTSIDE. FOR a few moments I stand completely still, stuffing bills into the pockets of my stiff black jeans. It's got to be several hundred dollars—more than I earned for both my commercials.

As I look around for a taxi, I spot Maggie only a couple blocks away. She's walking slowly, shoulders rising and falling like she's crying. Since just about everyone drives in L.A., I figure she must be going somewhere nearby.

I follow her. Block by block, the buildings become smaller. There's less glitz and glamour, and more apartment buildings with tiny pools.

Maggie never looks back. Not a single glance at the building she's left behind and the people inside who trusted her. Why didn't she just lie? I never could've proved that she leaked the story.

She stops before glass double doors and places a key in one of the mailboxes that run in rows against the wall—bottom row, far left. She retrieves her mail without looking at it, and goes inside a four-story building with stucco walls.

I run to catch up, but the door has already closed. The mailboxes have apartment numbers on them—hers is 17. There's an intercom beside the door for visitors, but what would I say to her? She did this for me. For herself too, I think. After Kris took cheap shots at us, it must have felt good to exact revenge so swiftly.

I turn away from the boxes. The street is quiet, empty except for a single car that idles along at walking pace. I'm distracted, so I don't recognize the vehicle until it pulls alongside me.

It's the forest-green Mazda.

I run toward it to get a look at the driver. When I'm a few yards away he floors the gas. Tires skid. I'm left stranded in the middle of the road.

Several seconds later, my phone chimes. There's another text message: *I'm still watching.*

A car door opens as I approach the entrance to the hotel. A black Porsche, no less. "Get in," a voice shouts.

I peer inside. Kris leans across the passenger seat. "We need to talk," he says. "Or we can have a conversation like this. Your choice."

I don't want to get in. But if he thinks it was me who leaked the information about him and Tamara, he's going to make my life miserable. At least this'll give me the chance to set the record straight.

As I slide onto the leather seat, a couple of women stop beside the car. "Oh my God," one shouts. "It's Kris Ellis. Hi!"

Kris gives a tired wave. "Merry Christmas." Then he whispers to me, "Close the door."

I shut it, separating us from the women and the sounds of L.A. traffic.

"Damn." Kris pulls onto Wilshire and hangs a left a couple blocks later. "That's annoying."

"Having fans is annoying?"

"After this morning's news, yeah." He regards me from the corner of his eye. "You heard, right?"

I nod.

"And now those *fans* are texting that they just saw me. It'll be on Twitter in seconds. Entertainment sites will catch my name moments after that. There'll be at least one photographer at the hotel within five minutes. By the time I drop you off, you'll find it hard to get in the door." He speaks in a kind of low-energy drone, resigned but not frustrated.

He checks his rearview mirror several times as he cuts a jagged path through Beverly Hills. I don't recognize the street where he stops, but the sidewalk is almost empty, even though there's a coffee shop right next to us. Tourists clearly don't bother with this block.

"Did you go home with Sabrina last night?" he asks.

"No. You saw her leave the party alone, same as I did."

"Sure. And I saw you leave right after her. Haven't seen her since, either." He peers through the window as if he's looking for something. Then he turns the engine off and unclips his seat belt. "Come on. This place makes seriously good coffee."

The shop is small and mostly empty, quiet except for soft jazz coming from a single speaker. Movie posters adorn every inch of wall space. Kris bumps fists with the barista, orders us lattes, and pays with a twenty. He doesn't wait for change.

We take a table at the back. Kris chooses a wicker chair that faces the entrance.

"Man, just look at us," he says. "I swear Hollywood works in crazy ways. One day you're dressed in a chicken suit outside of El Pollo Loco, the next you're Brad Pitt, movie star. It's kind of like you and Annaleigh, actually. Seems impossible, what's happened to you. Doesn't it?"

He's chosen that word—*impossible*—deliberately. "What do you mean?"

"I'm not trying to be a jerk. Just being honest. Fact is, you're bumbling around, all I-can't-believe-I'm-in-Hollywood. And that's your choice. But Sabrina's way too vulnerable to be hanging out with someone as naive as you."

"Says you."

"Says me," he agrees without a hint of embarrassment.

The coffees arrive. Kris wraps his large hands around the cup. "Look, you ever wondered why everyone knows so much more about Sabrina than they do about me? It's because I've had the same friends for the past ten years. I look after them, and I trust them to keep their mouths shut. Sabrina isn't like that. She isolates herself, then trusts anyone who's nice to her."

"Even a stranger?"

"Especially a stranger. And right now, that stranger is you. She probably likes that you're naive, actually—it's a luxury she's never had. Trouble is, Sabrina doesn't always know what's best for her."

I've heard other guys spout stuff like this, but I'm surprised to hear it from Kris. He seems too savvy for that. "The way I see it, Sabrina's got things figured out better than anyone."

A smile envelops his face. "Don't tell me—she shared her Gilda theory with you, right?" He mimics her. "The secret is the

105

separation of self into three equally valid yet distinct personas."

It's a crappy impersonation, and I wouldn't laugh anyway. I can't tell whether he's ridiculing Sabrina, or me for listening to her.

"Look," he says, growing serious again, "that right there is proof, she's messed up. You really think she can keep that shit straight in her head?" He takes a sip and puts the cup back down again quickly, like he doesn't want to lose momentum. "She doesn't know who she is half the time, let alone who she's meant to be. That's why she does crazy stuff like leaking the story about Tamara and me."

I try to stay calm. "Why would she do that?"

"To get back at me. Probably feels like I humiliated her last night. She was kind of out of it, running her mouth, saying a bunch of stupid crap to anyone who'd listen. I was trying to get her to leave when you showed up."

"And she'd ruin you over something like that?"

"She hasn't *ruined* me. This'll disappear soon enough. Compared to some guys, I'm a saint."

We both focus on our coffee. He's telling the truth about the "crap" Sabrina was saying—Annaleigh heard it firsthand—but I'm still not sure he's being up-front about his own feelings for her. Or why they broke up in the first place. All I know is that one moment Sabrina was sharing the red carpet with her boyfriend, and the next he was gone from her life.

Come to think of it, so was her best friend.

"Were you and Genevieve Barron ever together?" I ask.

He snorts into his coffee. "Hell no!" He wipes foam from his lips with the back of his hand. "Anyway, Gen was Sabrina's best friend."

"Exactly. *Was*. Now they're not talking."

"Come on. You know how girls are: One moment they're inseparable, the next they're not speaking. Gen changed when she got out of acting. She was always kind of needy, but got real preachy too. Pissed Sabrina off."

Silence. I figure Kris will have more questions, but he seems to be done. Was this really just about putting me on my guard? If so, I could've saved him the trouble. Maggie and my anonymous stalker have already done that.

"That stupid crap Sabrina was saying last night. Was any of it about me?" I ask.

"She said a lot of stuff about a lot of people."

"Including me?"

He stares at his coffee. Taps his index finger against the ceramic mug like he's playing for time. "She mentioned you, yeah. But it was only good stuff, you know?"

It's obvious that he's lying. But if he heard Sabrina insulting me, why not seize the opportunity to drive us even further apart?

"Look, can you do me a couple favors?" he asks.

"Like what?"

"Give me your number, and I'll give you mine. I want to stay in touch."

I can't think of a good reason to say no, so we exchange phones and enter our numbers. "What else?"

"That woman you were with last night—apologize for me, okay? I was pissed at Sabrina, and angry that you interrupted us.

But it was totally uncool, what I said." He gives a wan smile. "I guess Sabrina's not the only one who runs her mouth in public, you know?"

The expression may be practiced, but the way he reddens isn't. I give a halfhearted nod, the best I can offer under the circumstances.

It's strange, but his lie about what Sabrina said makes me take his other words more seriously. And as we leave the coffee shop, I realize I have no idea who Kris Ellis really is.

17

KRIS WAS RIGHT—PHOTOGRAPHERS HOVER AT
the hotel entrance, two rows deep. He drives right past and drops
me a hundred yards down the road. By the time the paparazzi
catch up to us, he's pulling away.

The photographers snap pictures, murmuring his name. Sabrina's
too. Finally they turn their attention to me, because any photo is
better than no photo at all.

I run inside and take the elevator. In front of my door, legs
pulled up, chin resting on her knees, is Sabrina.

She doesn't look like the same girl I kissed at the party last
night. She looks worn down, as if she hasn't slept. Her eyes are
glassy, unfocused.

"Hi," she says.

I unlock the door and she follows me inside. There's only one
reason for her visit: to hear me promise that I had nothing to do
with outing Kris and Tamara. From the way I'm avoiding eye contact, she has probably already worked out the truth.

Sabrina spreads her fingers across the patio door. "Did you
have a nice walk? Ryder said you left a couple hours ago."

I try to detect suspicion in her voice, but she sounds like

she's just making conversation. "What do you want, Sabrina?"

"To make sure we're still friends."

Last night she kissed me. Today she wants to be friends. Does she do this with every male costar? Which of her three personas does she draw on for that particular role? Which persona is she drawing on now?

How pathetic am I for wishing that I knew?

"Last night, at the bar, did you really call me a . . . mess?" I ask.

She bumps her head against the glass. "Probably. I wasn't exactly myself."

"What does that mean?" I wait for her to answer, but she doesn't. "What about the other times we've been together? Were you yourself *then*?"

"On the beach, yeah."

"Not the first time we met, though. Not at that party."

"It's complicated."

Actually, it doesn't seem complicated at all. Any time she flirts, she's not herself. "It's fine," I tell her.

She makes a little sound at the back of her throat like she's annoyed. "Don't be that way—all macho, like nothing can touch you. I remember sitting beside you on the sand. The way you listened."

For a few moments I feel myself being dragged back into her orbit. But then I remember: She ditched me for Kris. Ripped me in front of her entourage. I can't separate myself into different personas like she does. For me, failing as an actor is still failing.

"Look, I was angry at you, okay?" she growls. "For questioning me about getting Kris to sign on. And then you went after that guy."

"That *guy* was the one who tailed us the other night. He left in a green Mazda. And he's been sending me texts."

"How did he get your number?"

"You tell me!"

She's silent for a moment. "This is what I warned you about. You're always being watched. That's why you need a public persona. The moment you step outside—"

"It's not that easy for me."

"Or me. I've just had more practice." She runs a finger across the glass like she's tracing letters in air. "I'm sorry I said that stuff about you, though. It was mean. I get that way sometimes. Give me an audience, and I can't help running my mouth."

"Yeah, Kris told me."

Her finger stops moving. "So that's why it took you so long to get here, huh?" She flares her nostrils. "Well, screw you."

It was a mistake to mention Kris, but even so . . . "We were just talking."

"Oh, really? So what else did he tell you?"

"Nothing."

"I'm not going to let you gang up on me."

"We're not ganging up. I think he cares, is all."

"Yeah. He's all heart. You too. How lucky can one girl get?"

She pushes off and strides across the room. As she passes me, I touch her arm gently, but she swipes my hand away.

"Get the hell off me!" she yells.

I stagger back. Here's yet another new version of Sabrina—incandescent with rage—and it's not inspiring or alluring at all. Right now, she's just scary.

"Where did you go last night, Sabrina?"

She stops at the door. "Is that your question, or his?"

"Both, I guess."

"You're worried for me, huh?" She wears the glimmer of a smile, but it's humorless and cold. "Well, don't be. I'm just fine."

She slams the door behind her.

As I stand in the large, silent suite, a voice at the back of my head reminds me that I ought to be relieved. Sabrina doesn't have me pegged as the source of the leaked story. I can focus on the movie now, and put all the other stuff behind me.

But there's another voice too, louder and more insistent, that demands to know what the hell just happened. In what parallel universe does Sabrina Layton kiss me one day and ditch me the next?

I head out after her. Take the elevator downstairs as the first voice warns me that I might be doing exactly what she wants. That she's playing me like a chess piece—me and Kris and Ryder and the Hollywood press and pretty much the whole freaking world, all hanging on her every word and whim.

But even Annaleigh admitted that there was only one true star in this movie. If Sabrina pulls out, will there be a movie at all?

I hustle through the lobby, past large vases of fresh-cut flowers and loitering Christmas Eve couples. Outside, Sabrina is climbing into a taxi. She's only ten yards away from me, but an impenetrable wall of paparazzi separates us. They jostle her, stubborn as bloodhounds in the hunt.

"Sabrina," I shout.

Faces turn toward me, including Sabrina's. Cameras flash at

me as well as her now, and she hesitates. Is she pleased that I'm distracting them, or angry that I'm stealing the spotlight?

"Seth?" A familiar voice distracts me. I turn to find two figures standing beside a just-arrived taxi. They carry mismatched duffel bags and wear identical puzzled expressions, like they're not sure they belong.

Me, I'm certain they don't belong. Not here. Not now.

As Sabrina's taxi pulls away, Dad and Gant wave.

18

"HEY, SETH," ONE OF THE PHOTOGRAPHERS calls out. "What's the latest with you and Sabrina?"

It's pathetic, but my first instinct is to glance at my brother just to catch his reaction—satisfyingly openmouthed, his eyebrows raised almost an inch. But then I notice Dad frowning, and I just want to get away.

I hurry them inside the hotel, and the cacophony of voices grows quieter behind us. "I wasn't expecting you," I say.

Dad's mouth twitches. "R-Ry—"

"Ryder? He brought you here?"

Dad nods.

"Called us this morning," says Gant. "Told us your room is plenty big enough for three. Even got us a taxi." He whistles. "We stopped by his office on the way here. He wanted us to sign waivers, in case we're around during filming. Hey, maybe we'll be movie stars too."

I press the elevator call button. "Lucky you."

On the fifth floor, I walk them to my room. Dad goes straight inside and heads for the patio doors and the perfect pool view, while Gant lingers in the corridor.

"So, you and Sabrina, huh?" he says.

"Yeah. I mean, no. Nothing's going on."

"You sure about that? She just ran out of the hotel in tears, and you were right after her. Seems like plenty to me. And then there's the photos."

"What photos?"

"What do you mean—*what photos*? You and Sabrina getting cozy on a beach. Came out this afternoon. Haven't you seen them?"

The beach. Sabrina warned me we were being photographed and I didn't believe her. Now the pictures are out there, just as she predicted. But if she was so sure, why didn't she make us leave? Was I a prop? Another way for her to control the story of who she is?

I shrug. It's a meaningless response, but for once, Gant doesn't push it. "Hey," he says, brightening. "I'm not saying I blame you. This is Sabrina Layton, right? Most guys in America would kill to be in your shoes right now."

"It's not how it seems," I tell him.

He wanders inside. "Try telling Dad that."

Half an hour later, Gant and I are throwing a foam football across the pool, while Dad sits on one of the deck chairs, head tilted back as he takes in the majestic hotel. I glance at him from time to time, hoping to see him smile. But instead he knits his brow like he can't make all the puzzle pieces fit. Or maybe it's that the most important piece is missing. There's nothing I can do about it, either. Mom's never coming back.

"Isn't she in the movie too?" asks Gant, pointing behind me.

I turn around. Beyond the pool deck, a familiar figure in a red vest is running on a treadmill. "That's Annaleigh," I say.

"What's she like?"

"She's nice."

"Nice?" He gives the ball a little extra velocity. "She's been watching us."

I fight the urge to look again. "Actually, I should go talk to her."

"*Should?*" Detective Gant smells something fishy.

"I'll see you back in the room."

Gant hurls the ball at me anyway.

I climb out of the pool and throw on a T-shirt. Enter the gym from the back, which means that Annaleigh can't see me. Her triceps flex with every arm swing. Her stride rate is high, footsteps light.

As I pull up alongside her, she startles. "What's up?" she asks, looking worried.

"Can we talk?"

She places her feet on either side of the rubber track but doesn't turn it off. "Right now?"

"Just . . . whenever."

She presses the red stop button. A middle-aged guy on the neighboring treadmill stares at the overhead TV screens with such focus that I'm sure he's eavesdropping. Annaleigh must think so too, because she tilts her head toward the exit.

I follow her along the corridor to the elevator. We get off on the fourth floor and she leads me to her suite. Coincidentally, it's directly underneath mine, but her room is tidier—clothes packed neatly away, bags out of sight.

She sits on the edge of her bed. "What do you want to talk about?"

"I want to say I'm sorry."

"For what?"

"For not listening when you said that Sabrina was taking over this movie."

"So you think she *is* trying to take over?"

"I don't know. But something weird is going on and . . . I guess I don't trust her."

Annaleigh reaches for the video camera on her nightstand. "Actually, I kind of wonder if all of this is my fault."

"Why?"

"I should've held my own at the junket. And I totally overreacted about Kris joining us. He and Sabrina are big-time. It's no wonder Ryder wants them in the movie." She turns on the camera and points it at herself. "Yeah, Sabrina, I got jealous. There, I said it." She directs the camera at me. "It's not surprising you trusted her. You have pretty good chemistry."

Reddening, I try to take the camera from her, but she rolls away. As I make another grab for it, she turns back toward me and we're only inches apart. She's still flushed from the treadmill. Where Sabrina is cool, detached beauty, Annaleigh is all fire.

"You know," she says, waving the camera tantalizingly close, "you need to get used to being filmed."

"You know," I say, taking it from her, "so do you."

I move around the bed. Sit on the desk chair and zoom in on her. "My turn to embarrass you now."

"Go ahead and try."

"Do you have a crush on Kris Ellis?"

She rolls her eyes. "I'm a girl with twenty-twenty vision. Yeah, I have a crush. But nothing like the way you crush on Sabrina."

I'm turning red again. "Crush*ed*," I say quietly. "Not crush."

"So no Christmas Day celebrations with Sabrina, then? No prezzies? Not even some mistletoe?" She puts on a sad face. "TMZ viewers *will* be disappointed."

I'm so glad I'm behind the camera right now. "Actually, my family's in town. When's yours coming?"

"They're not. Dad's stuck in Arkansas. Mom's staying with him."

"So what are you doing for Christmas?"

She shrugs. "Give me that," she says, reaching for the camera.

I wish she'd turn it off, but I play along. Pretend that it doesn't bother me to have a camera in my face.

"You should spend Christmas with us," I say.

"Why? So you can prove that you're over Sabrina?"

"No. I mean, yeah. Look, I don't care about Sabrina right now. She'll be fine, no matter what happens. Same with Kris. But you and me . . ." The camera lens turns. Is she zooming in for a close-up? "For a while there, I honestly thought we were going to get cut. Now we've gotten a second chance, there's no way I'm going down without a fight. You know what I'm saying?"

"Yeah. I know."

"So you'll join us tomorrow?"

She lowers the camera and turns it off. "Okay. Actually, I'd like that very much."

19

CHRISTMAS DAY. WE DON'T HAVE A tree, so I steal a potted plant and set it on the coffee table beside Dad. He stifles a laugh.

Annaleigh comes over at five o'clock. She's wearing three strings of red-and-silver tinsel around her shoulders. "I liberated them from a stairwell," she says. "Tinsel this pretty has no business being hidden away."

As she adds them to my plant, there's a knock on the door. Waiters wheel in two trays and four sets of plates and cutlery.

"Seriously?" says Gant. "Room-service turkey?"

"Mmm-hmm," I reply. "Enjoy it now. When Brian gets the bill, he might ask for it back."

"That could be messy."

Annaleigh chuckles. "You're a family of guys. I'd expect nothing less."

It's an innocent comment, but also a reminder that Mom is gone. "Time to eat," I say quickly.

Dad claims the carving knife and attempts to cut the turkey. He does okay at first, but his hands shake the harder he concentrates, so I step around the table and take the knife from him. He gives it up without complaint, but his shoulders slump.

"Look at y-you all," he says. "Doing so . . . so well."

Annaleigh gives an appreciative smile, but I can hear the sadness in his voice. I'd thought that feasting on a too-large turkey in a fancy hotel room would make him happy. Trouble is, all of it is because of me, not him, as if I'm the head of house. Dad wants to provide for us, to be the one we depend on. I should've let him carve the turkey.

When I'm done serving, and the four plates are overflowing with food, I raise my water glass. "A toast to Brian and Ryder, for bringing us together."

It's not until the words are out that I remember Annaleigh's parents, conspicuously absent from the festivities. She's the first to clink glasses with me, though.

"To turkey," says Gant.

"And . . . and . . . t-to all of you," concludes Dad, raising his glass with a shaking hand. "I'm pr-proud."

Proud. I'm not sure I deserve that right now, but it wasn't just directed at me, and I don't think he's talking about the movie. As I look at Gant and Annaleigh, I realize that each of us is trying to get by. We may never be stars like Sabrina and Kris, but we're not quitters either, so maybe Dad's right.

I raise my glass too.

After dinner, Annaleigh and I go out for a walk. She tells me to take the headcam. Says we need to practice wearing it, and anyway, it'll be kind of funny. I slide it on and check out my reflection in the mirror. I look funny, all right, and not in a good way.

Rodeo Drive is busy, but everyone moves slower than usual. The lights, so bright yesterday, feel tired now, like they're clinging to Christmas rather than welcoming it. The piped-in Christmas hits of Frank Sinatra seem to follow us like a deranged stalker, promising snow and white Christmases and a million other things that Los Angeles can never deliver.

"Your dad," she begins.

"Stroke."

"I was going to say, he seems kind."

"Oh, right. Yeah, he is. I'm sorry your parents couldn't be here too."

"I'm not. Life is easier when they're not around."

"Why?"

She peers up at me. Seeing her in the glow of the streetlights, I can't help noticing that her face is rounder, less dramatic than Sabrina's. Her expressions are spontaneous and unguarded. Annaleigh hasn't divided herself into three separate personas. Her unhappiness is written in every word, every muscle. But she still isn't answering my question.

"What's the story with your parents?" I ask.

Her steps become slower. Her eyes flicker between my eyes and the camera perched a couple inches higher. "Would it be all right if I don't answer that right now?"

"Okay."

"It's just . . . this is Christmas, you know? And I'm happy."

She links our arms and we stroll along in silence. Passersby stare at my camera and smile.

"I think it's your turn to film now," I say.

"No. I feel full of profound thoughts, and I'd hate for our viewers to miss out on them."

"Like what?"

"Like why does everyone in L.A. wear full winter gear even though it's sixty degrees? Look at them. Coats, hats, gloves, scarves. Your city's just weird."

She's right: This is my city, although it doesn't feel that way right now. Christmas trees and garlands adorn Rodeo Drive. Lights dangle from the roof of the Beverly Wilshire like cascading diamonds. Everything is bigger, brighter, and bolder here.

"Penny for your thoughts?" Annaleigh asks.

"Just a penny?"

"Or an IOU for a buck. You'll get it when we're paid." She clicks her tongue. "Maybe."

"I was just thinking, we're going to be okay, you and me. We'll stick together."

My phone chimes. Annaleigh lets go of me so I can read the text, and I feel the breeze where her arm has been.

The message is short: *You shouldn't play the field*.

"What is it, Seth?" she asks, watching me.

"Nothing."

She continues toward the hotel. I don't follow right away, though. Instead, I stare at the lamp-lit streets and wonder where our stalker is, and what the hell he wants.

20

THE ITINERARY SAYS *PHOTO SHOOT—LOCATIONS TBD*. There's an instruction to "dress in character," which ought to feel freeing, but doesn't. Ryder has remade my entire wardrobe. Which of the many possible versions of Seth-Andrew does he want me to impersonate today?

He picks us up at ten a.m. Compliments Annaleigh on her print dress and cardigan combo and turns to me.

"Nice shirt," he says. "Someone has good taste."

"You bought it, not me," I say.

"Exactly."

We travel east on Santa Monica Boulevard. North on Fairfax. East on Hollywood Boulevard. I visualize a map of L.A. and mark off each turn. Half an hour passes before we stop beside Hollywood Reservoir. To one end of the large park, the gray concrete of Mulholland Dam peeks above the still, glassy water. To the other, the Hollywood sign stares down from its hillside perch a mile away.

Two guys emerge from a minivan in the next parking space. One carries a long-lens camera that would make Gant envious, while the other shoulders a video camera.

Ryder notices me watching the videographer. "As well as publicity shots, we need footage for the DVD extras, that sort of thing," he explains. "Figure we might as well do it now. When you're in the thick of filming, you'll be too tired to worry about that stuff."

As Ryder issues instructions to his crew, Annaleigh points at the Hollywood sign. "It's kind of stupid," she says, "but seeing that thing gives me goose bumps."

"Not stupid at all." I've seen it too often to feel the same way, but I can remember a time when I did.

"I wonder how many people have come to Hollywood thinking they're going to make it big."

"Thousands. Maybe millions."

"Doesn't it freak you out?"

"Not as much as it did a couple days ago."

She cocks an eyebrow. "What changed?"

"They're photographing you and me for the promo materials, not Sabrina and Kris."

She slides her fingers through the chain-link fence that separates us from the water, and glances at the Hollywood sign again. "I hadn't thought of it like that," she says.

"Okay, let's get moving," Ryder shouts.

Like the Pied Piper, he leads his posse of actors and cameramen toward the middle of the dam. There's water to one side and a massive drop on the other.

"We're doing this without permits, so we need a quick turnaround," he says. "Imagine this is the lake scene from early in the movie. You're just walking across the bridge, chatting, smiling.

No one's getting in your way, and things are good. Got it?" We nod. "Good. Turn your cell phones off. We don't want any interruptions."

Annaleigh and I exchange a glance and begin walking.

We've only taken a few steps when Ryder raises a hand. "No. We're looking for quiet understanding, not detachment. You're falling in love, remember?"

Annaleigh pulls her cardigan closer. It's soft—cashmere, or something like that. She looks really pretty.

I offer her my arm and she laughs. "What is this, the nineteenth century? Next you'll be writing me poetry." She takes my hand and we twine fingers. "Trust me, this is what we'll want."

Ryder gives a signal and we resume walking.

"So," she says. "What's your favorite kindergarten moment?"

"Hmm. The day I finally made contact in T-ball. You?"

"The day my parents gave me a packed lunch instead of the free school meal."

"That's kind of a sad highlight."

"You never saw our school lunches. What about elementary school?"

"That's easy. Getting cast in *The Greatest Christmas Pageant Ever*. I was one of the Herdman kids, and I was badass. Maybe a little too badass."

She rests her head against my shoulder. "Like how?"

"They gave us rolled-up newspapers and told us to pretend fight onstage. You know, to show how bad we were. But I'd never been in front of an audience before, and I was pumped, so I swung that thing *smack* against the littlest kid's face. I knew he

126

was in pain, but he refused to start bawling onstage, so no one in the audience realized what was happening. After that, he kept flubbing his lines, and everyone must've figured he was nervous, 'cause at the end they gave him this sorry, sympathetic applause. Even worse, I got a standing ovation. I guess compared to him, I was awesome."

"That's horrible," says Annaleigh, grinning.

"No kidding. The kid transferred to a new elementary school the next year. I've always wondered if it was my fault."

"Was that when you decided to become an actor?"

"I think so. I was supposed to be a bad kid in the play, and sure enough, I messed this poor kid up. It was like Bruce Banner unleashing the Hulk. If I'd done that to a kid in school, I would've been in so much trouble. But because it was onstage, everyone applauded. It got me thinking: Who else could I be? Everyone wishes they could be someone else from time to time, right?"

"I know I do." She takes a deep breath. "Is that your *thing*, then—taking out cast members?"

"Absolutely. One actor per production, by whatever means necessary."

"Wow." Annaleigh gives me a funny sideways look. "Thanks for giving me a heads-up. So who's it going to be this time—me or Sabrina?"

"Neither. Kris is already gone, right?" I open my eyes super-wide so she'll know I'm kidding, but she's not looking at me.

"Cut!" Ryder claps his hands together. He's smiling. "That's exactly what I'm looking for, guys. Just ad-lib. See where the conversation takes you."

He turns to his crewmen. "Did you get everything?" They give an emphatic nod. "Let's move to the next location, then."

The men lower their cameras and traipse back to the van. With the cameras off, Annaleigh and I could ease apart. Instead we remain exactly as we are, hand in hand, her head against my shoulder.

"Is that story true?" she asks softly.

"Which one? Hitting the little kid, or taking out Kris?"

She knows I'm kidding, and pretends to punch my arm.

"Yeah," I say. "It's all true. Did you think I was making it up?"

"I just wondered if I was talking to Seth or Andrew."

"You were talking to me," I tell her. "Were you Annaleigh or Lana, then?"

Now she loosens our hands. "I'll let you in on a secret. Lana and I have so much in common, it may not make any difference."

We make stops at Santa Monica pier and downtown before returning to Hollywood. It's late afternoon and the streets are busy, and Annaleigh seems captivated by the restlessness of it all.

We park near the Chinese Theatre on Hollywood Boulevard. It's a landmark, and a large crowd has gathered before the giant pagoda. Tourists stroll along the Hollywood Walk of Fame, snapping pictures of actors' and actresses' hand- and footprints.

Ryder has saved the interview questions for last. With the theater as backdrop, he tosses softball questions that give us room to say whatever is on our minds.

Annaleigh waves her thumb at the theater and says she can't believe her good fortune in being here, part of a real movie. I talk about how unique the project is, and the challenge of making it work. It all feels so wooden, though. If Ryder really wants me to open up, he should let Annaleigh do the interviewing.

He's halfway through a question when his phone rings. He raises a hand apologetically and turns away to speak.

Seeing him leave, a group of girls shuffles toward us. "Are you in that movie with Sabrina Layton?" one of them asks me.

Annaleigh flashes me a grin, eyebrows raised.

"Yeah," I say. "We both are."

"Can we have your autographs?"

"Uh, sure."

It feels strange to give autographs. I don't get to take it too seriously, though, as Annaleigh keeps nudging my arm. She does it really gently so that no one sees, but my signature changes every time.

When the first group leaves, another takes its place. Annaleigh surveys the growing crowd with disbelief. "I guess this is what you were talking about at the party the other night, huh? How it feels to be noticed. To *matter*."

This isn't exactly what I had in mind, but we're definitely getting noticed.

"Do you think we'll get to put our footprints here too?" she whispers, pointing to a concrete slab imprinted with two hands, two feet, and Marilyn Monroe's autograph.

"Sure," I say. "If we screw up this movie, I could definitely see Brian sticking our feet in concrete and tossing us into Long Beach Harbor."

Annaleigh frowns. "That's not the way I want to be remembered. Plus," she adds, tapping another slab with the toe of her shoe—this time, the tiny hands and feet of Shirley Temple—"teen stars are supposed to mess up, right? It's part of the stereotype."

"Seth!" Ryder holds out his phone. "Brian wants a word."

I take the phone from Ryder and walk several yards before speaking. Rita Hayworth's prints are on a slab to my right, which reminds me of Sabrina: *They go to bed with Gilda. They wake up with me.*

"Hi Brian," I say.

"I'm sending a picture through," he replies.

A photograph appears on the phone—Sabrina and me again, but we're not on the beach anymore. This time we're in the darkened surroundings of Machinus Media Enterprises. Her arms are draped over my shoulders. Our lips are pressed tight together.

If I'm getting autograph requests now, wait till everyone gets a load of this.

"First you go and tell Maggie about Kris and Tamara," says Brian. "Now you're making out with Kris's ex-girlfriend. I have to tell you, Seth, you're not making life easy for yourself."

That might be true, but as I stare at the photo, Kris is the last thing on my mind. What I'm trying to work out is why Sabrina and I let it happen in the first place. We both knew the curly-haired guy with the cell phone was trying to film us. We knew how it would look if he succeeded in getting an intimate photograph. But we kissed anyway.

"It won't happen again," I say, like that's going to make any difference.

Brian sighs. "Just be smart, Seth. Actors are big business. Don't make yourself a target."

He hangs up, and I stand there, staring at Rita Hayworth's prints.

"Over here, Seth." Ryder waves from the most crowded spot on the sidewalk, where Annaleigh is waiting for me, eyes wide, smile wider.

I take a deep breath and join her. The photographer wants to snap away, but people are getting in the way of the picture. At the junket, Sabrina suggested that this might happen. Encouraged it, even. It's not random passersby that have me tense, though—it's Sabrina herself.

"Closer," the photographer says, pressing his palms together.

This time, a whole group of guys steps in front of the camera. They look like they're college students, a frat on a field trip.

"What's the scene?" one of them asks. He's large and red-cheeked. "You want us to be part of this movie, right?"

His friends bump fists.

"Are you two going to make out?" another asks Annaleigh. "You should totally make out."

A third steps forward and kneels before her like he's about to propose. "If you need someone to make out with you on camera," his says, words slurred, "I'm here for you."

Standing, he reaches for her hand. As Annaleigh shrinks back I push the guy away. Off-balance and probably drunk, he topples over. A moment later, he bounces back up, arms outstretched like he's ready to fight.

"That's a wrap," yells Ryder, stepping between us. He turns to the guy challenging me. "You were awesome," he says, patting him on the shoulder. He gives appreciative nods to the others too.

131

"All of you were great. Thanks for being part of this."

They all wear matching confused expressions, like they're not sure if he's serious, or just trying to avoid a bad scene. Ryder points to his crewmen, still shooting from nearby. Then, to reassure the students further, he produces a clipboard and asks each of them to sign a waiver. He's doing anything, saying anything, in a desperate attempt to defuse the situation.

As the energized crowd closes in once more, Annaleigh and I hold each other, like anchors restraining rudderless boats. There's no orderly line for autographs anymore and no respect for our personal space. I look beyond the crowd, hoping for a way to escape.

Instead I see other passersby stopping, drawn by the crowd and the noise. Some of them clearly recognize Annaleigh and me, while others behave as if they're trying to remember where they've seen us before. Plenty more turn quickly away like we're a nuisance. Or just invisible.

Maybe we are a nuisance, but we're not invisible anymore.

Not by a long shot.

21

AN HOUR LATER, I ARRIVE BACK in my room. Gant's working on my laptop. Dad is on his too, trawling through job listings while he listens to a piece of soothing classical music. When he realizes that I'm watching, he hides the browser window.

"How d-did it go?" he asks.

Images run through my mind, of leering students, an intrusive crowd, and a scandalous photo of Sabrina and me.

"Fine," I say.

"Who were you w-with this time?"

"Huh?"

"Which girl?"

His left eye is twitching even more than usual. I don't ask if he has seen the new photo—it's obvious he has.

"Annaleigh," I say.

He purses his lips, but they continue to twitch. "Be a . . . a good man, Seth."

Before I can reply, he resumes his online job hunting. Maybe it's just as well. After the scene at the Chinese Theatre, I don't know what a good man is supposed to do.

Over at the desk, Gant is taking in the newest photo of Sabrina and me. I join him there.

"Looks like someone hit the jackpot," he says.

"Not you as well. I already told Dad—"

"I'm not talking about you, Seth. I'm talking about whoever took it."

"Oh." I crouch next to him. The photo is clearer on my computer screen: Sabrina and me framed perfectly, her lips parted against mine. "It was only a couple seconds."

"Well, kudos to the photographer, then. This is much higher quality than the beach photo. When was it taken?"

"At the Machinus party a few days ago."

"A few *days* ago?" He studies the image again. It feels skeevy the way he's staring at me, mid-kiss, but something's clearly bothering him.

"What's wrong?"

"You know those photos I took of *Romeo and Juliet*? Even though I worked on them the first chance I got, someone uploaded footage to YouTube before I was done."

"Yeah. I remember."

"Lesson is: If you have something valuable, don't sit on it. Most paparazzi would want to sell quickly, while you two are big news."

"Paparazzi are freaking parasites."

Gant bristles. "No way. They're artists, producing stuff on the fly."

"Not this one. It was just a guy with a cell phone. Left the party straight after he took this shot. He's been stalking me ever since I got here."

Gant's mouth hangs open. "Someone's been *stalking* you?"

I check that Dad didn't hear, and shoot Gant a warning look. "Not just me. Sabrina too. She says it comes with the territory."

"When did she say that?"

"When we were on the beach. There was a guy with a camera there too. Really long lens."

"And she stuck around and let him shoot anyway? That's pretty weird behavior for a celebrity. Normally they're fighting paparazzi off like flies." He resumes looking at the party photo—Sabrina and me, lip-locked. "Something's not right here."

"Apart from the invasion of privacy, you mean."

"No. The shot . . . the way it's framed, the lighting, the resolution—you don't get that by holding a cell phone in the air and crossing your fingers."

"Well, no one else was around. I would've noticed if there was another photographer."

He taps the screen at the exact place that our lips are joined. "You sure about that? You look kind of busy." He chews the inside of his cheek methodically. "All I'm saying is, your stalker guy didn't take this photo with a cell phone. So who did?"

I don't have an answer for that. "Seems like you know a lot about this stuff."

"Photography's my thing."

He leans back like a self-satisfied attorney, evidence presented, reasonable doubt established. But if he's right, he's missing an even bigger point: If our stalker isn't in the business of selling photos, why is he following Sabrina and me at all?

22

RYDER CALLS JUST BEFORE LUNCH THE next day. "Good news," he says. "I've got tickets for the Lakers-Clippers game this evening." I wait for him to mention the new photo of Sabrina and me—he must have an opinion about it—but he doesn't. "They're prime seats. I was going to offer one to Sabrina, but she's not answering her phone."

"I'd prefer to go with Annaleigh."

"Oh. Okay."

"Do you think Annaleigh wants to go?"

"I guess we'll find out," he says.

Apparently Annaleigh wants to go. It's just her and me, a private chauffeur, and a too-large limo. Ryder's all in favor of the grand gesture, but sometimes I wish he'd stick to a taxi.

I wear black jeans and a plain white shirt so I can blend in. Annaleigh counters with a flower-print halter top and beret combo that's so cute I figure she'll own every eye in the arena.

The seats aren't courtside, but are close enough to get an awesome view of the action, the sweat, the dunks, and the floor burns. Close enough to notice every time the TV cameras turn to us for a reaction shot.

"Look," I say, "about that photo."

Annaleigh tilts her head and watches me closely. She's wearing more makeup than usual, her blue eyes accented with liner and mascara, as if she's veering toward Sabrina territory. "Hooking up with a movie star doesn't make you a player, Seth."

"Yeah, but—"

"It was before you found out about Kris getting back in the movie. You never would've kissed her if you knew what Sabrina was up to." Having provided me with an excuse, she smiles.

She's wrong—the photo was taken *after* I knew about Kris—but I smile too. Annaleigh wants to move on, and that's fine by me.

A cheer goes up from the crowd. "So which team are we supporting?" Annaleigh shouts.

"The one from L.A."

"Aren't they both from L.A.?"

"Yeah. I think our team is going to win tonight."

She rolls her eyes, but she's smiling too. "Oh, we're up." She elbows me in the ribs.

As the players leave the court for a time-out, she points at the jumbotron. An image of us fills the screen, along with the words *kiss cam*. It takes me a moment to catch up with what's happening, but only a split second more to turn bright red.

Annaleigh bites her lip and shrinks down like a turtle hiding in its shell. Then, fixing her eyes on me, she reaches behind my head and pulls me toward her. Gives me a full-on movie kiss—lots of lips on lips, and hands gliding over skin, and mouths slightly open so that I can feel her short breaths punching the air.

The crowd grows louder, crazier than at any point during the game, but I shut them out. With Sabrina, I had no idea what our kiss meant. With Annaleigh, I know exactly where things stand—we're acting, and we have an audience of eighteen thousand. It ought to feel uncomfortable, but it doesn't. It feels good.

When we stop, people continue to whoop and shout. One section gives us a standing ovation. Annaleigh doesn't miss a beat. She drags me off my seat and leads me in a low bow as every remaining TV camera turns toward us. By the time we sit down, several hundred cell phones are turned in our direction. People who aren't taking photos are texting friends. For a few minutes after play resumes, the game is an afterthought.

Kris told me that news travels fast. Seeing that wall of cameras, I finally grasp *how* a situation can take on a life of its own. The sum of my achievements—acted in a couple commercials and a bunch of plays—cannot explain what I'm seeing. I'm just a creation, an unproven actor in a movie with no director and a fluctuating cast. It's like I've reversed the natural order of celebrity.

Or maybe I'm missing the point. The crowd isn't seeing Seth Crane. They're watching the boy who appeared as Sabrina's sidekick in two now-famous photos. And who, a few days later, is making out with Annaleigh on a kiss cam.

I'm so distracted it takes me a moment to realize that Annaleigh's hand is resting on my leg. Probably has been ever since we sat down. There's something comforting about it, kind of like the way she gazes at me. There's nothing unfocused about that look, and nothing mercurial about her behavior. Annaleigh is my partner in a way that Sabrina can never be, because I trust her.

"This is pretty freaking crazy, huh?" I say.

"I don't know," she says. "I think I could kind of get used to it."

"What? Seats to Lakers games?"

She shakes her head. "Going out with you."

People shove cell phones in our faces as we leave our row and head for the exit. It's like a receiving line, and no one is respecting our personal space.

"Seth! Seth!" A heavyset guy with a cue-ball head yells my name as he takes photo after photo. His camera is expensive, his attitude confrontational. "Is it over between you and Sabrina?"

I take Annaleigh's hand and move faster.

"Annaleigh!" Another photographer barrels through the crowd. His momentum carries him straight into her, and for a moment, she loses her balance and our hands disconnect.

It's like we're fighting a riptide. I need to get back to her. I don't even push the guy hard, but one moment he's standing, the next he's on his butt, asking for witnesses.

Witnesses. It's a joke, but like the incident at the Chinese Theatre, there's nothing funny about this situation. I grasp Annaleigh's hand and we run. Photographers hound us, but I'm with a natural-born runner. The fight-or-flight instinct carries us all the way to the waiting limo.

I slam the door behind us. "Go!" I shout.

The driver throws us into heavy traffic. Two cars tail us.

On the Santa Monica Freeway, one of the vehicles draws alongside us on the outside lane, perfectly matching our speed. When I peer over, a camera flashes.

There's no way anyone can get a decent picture through tinted glass. This is harassment.

I scoot away from the window and bump into Annaleigh. "Why are they doing this?" she asks.

The limo driver growls something unintelligible and leans on the gas. Horns sound, but the noise is muted by the car's plush interior.

My cell phone chimes—an incoming text from Ryder. He must know we're busy, so I figure it's important. I click on the link.

Now I know why we're being pursued.

An entertainment website has published a gallery of photos of Sabrina and me, all of them from the Machinus party. It's like looking at the individual frames of a movie, as Sabrina coils her leg around me, and we come together, and kiss. I shut it down, but not before Annaleigh sees it too.

As enthusiastically as he used the gas, now the driver brakes. We careen across lanes as the pursuing cars fly by, and peel off at La Cienega.

The first traffic signal is red. No one is following us. Annaleigh stares straight ahead, fingertips teasing her hair into sweaty spikes.

"I lost my beret," she murmurs.

We hang a left on Wilshire. At the hotel, we thank the driver and head inside. Don't stop until the main doors close behind us.

We ride the elevator to Annaleigh's floor in silence. I walk her to her room. Earlier, I felt like we'd reached a kind of quiet under-standing. Now everything is messed up again.

"Can we talk, Annaleigh?"

"Okay."

She opens the door and kicks off her platform shoes. Sits on the bed and rubs her feet.

"You were running in *those?*" I ask.

"I save my Nikes for special occasions. You can sit down if you want." She pats the space beside her.

I join her. Even though this is a perfect copy of my room, it feels different—larger, or maybe just emptier.

She turns the video camera on the nightstand so that it's facing us.

"You're really doing that?" I say.

"If I can face a camera feeling like I do now, I can do it any-time." She presses a key, and a tiny light comes on. "So, you want to talk."

Yes, I do. But not like this. Not with the camera on, and only a few inches of bed between us. Trouble is, silence is uncomfortable too.

"Those photos Ryder sent me all came from the same party," I explain. "From the same moment, practically."

She looks bored, like she wishes this would all just go away. "I know," she says.

"It was a mistake."

"A *mistake?*"

"Sabrina wasn't even my first choice for a hookup."

Annaleigh hesitates. "She wasn't?"

141

"No. But Kris was already taken."

She hits me with a pillow, but she's kind of laughing too. "You're such an idiot."

"Yeah, I am."

She looks at our hands, side by side on the bed. "When we showed up on the kiss cam tonight, that was crazy."

"Kind of, yeah . . . being so public and all. But nice too." It comes out sounding like a question.

"Definitely nice." Annaleigh gives a tight-lipped smile. "You're being very agreeable tonight."

"Uh-huh."

She moves her hand so that our fingertips touch. Every fiber of my body, every nerve ending feels like it's being redirected to that one place.

"I guess we should get some sleep," she whispers. "After all the camera flashes we just saw, tomorrow's pictures might be hard to take."

I don't want to move, but I have to. Annaleigh and I were costars and acquaintances. Now we're partners and friends. I need her to see that she can trust me. That I'm everything she thinks I should be.

I stop beside the door. "We're going to be okay. I really believe that."

She nods, but her expression is serious. "I hope you're right."

23

I WAKE EARLY. GANT IS FAST asleep on the other side of the bed. Kind of a bummer that the first time I share a fancy bed with someone, it's my brother.

Dad opted to sleep on the sofa, but he's up too. He's even showered and dressed already. He leans against the sofa, his battered duffel bag packed beside him.

"Where are you going?" I ask him.

"Interview," he says.

I'm about to remind him that he doesn't need to put himself through this—I get fifty grand in less than a week—but he looks different than usual. He's smiling, for one thing. More than that, he seems confident.

I throw on some clothes and head out with him.

In the foyer he picks up a complimentary newspaper. "I-I've been reading things," he says, waving it.

"It's just stupid stuff, Dad. Comes with the territory."

He nods, but doesn't smile. "You'd t-tell me if something was . . . wrong."

"Yeah. I'm just finding my way still."

Now he smiles. "You and me both, son."

We walk toward the main entrance. It's early, but several people are milling around.

"So," he says. "K-kiss cam, hmm?"

I try to laugh it off.

"Y-you were one of *SportsCenter*'s Top Ten Plays."

"*What?*"

He ruffles my hair. "Just kidding. Annale-leigh is nice, though. Your mother . . . she would've liked her."

Two paparazzi hover on the street outside the hotel. The first gets up in our faces as soon as we hit the sidewalk. He's like a school bully, invading our personal space, daring us to push back.

Dad, visibly uncomfortable, climbs into a taxi. I want to hug him and wish him good luck, but there's nothing personal about this moment anymore. Even as I wave good-bye, I feel observed.

"Want to make a comment, Seth?" says the second paparazzo, microphone in hand.

"About what?"

"Annaleigh."

"What about her?"

He acts like I'm joking. Then, as it dawns on him that I'm serious, he tosses a newspaper to me.

I glance at the front page, and freeze.

There are two photographs. The first is of Annaleigh, but she looks different—long hair, and baggy sweatshirt that hangs off one shoulder. The second is of a middle-aged guy with short hair and thick wire glasses, and it's no ordinary photograph.

It's a mug shot.

The two guys photograph my reaction, so I turn away. Inside

the hotel, I continue reading. Words leap off the page, a laundry list of indictments that set my heart pounding: father . . . stolen goods . . . repeat offender . . . awaiting sentencing. But all of them fade away as soon as I read the phrase *first-degree assault*.

Annaleigh's family has distanced themselves from him, according to the report, but none of their neighbors has anything good to say about either parent. Even Annaleigh's boyfriend is quoted as saying that her father is better off behind bars.

Of all the words on the page, *boyfriend* should be the least problematic for me. I can't stop reading it, though.

There are two more photographs at the bottom of the page, both of Annaleigh and me. One is of the kiss cam. In the other, we're walking along Rodeo Drive on Christmas Day. The pictures feel tagged on, irrelevant, but they bring me into Annaleigh's story—make me a character in a drama that I didn't even know existed.

I thought I knew her, this girl I kissed in front of eighteen thousand witnesses.

Turns out, I don't know anything.

I'm early for the rehearsal, but I'm not the first to arrive. Brian welcomes me with half a nod and a whole frown, and I head back to the rehearsal room.

The door is closed, but I can make out Annaleigh's voice. Sabrina's too. They're keeping the volume low, but there's no doubt they're arguing. I stay outside and try to catch a little of their conversation.

"No need to wait," says Ryder, joining me. "We may as well get started."

The argument stops as soon as I open the door. Annaleigh sinks lower in her chair. Sabrina returns to her place on the opposite side of the table.

For a while, we focus on the new script, complete with expanded role for Andrew's *best friend*. But no one's in the mood to improvise and the scripted dialogue sounds trite against the backdrop of Annaleigh's truly dramatic home life.

Thirty minutes in, Annaleigh's phone rings. She rummages in her bag and pulls out two phones—one old, one new. The old one is ringing. She looks at the number on the screen, and at us. I can't tell if she wants permission to answer it, or for someone to tell her to turn it off. Which would be kinder?

She takes the call as we pretend not to listen. The woman's voice on the other end is loud and insistent. When there's a break, Annaleigh doesn't offer a word in self-defense, so the woman resumes yelling.

Finally Annaleigh speaks up. "I didn't tell anyone, Mom," she says quietly. "I don't know how they found out."

Her mother takes over again. This isn't supposed to be a conversation. This is judgment and punishment in one.

"In case you haven't noticed," Annaleigh fights back, "Dad's charges aren't exactly the kind of publicity we want right now!"

For a few seconds Annaleigh keeps the phone pressed against her ear, but it's clear her mother has hung up. Then she stands abruptly and leaves the room. Ryder follows her.

I push my chair back.

"Let her go," says Sabrina.

"She's freaking out."

"Ryder can handle it."

"So can I."

I head along the corridor and out into the sun-smog L.A. air. When she sees me, Annaleigh wraps her arms around me and buries her face in my chest.

"I'm sorry," she says.

"This isn't your fault."

She doesn't say anything after that, just holds on to me, her whole body shaking.

"Let's get you back to the hotel," says Ryder gently. Then, turning to me, he adds, "Stay here. Work on those new scenes."

What he means are the scenes with my new best friend, Sabrina. He's several days too late for that relationship to ring true.

Annaleigh slopes toward his car like she's sleepwalking, and Ryder follows, seemingly as dazed as she is. He's probably calculating how much this news will affect the movie. Hard to put a positive spin on a story like this.

The car pulls away. I can't see Annaleigh through the glare on the windshield, but I imagine her sitting inside, quiet and pensive. I feel like I did when Maggie leaked the story about Kris and Tamara—worried and frustrated and lost. Difference is, there's no one to blame this time, and I really want to blame someone.

A door closes behind me. Sabrina leans against the wall, lighting a cigarette. She blows a stream of smoke high into the air.

"How's she doing?" she asks.

"How do you think?"

"Well, it was an intense scene, but all things considered, she did pretty good." She takes a long drag on the cigarette. "I'd give her seven out of ten. Timing's a little off, but the instincts are there. Probably just needs practice."

I never thought that Sabrina could say something so cruel.

"She must've known this would come out, right?" Sabrina murmurs. "That's a lot of time to prepare a reaction."

"Not everyone prepares for bad news."

"Then she's crazy. Or delusional. And I don't think she's either."

I want to fight back. I want to say how unfair it is that Sabrina emerges from her dysfunctional home life stronger than ever while Annaleigh suffers for her father's crimes. But I can feel the entire movie hanging in the balance. It's no secret that Sabrina and Annaleigh aren't getting along. One angry word from me, and Sabrina might pull out completely. Without her, who knows if there'll be any movie left at all?

24

I KNOCK ON ANNALEIGH'S DOOR, BUT she isn't answering. I try her phone but go to voicemail. Call Ryder, who assures me that he saw her to her room before leaving.

I ask the desk clerk if there's any way to check on her. "I'm worried," I explain.

"She looked okay on her way to the fitness center earlier," he replies.

Sure enough, Annaleigh is on a treadmill. She told me this relentless need to run is an attempt to escape her home life. One week in L.A. and it has caught up with her.

The display reads 9.2 miles. She's been running for an hour and twenty minutes. She should be coated in sweat, but she isn't. She should hear me approach, see me standing right beside her, but she doesn't. She just stares at the TV screens above her—a talk show wading through the day's juiciest gossip.

There are familiar photos of Annaleigh and her father. Annaleigh and me on the kiss cam. Then pictures of me: stills from *Romeo and Juliet,* a short clip from my first commercial, with Kris at the party, all moody looks and fancy clothes. The sound isn't on, but it's obviously an attempt to show that we've grown up on opposite sides of the tracks.

"Annaleigh?"

My voice seems to awaken her, but she keeps moving. She must be dehydrated. I wasn't able to face breakfast. What's the likelihood that she has eaten today?

"Annaleigh," I say, firmer this time.

She blinks, but doesn't stop. So I press the stop button for her, and watch her strides contract until she's only walking, then standing. When she steps off the machine, she almost falls.

I wrap an arm around her and lead her away. She should feel hot against me, but she doesn't. All the way to her room she leans against me for support. I'm certain that if I let her go, she'll collapse.

I tell her to lie down on the bed. Remove her shoes and socks, and cover her with the sheet. She pulls it tight against her—more for the feeling of security than need of warmth, probably.

"My full name is Rebecca Annaleigh Ware," she says. "But I always wanted to go by Annaleigh."

I sit beside her. Her eyes are open, but she isn't looking at me.

"I hoped it would be enough, using my middle name. Figured that with a new haircut and clothes, there was a chance no one would make the connection. I even kept my new cell phone number a secret from everyone back home, like I could make that life go away. Start over. How stupid does that sound?"

"This isn't your fault."

"Yes, it is. I should've used a completely different name, but I wanted it to be *my* name in lights. I wanted something to be proud of. Why wasn't I satisfied with just getting away?" She clicks her tongue—dry, parched. "At home, it never matters what I do. Nothing ever changes. But this movie could've made all the difference." Anger flares across her face, but it's quickly extinguished. "Now I don't know what's going to happen."

I fetch a glass of water. "You should've told me."

"About my father? How he lost his job and started dealing stolen goods to make ends meet? How sometimes he'd come home with injuries he couldn't explain? I was afraid that if Ryder and Brian found out, they wouldn't want me anymore. Especially not once I told them I'm using the money to pay for his lawyer."

It never occurred to me that she might still feel connected to her father.

"He's family," she says, interpreting my silence. "I hate my parents, and I'm so angry at my dad. But he wouldn't hurt someone like they say he did."

As she takes the glass from me, our fingers brush together. "Did Brian tell you to check on me?"

"No."

"He already called. Wanted to know how long I'll need to get my head straight. That's how he said it, like I'm some kind of flake. It's only a matter of time before Sabrina gets my role."

"That's not going to happen."

"Oh yeah? How are you going to stop her?"

"I don't know. But you and me, we've dealt with too much crap to give up fighting now."

Annaleigh shrugs. "You'd be really good together."

"No, we wouldn't! Look, I'm not who you think I am."

"So who are you? I don't know anything about you, either. Where do you live? Where's your mom? What *crap* have you dealt with?"

I don't want to talk about me—the timing doesn't feel right—but there's no camera recording us now. As Annaleigh squeezes my hand, I realize that maybe the right time to open up is when someone cares enough to listen.

"I grew up in Ohio," I begin. "Summer before high school, Mom got a job at UC–Northridge. Something big in human resources. She had a month between jobs, so we took a road trip. We were in New Mexico when she got sick. Stomach pain. We tried to get her to go to the hospital, but she wouldn't. Toughed it out for three more days. Turned out, her appendix had perforated. They operated immediately. She seemed to be getting better when she became septic. She died the next day."

I've told the story so many times that it has an almost clinical efficiency, like the synopsis to a play. I don't even cry anymore. But then, I don't need to. Annaleigh is crying for me.

"Why didn't your mom listen to you?"

It's what everyone asks—the seventy-eight-thousand-dollar question. "Because her new health insurance didn't kick in for another couple weeks. We were supposed to close on a house in Encino, but the bank pulled out when they realized we were on the hook for the hospital bills. Dad's stroke happened a few weeks later. He wasn't insured either. Gave it up when he quit his old job, because he was going to be covered by hers."

Annaleigh runs her thumb in slow circles across my wrist. "I'm sorry. I had no idea."

"How could you? Like you say, it's not something I talk about."

152

"How did you get over it? I mean, something like that . . . I just can't imagine."

"I didn't. Not at first. But then I realized, you can't control everything. Stuff happens, and it'll happen again. There's nothing you can do about it. You just have to keep going." I savor the feel of her thumb against my skin. "This movie isn't over, Annaleigh. It's a dark moment, but we'll survive."

Annaleigh stares deep into me. "We?"

"Yeah. *We.*"

Her thumb stops moving. Her bare arm rests on the sheets, fading summer tan against bright white. She watches me watching her.

I want to hold her. She's beautiful and strong and determined, and she cares about me. I care about her too.

"I'm sorry I didn't tell you the truth," she whispers. "I was going to, at the party, but then Sabrina arrived . . ." She takes my hand and we twine fingers. "I won't compete with her, Seth."

"I don't want you to."

"I'm just saying, I'll never be Sabrina Layton." She rolls away, so that I can't see her face. "I don't have a boyfriend, just so you know. The guy in the article, he dumped me last summer. Did it by text. Hasn't said a word to me since. But I guess I'm worth knowing again now."

Our hands, still joined, rest on her hip. Her skin is warm beneath the sheet and the thin material of her shorts.

"Yes," I say. "You are."

25

DAD CALLS ME AROUND DINNERTIME. I expected him to be back already. Job interviews don't usually take all day.

"I g-got it," he says.

I've already prepared a sympathetic response, and it takes me a moment to switch gears. "That's . . . amazing!"

Amazing might not be the best choice of adjective, but Dad makes nothing of it. "I worked this afternoon. Tomorrow I'll be f-full time."

"So what's the job? Where're you working?"

"UC–Northridge."

The words just sit there. Mom was supposed to work at UC–Northridge. It's why we moved out west. We always figured that Dad would get an accounting job there too, sooner or later, but after the stroke, all bets were off. Now we've come full circle.

"Which department?" I ask.

"A f-few of them. Wherever they . . . need me most."

It can't be easy to manage accounts in several departments, so maybe he's doing audits. Not his favorite work, but between his income and mine, we'll be comfortable for the first time in years.

"I'm so proud of you, Dad. I mean it."

"Thanks, son. Is G-Gant there?"

I pass the phone to my brother. As usual, he's sitting at the desk, studying photos of me and Annaleigh and Sabrina. He must already know Dad's news from my response, but he bubbles with excitement when he hears it firsthand.

A few seconds later, he turns to me. "Dad says I can stay here, if it's okay with you."

"Sure, as long as you move to the sofa."

Gant relays the information. "Seth's even letting me have the bed!"

My brother has a weird sense of humor.

Ryder goes ahead with the rehearsal the next morning, even without Annaleigh. She says she doesn't feel well, but we all know what the real problem is, and there isn't a pill to fix it.

Sabrina and I sit on opposite sides of the table and read aloud the latest version of Ryder's script. She warns me—her best friend, Andrew—not to get too involved with Lana. She tells me that I'm being irrational. She wonders why I don't trust her anymore. As Andrew, I assure her that she's wrong about everything. As Seth, I want to add that it's none of her business.

After half an hour, Ryder offers us headcams.

"No way," says Sabrina. "Not now."

Startled, Ryder turns to me. "You're going to be wearing them during filming," he says.

I don't want to wear one either. I just want the rehearsal to end so I can check on Annaleigh. Then again, isn't it time Ryder got to call the shots?

Sabrina watches intently as I pull the strap over my head and adjust the camera.

"Remember," says Ryder, "you can improvise. I *want* you to improvise. Scenes like this are tough and emotional, I get that, but the script is only a starting point. Let the dialogue flow."

Sabrina reaches for the other headcam. It ought to be comical, watching Sabrina Layton strap a camera to her forehead, but she's not smiling. Like adversaries choosing pistols at dawn, we use the cameras as weapons in our duel.

"Only one headcam at a time, please," says Ryder. "Seth, just put yours on the table facing Sabrina."

It would seem petulant to point out that I was wearing my camera first, so I do as I'm told. All the same, the message feels familiar: *There's only one real star here.*

"Do you love her?" asks Sabrina.

"What?" I reply.

"Lana. Seems to me, she's hooked you good."

Earlier, Sabrina was reading the lines straight off the page. Now she's ignoring the script altogether. She stares at me, bristling with impatience and frustration and maybe even anger.

"I . . . yeah, she's special."

"Special?" Sabrina makes the word sound trivial, childish.

"I like her."

"Is that why you're shutting me out?"

"I'm not. Things are different now, that's all."

"They sure are. You don't want to hear a word I say. Don't even want to look at me."

I return my focus to her camera, unaware that I was even looking away. "It'd help if you could just be normal for a change."

Sabrina flares her nostrils. "So I'm right—you are shutting me out."

"Not everything has to be about you."

"Why can't you admit you hate me? Just *say* it!"

Silence hangs between us. A minute ago, she came out firing, but she's out of ammo now and vulnerable. I could go for the kill right here, but I'm not Andrew and Sabrina's not my best friend and this is feeling way too real.

"I don't hate you," I say. "I just feel like things would be easier if you weren't around."

She doesn't respond for several moments. Then she removes the headcam and places it gently on the table. "Good luck with that." She stands, so that I'm staring up at her. "'Cause this is my story too, and I'm not going anywhere."

As if to prove her point, she lights a cigarette and blows a stream of smoke across the table. I wait for Ryder to intervene, to chasten her for being out of line, but he doesn't say a word. It's like he's our audience, not a director at all, and he's afraid to break the spell.

Scripted reality has never felt more real.

Gant's waiting for me in my room. "Let's get out of here," he says.

I don't argue. I want to get away too.

We leave the hotel, walking north on Rodeo. Then Beverly Drive. "Where are we going?" I ask.

"Franklin Canyon."

"Ever heard of taxis?"

"Ever heard of legs?" He glances over his shoulder. "So far, so good."

I look too. "What's back there?"

"Nothing," he replies enigmatically. "That's the point."

He knows the canyons well. Not just Franklin, but Dixie, Fryman, Coldwater, Laurel. They run like fingers—some slender, some stubby—from the Santa Monica mountains. He used to bring his camera here and photograph the landscape. Then he'd put the pictures on a website. It's how he landed his first paid work.

He hasn't brought his camera today, though.

We don't have to go far into the park to feel apart from the city. One moment it's spread below us, the next it's disappearing. Gant stands on the threshold and surveys the gray concrete landscape under the steel-gray sky.

"Your stalker's taking the day off," he says.

I follow his gaze back down the path. It's true—no one else is there. Which pretty much confirms what I already suspected: The stalker is more interested in Sabrina than me. What I still don't understand is why Sabrina doesn't seem to care.

We take Hastain Trail, a wide dirt path that slices up the east side of the canyon. Scrub smothers the hills, and it's quiet here. I feel like I could walk straight out the other end of the canyon, all the way home to Van Nuys, and discover that the past two weeks have been a dream.

After a mile, we stop to take in the view. A sliver of downtown L.A. is visible again, and my heartbeat quickens. "Let's keep going," I say.

Gant follows, but stops a short distance later. "It's gone," he says.

"What is?"

"The city. That's what was freaking you out, right?" I expect him to laugh—it's kind of ridiculous for me to get paranoid about an entire city—but he doesn't. "Did you know that someone dies in these canyons almost every year?"

I shake my head.

"Yeah," he continues. "It's usually dehydration, or heat exposure. They can be two hundred yards from a road, but it still takes hours for rescue teams to find the body. Sometimes days. Even with four million people in the city. Ten million people in L.A. County. *Days*." He runs a hand through his hair. "But the cast of *Whirlwind* can't stay out of the news for even one day."

I get the feeling this is why he's brought me here—to talk about the movie. "Sabrina says it's not really news, most of the time. When people can't find anything to write about, they just make stuff up."

"But they're not making it up, right? That's the whole point. It's like there's this huge file of photographs and fresh-squeezed gossip just waiting for the right moment to come out. First, it was a picture of you and Sabrina on the beach. Then the story about Kris and Tamara. Then you and Sabrina, redux. Then you and Annaleigh making out on the kiss cam. Then *bam!* Suddenly her father is front-page news too." He watches me from the corner of his eye. "It's almost like someone has an agenda against all of you."

I resist the temptation to roll my eyes. "It's called making

159

money. Selling stories and photographs to tabloids and magazines. How else do you think Kris and Tamara's story got leaked?"

It's a throwaway remark, but Gant latches on to it. "*Leaked? What do you know about it?*"

"At the Machinus party, Sabrina told me that Kris and Tamara were dating in secret. Later on, I told Maggie."

"Who's Maggie?"

"She was Ryder and Brian's intern. They fired her when she leaked the story to some magazine."

"Does Kris know that?"

"No. He thinks it was Sabrina."

Gant takes a water bottle from his backpack. "Let me get this straight. Kris thinks Sabrina ratted him out. Then he sees a picture of you two making out at the same party *he* was attending." He takes a swig. "You can see why he might want to bring you all down, right?"

"Kris is an actor, not a mafia kingpin."

"Do your research, Seth. He's a rich, powerful actor with very loyal friends. An actor no one is talking about anymore, because they're too busy talking about Seth Crane, the unknown guy who took his role *and* his ex-girlfriend."

"Then why wouldn't Kris go after *me*? What's Annaleigh done?"

"She's part of the movie too. Maybe he's trying to shut the whole thing down. If the movie folds, you disappear along with it." He hands me the bottle. "Look, there's no way your stalker took that photo of you and Sabrina at the party, not with a cell phone. Kris could've done it, though. That's probably why there are photos of you and Annaleigh and Sabrina, but none of him. It'd also explain why he didn't sell the picture right away. He wanted to wait until it could do the most damage."

"If Kris took those photos of Sabrina and me kissing, I would've seen him."

"No, you wouldn't." Gant finds a twig and sketches in the orange dirt: two stick figures, and a camera positioned high above us. "The downward angle of the photo was steep, like someone was shooting from above, right? I'm guessing whoever took it was camped out on a balcony. In the low light, you never would've seen him."

He's all confidence and thinly disguised excitement. It may not be JFK and a rogue shooter and a grassy knoll, but Gant has a theory, and he's clearly given it a lot of thought. He has no idea that his account is completely implausible.

"There was no balcony."

He brushes the objection aside. "A second floor, then."

"The building was one story."

"Well, *someone* took it." He flicks the twig away.

This isn't about solving a problem— it's about holding someone responsible. Finding the cause of this bad luck, because bad luck has to have a cause. Gant looks like he did after Mom died, a preteen standing outside our father's hospital room, teeth gritted and fists clenched at his sides, waiting for someone to explain *why* it was happening. He still doesn't understand that bad stuff happens, and all you can do is pick yourself up and carry on.

"Maybe it was a security camera," I say. "Mounted to the ceiling."

He stares at me from under heavy brows. He thinks I'm trying to placate him, the little brother with the crazy theories. "You and Dad, you're just the same."

"Yeah, we both have jobs."

"You don't even know what he's doing, do you?"

"He's doing accounting at UC–Northridge."

"Is that what he told you?"

"Yeah. He said he's working in a few different departments."

"Sure, as a *custodian*." He gives the word time to sink in. "Not an accountant. He'll be cleaning toilets and polishing the freakin' sinks."

I could say that someone has to do it, and that Dad sounded more excited last night than he has in a year, but Gant has made his point. I don't ask the important questions. I just want to see the silver lining. Want the future to look better than the past.

Even if that means closing my eyes.

26

THE NEXT MORNING, I BUY ANNALEIGH a latte and a
Danish pastry and take it to her room. She answers the door in
faded cotton pj's.

"How are you doing?" I ask.

She returns to the bed and sits cross-legged on the comforter,
eyeing the pastry. "You know those fishing shows on TV? The
ones where guys trash-talk about the size of their bass catch?"

"No."

"Well, you would, if you lived in Arkansas. Anyway, they always
hold the fish up like a trophy, and you see it trying to breathe, but
it knows it's dying. Right now, I feel like that fish."

I think she's trying to be funny, but it's hard to tell.

"Look, I'm not going to flake out on you, okay?" she says suddenly. "So stop worrying."

"Who said anything about flaking out?"

"Trust me, I get it. If I were you, I'd be worried too. But I won't
screw this up for you."

Maybe I ought to be touched that she cares. Instead, I'm
annoyed that she thinks this conversation is about me. "I'm worried about *you*, Annaleigh. Not the movie."

"Oh. Well then," she says, holding up the pastry, "you're doing a good job of looking after me. Five more of these and I'll be ready for anything. Including a new wardrobe."

"With all the running you've been doing, I don't think you need to worry."

She's about to take a bite when she notices the backpack slung over my shoulder. "What's that for?"

"There's something we need to do. You should probably get dressed first."

"What's going on?"

I fold my arms. "You're just going to have to trust me."

She opens her mouth, and closes it again. "Fine," she says, heading for the bathroom. "Give me five minutes."

I press the key for the top floor. Annaleigh leans against the elevator wall and tugs at the strap of her running vest. It's tight against her. Every curve, every muscle is visible.

The doors open, but she doesn't step out. It's eerily quiet. "Are we allowed up here?" she asks.

I press a finger to my lips and whisper, "Definitely not."

The door to the suite is very slightly ajar, just as planned. I nudge it open.

"Okay," she says. "Now I'm getting nervous."

"Nervous is good. This room costs twenty-five thousand dollars per night."

"You're kidding."

"Never been more serious."

There's a tray beside the door. A couple plates of largely

untouched food. A jar of caviar. An empty bottle of champagne. Last night's guests have been enjoying themselves.

I close and lock the door behind us.

"What are you doing, Seth?"

"We don't want to be interrupted. Trust me."

She's been trying to play it cool, but now she blushes. "Exactly what do you have in mind?"

I beckon her farther inside.

She follows me along the marble hallway. "Wait a minute. Is this the *Pretty Woman* suite?"

"Uh-huh."

She stares at the floor-to-ceiling windows. Los Angeles is spread out before us, an urban ocean stretching to the horizon.

"You're not about to drop three grand on the bed and ask me to stick around for the week, like Julia Roberts, are you?" she asks.

"No, I don't have three grand. Plus, security will drag us off a long time before that. But don't worry. I gave housekeeping fifty bucks to clean this room last." I place my backpack on the floor and pull out a couple bottles. Hand one to Annaleigh and glance at my watch. "We've got another forty-five minutes to enjoy the view. And we're going to do it in style."

"Gatorade? Seriously?"

"It's important to stay hydrated."

We clink plastic bottles. Annaleigh takes a swig, and continues to explore the suite, which is at least twice as large as my house. She runs her free hand along the columns that line the hallway, and stops beside double doors. "Forty-five minutes, right?"

"More like forty-two."

"You're *sure*?"

"Yeah. Why?"

She opens the doors and wanders inside. I join her. It's the largest bathroom I've ever seen. Dark marble floor. Fresh bouquets of flowers on either end of the deep tub. There's even a TV built into the wall.

"In *Pretty Woman*, Julia Roberts got a bath," she says.

I follow her eyes to the tub. "Yeah. Wait . . . no way!"

"Why not?"

"Because it's crazy."

"You said no one would interrupt us."

"Sure, but . . ."

Her thumb drifts up to her mouth. She almost bites the nail, but stops herself. "So what if they *do* interrupt us? They kick us out, right? Maybe take photographs and sell the story to TMZ. Tell me how that's any worse than all the other crap that's been happening."

I want to say that it can always be worse, and that I carefully organized this episode *inside* the hotel so that we wouldn't risk generating publicity *outside*. But that's not really her point. She's tired of paying for other people's mistakes. Why shouldn't she go crazy herself?

"Forty minutes," I tell her. "I'll keep guard."

I check the corridor for signs of unwanted visitors. As I lock the door again my cell phone chimes. It's a text from Sabrina: *Need 2 meet. 3PM. Back of hotel.*

I almost delete the message, but I have things I want to say to

Sabrina too, about photographs and a mysterious stalker. Things that are best discussed away from the rehearsal room.

I text back that I'll be there.

Five minutes later, Annaleigh shuts off the water. It sloshes as she slides into the bath. "You can come in now," she calls out.

I hesitate. "Really?"

"Really."

I open the doors. She's submerged beneath a nest of bubbles. Only her left leg rises above the surface.

"I just realized that a bath is kind of boring if you don't have someone to talk to," she says.

"Yeah."

"You're letting the warmth out, by the way."

"Oh." I close the doors behind me.

When I turn around again, she's got a smile on her face like she's teasing. It's not the smile that draws me in, though. It's her wet hair, and the color in her cheeks and lips, as if she's radiating heat.

"So we've got about thirty-five minutes," she says.

"Unless housekeeping comes early."

"True." She lifts a finger to her lips. "I've been thinking—if we get kicked out, Brian'll have to find someplace else for us. I vote for the Chateau Marmont. Or maybe the Four Seasons." She tilts her head to the side. "Are you planning to stay over there? This long-distance conversation feels kind of weird."

"Unlike taking a bath in someone else's suite, you mean?"

"It's no one's suite until someone checks in."

I pad over to the tub and sit at the end. She places one dripping foot in my lap and points her toes like a ballerina. "Julia Roberts got a foot massage," she says.

"Do I look like Richard Gere?"

"No. You look like his cute grandson."

I run my hands over her foot. Press my thumbs into the pad of every toe, and slide a finger between them. She watches me intently, her breathing slow and deep. I love the sound of it, and the way she bites her lower lip.

"You haven't tickled me yet," she says. "Must be all that practice. You probably bring all your girlfriends to the *Pretty Woman* suite, huh?"

I nod. "Every one of them. I always figure, what's twenty-five grand for a decent foot massage, right?"

"Don't exaggerate. You told me you bribed the cleaning staff with fifty bucks. You cheapskate, you."

"Ah, you've seen through me already."

She opens her mouth as if to reply, but hesitates. "Not *through* you, no. Just seeing the real you, I think." She cups her hands and lifts a cloud of bubbles. "Why are you being nice to me, Seth?"

"Why shouldn't I be?"

"I don't want you to feel sorry for me."

My thumbs come to rest on the top of her foot. "I'm being nice because you deserve it. Because you're the one person in this whole place who's real."

"Real," she murmurs, like it's a funny concept. "Is any of this real? At home I spend every day just trying to get by. My last boyfriend wasn't nice to me. Be honest. Is this just one of those summer camp moments where everything is magical because it can't last?"

It's a good question. I thought that being on the beach with Sabrina was real, and I was wrong. What makes this situation any different?

"It's real if we want it to be, right?" I reply.

She closes her eyes momentarily. I figure this is the end, and the reality we suspended the moment we walked into the bathroom is about to return with a vengeance. But then Annaleigh slides along the tub and kneels so that we're eye to eye. Drops of water run down her neck and over her shoulders.

She smells of soap and shampoo. I know exactly what I want to do but I'm too afraid to do it.

"Will you go out with me tonight?" I ask, stalling.

Her already pink cheeks grow rosier still. "Yeah. I'd like that."

I run my fingers through her hair. She cups my chin and leans forward, closes her eyes, and kisses me. Her lips are soft. Every brush of her tongue is pure electricity.

I don't need to ask if she's in character now. There are no cameras and no audience here. There's just the two of us, holding tight to each other.

27

SABRINA PULLS UP AT THREE O'CLOCK SHARP.

"Thanks for coming," she says as I climb into her car.

Her makeup is perfect. Not a hair is out of place. The outside world may ruffle Annaleigh's feathers, but not Sabrina's.

We get onto Santa Monica Boulevard, heading east. "So how are you doing?" she asks brightly, as if she has already forgotten yesterday's awkward rehearsal.

"Why do you want to see me, Sabrina?"

She fingers the ends of her hair. Whatever expectations she had for this meeting clearly didn't include me being short with her.

"Sabrina?"

She peers at the rearview mirror and her shoulders slump. When I check the side mirror, I see why. The green Mazda is right behind us.

"Who is he?" I ask.

"I don't know. Probably a paparazzo."

"Uh-uh. He didn't take that photo of us at the party. He *wants* us to know he's watching too. Even sends stupid texts." I check him out in the side mirror, but I can't get a good look. "Stop at this traffic signal."

"The light's green."

"Just do it."

She brakes suddenly. Our stalker is tailing us so close that we're bumper to bumper as we stop. We're two rocks in a creek, and traffic flows around us like water.

I step out to the sound of blaring horns. It's a crazy thing to do, but I want the guy to know how it feels to be trapped. To feel like the one being pursued.

I can just make him out, jamming the lock on his door. I hold up my cell phone and he covers his face with his hands. Doesn't matter. There's nothing he can do to stop me from taking a picture of his license plate.

Then I'm back in Sabrina's car. "Wait until the light turns red, and floor it," I tell her.

Seconds tick by, and the light switches from green to yellow, and yellow to—

Sabrina guns the gas. The cross traffic doesn't even move before we careen across the intersection. Behind us, the Mazda is stuck at the light.

"We need to get off this street," I say. "He'll catch up again."

She takes the next left. A few blocks later, she turns right.

I email the photograph to Gant. He said I needed to find out who this guy was. Well, now we've got his license plate. It's a start.

For a minute, neither of us speaks. Sabrina still looks tense, though.

"Are you going to tell me what this is about?" I ask.

She's gripping the steering wheel so tightly that her knuckles are white. "I know this entertainment reporter," she begins.

"We've done a couple interviews. I've told her stuff off the record, and she's never used it, so I trust her. Anyway, I asked her about the story on Annaleigh's father. She did some rooting around and . . . well, there's something weird about it."

"Like what?"

"Someone went to a lot of trouble to hide all that stuff about Annaleigh's family. I mean, the moment she was cast, every gossip columnist worth their dime would've started digging. My contact did, and she said she couldn't find anything."

"Maybe she wasn't looking hard enough."

"No way. Whoever dug up the info knew what they were looking for. Must've had details—where she's from, contact information, that sort of thing."

Could Kris have paid someone to find this stuff out? It's possible, but unlikely.

"*You* know Annaleigh's contact info," I point out. "And you just said you know a reporter."

"Wait. You don't think that I did this, do you?" Sabrina stares straight ahead, shoulders rigid. "That *is* what you think, isn't it?"

I don't answer because I'm not sure. It'd be crazy for her to tell me all this if she's the one pulling the strings, but then, I don't know who took and sold those photos of Sabrina and me at the party either. Fact is, some of those pictures came out immediately after the kiss cam, almost like someone was trying to divert attention back to Sabrina. If there's a list of suspects, Sabrina's on it.

I stare out the window at the city to my right and the hills to my left. We're in the vicinity of Hollywood Reservoir. Does Sabrina know that Annaleigh and I came here for the photo shoot? Is this another clue?

"How does anyone really have friends?" she murmurs, although I can't tell if she's talking to me, or herself. "I really wanted us to be friends."

"Yeah, well, so did I. But friends don't bring their ex-boyfriends back into the movie without warning. Friends don't make out in a dark corner one minute and then bad-mouth each other the next. How am I supposed to feel about that?"

"You're right," she says. "I wasn't thinking straight."

It's not even an explanation, let alone an apology. Maybe she doesn't know the answer herself.

"Why do you want us to be friends when you hardly know me?" I ask.

"I know that evening on the beach, you really *listened* to me and seemed to care. Being with you was like starting over, seeing everything for the first time, without all the bad stuff. You don't know how long it's been since I felt like I could open up."

Her words pull me back to the beach. But instead of reliving the roller-coaster emotion of the encounter, I just feel confused.

"You wouldn't even let on which version of you I was talking to," I remind her. "How can I trust you when I don't even know who you are?"

For a while she doesn't answer. Then she begins to nod, slow at first and then faster. "Okay, then," she says. "I'll tell you the truth. If we can't even be friends, at least I'll set the record straight."

Sabrina turns off the street and we begin the climb into the Hollywood Hills. We're heading away from Beverly Hills, and the hotel, and Annaleigh.

"Where are we going?" I ask her.

She doesn't look at me. "Somewhere no one can hear us."

28

WE PASS THE TURN FOR THE reservoir and head on to Griffith Park, within sight of the city but somehow removed from it too. Barely a day goes by there isn't a film crew somewhere in the massive grounds.

Sabrina parks the car and gets out. "Come on," she says.

"Where?"

"Please, just come."

She leads me into nearby woods, secluded and quiet, and sits on a patch of grass. I join her so that we're side by side, close but not touching.

She undoes the clasp of her bag and removes a pouch of tobacco. Opens it, and stops. The internal debate plays out on her face: the need to smoke versus the fact that I don't like it. When she puts it away, I'm surprised.

Sabrina faces forward, not blinking, loose hair whipped about by the breeze. "No," she says suddenly. "No, I can't do this."

She grabs her bag and strides quickly away.

Is this Sabrina the actress? Or Sabrina the public figure? I can't believe the real Sabrina would resort to something so melodramatic.

I wait for her to drop the act. It's got to be hard to maintain that kind of energy without an audience. But she doesn't stop, and her shoulders are shaking.

I follow her at a jog. When I catch up, she's crying—not delicate tears either, but sobs that rack her body. Mascara streaks angry lines down her face.

I don't know this version of Sabrina at all. It's not a persona she'd want anyone to see, though. Not ever.

"Sabrina?" I sit down, and coax her to join me on the grass.

She crosses her legs, Indian-style. "The other night at the party," she begins, "I didn't mean to be rude about you. That was stupid of me. Hurtful. But Kris said something at the bar, and I . . . I just panicked."

"Go on."

"He knew I kissed you. I don't know how he knew, but he did, and he told me I was embarrassing myself. That I needed to get a grip on my life. He said what I was doing to you was cruel."

"So you were leading me on."

"No. That's not it. He meant that, you know, things are complicated for me. And maybe you're not the best person to handle it."

"Handle *what*?"

I wait for her to put the pieces together, and reveal the picture once and for all. Instead, she grabs fistfuls of hair and leans forward until her face is almost in her lap.

"I ruined everything," she cries. "With you. With Annaleigh. I shouldn't have said that stuff about her. That was stupid."

"So why did you?"

"Because I was jealous." She takes a rasping breath. "It's not fair what happened to her. But no matter what people say, she knows deep down that her father was the one who messed up. Not her. She's innocent."

"And what about you?"

Slowly, she pulls herself upright. She looks me straight in the eye, but then turns away as if holding my gaze is too much. "I . . . I'm an addict," she says quietly. "Pills mostly. Amphetamines to get up. Vicodin when I'm flying and need to come down. Other stuff too. Sometimes . . . *anything*."

I feel the words as much as I hear them—icy fingers around my heart, a hand pressed tight around my neck. I want her to take them back. Start over.

"I've been trying to quit for over a year now, but . . ." She shakes her head sharply. "No, that's bullshit. I say I want to quit, but I don't. Not really."

I don't know what to say. I feel like I can help Annaleigh because I know what we're up against. Drugs are different, though—a moving target, something that happens to other people, not the ones close to me.

"Does Kris know?"

Sabrina seems to have been expecting the question. Either that, or she has steeled herself to answer anything. "It's why we broke up. He gave me an ultimatum: him or the pills."

"And then he left you."

She pauses, and a sickening smile pulls at her lips. "No. I chose the pills."

I try to imagine how such a conversation could play out, but what sane person could ever say those words?

"I don't know who I am anymore," she says. "I imagine that I'm watching myself, trying to work out which version of me is real. I can't stand it, so I take something to make the doubt go away. And then I take more to keep it away."

I think about Sabrina's weird behavior. How I never knew which version of her I was getting. "That evening on the beach—"

"I was clean, I swear. I wanted to prove to myself that I was in control. You helped me too. Kept me real for a few hours. But it was so *tiring*. You have no idea. And then, when I got home . . ." She doesn't finish the thought. She doesn't need to.

"Why are you telling me this now?"

"Because I want you to know the real me. Instead of being pissed, you should be pleased you get to walk away." She stares at her nails, bold red and manicured, a perfect exterior to distract from what's inside. "I don't want you to walk away, though. I think, deep down, you still care, and I need to open up to someone. It's been so long since I could just . . . *talk*."

"What about Genevieve?"

She pulls a strand of hair across her mouth. "No. I can't talk to her."

"Sure you can. Ask her to visit. She'll come."

"No, she won't. She'll never come again." She sounds maddeningly certain. "Something happened. Something I can't take back."

Another clue to the puzzle, but this piece will stay hidden. Friend or not, real Sabrina can't trust me with everything.

She told me not to believe the hype, the fiction of who she is. She *warned* me, even. But I thought I knew better. Hard to unlearn assumptions accumulated over years of seeing her on film. But the truth is that Sabrina is more alone and confused than anyone I've ever met.

Three years ago, I watched helpless as Mom's insides were liquefied by infection. It was so all-consuming that I didn't notice what was happening to Dad until it was too late. I swore then that I would take care of Dad and Gant. Others too, if I could. But as Sabrina leans against me, crying warm tears into my hair, I feel lost. I try to tell myself that I'm being the friend she needs simply by being here. But I'm not. I'm just a spectator, as irrelevant now as I was at the beach.

What use is a friend who has no idea how to help?

29

GANT BOUNDS UP FROM THE DESK CHAIR. "Where have you been?"

"Just . . . out. Why?"

He jabs a finger at my laptop. "You were right. The photo of you and Sabrina at the party was from a security camera." He practically trips over the words.

The party. Sabrina seemed invincible that evening, sultry and seductive in a little black dress. I remember the way she looked at me, dark eyes constantly moving, like she was drinking me in. How much of it was real? How much was drugs?

"I didn't believe it at first," Gant continues. "The image is too good. But then I realized, it's in a dark corner, so the camera would be calibrated for low light. A security camera would be mounted to the wall too, so there's no problem with shake. Suddenly you've got yourself some very valuable footage of Sabrina and Seth making out."

"The party was at Machinus Media Enterprises," I remind him. "Who could've gotten hold of security film?"

"I've got a theory about that," he says. But instead of sharing it, he sits down and taps the keyboard. "Now take a look at this one."

I join him at the desk. Another photo fills my laptop screen—Sabrina and me at the beach. A beautiful girl and her doting boy. A cigarette and a secret.

"I couldn't work out why the quality was so bad," he says. "But then I thought about the security camera, and it hit me: This isn't a photograph. It's a captured image, like a still frame from a movie. I think you two were being filmed on that beach."

"No. I already told you, I saw the guy. He had a camera with a long lens—"

"And I'm telling you that no self-respecting paparazzo produces an image this grainy. This is low resolution."

"He was a hundred yards away. It was twilight."

Gant's leg is bouncing up and down beneath the desk. "Doesn't matter. These guys are pros. They can get nude pics of celebs a mile offshore on a yacht, and the image is so clear you can recognize the actor's face. What angle was the guy shooting from, anyway?"

I think back to that evening. How Sabrina tilted her head toward the guy with the camera. Then she sat on the rock with her back to him.

"He was behind us," I say.

"Behind you," repeats Gant, leaving me to recognize the impossibility of the shot for myself.

"There weren't any other cameras, Gant. I would've noticed."

"Really? Sounds to me like Sabrina had you fully focused on the guy behind you."

He's got that look again—the one that says he's uncovered something important.

"You don't think Sabrina's behind this, do you?"

"It's possible."

"No, it's not. Anyway, yesterday you said it was Kris. Now Sabrina. Why would she do that, huh?"

He can tell he's touched a nerve, even if he's not sure why. "To get people talking about you as a couple." He laces his fingers behind his head. "Look, her ex-boyfriend is out of the picture, and Annaleigh's reeling because of her dad. But who's still standing? You and Sabrina, that's who. She's the common denominator. You see that, right?"

"Trust me, it's not her. Today she told me stuff . . . things she can't afford anyone else to know."

"Like the story about Kris and Tamara? She told you that too, right? And then you shared it, just like she figured you would." I shoot him a warning glance, but he plows on. "Worked out pretty well for her. A couple months ago, the press blamed her for breaking up with Kris. But in the past week, everything's changed. Kris looks like a lowlife, and Sabrina's the kindhearted star helping out the Hollywood newbie. And how do you repay her kindness? You hook up with Annaleigh as well." He points at the photo again and wags his finger. "Sabrina's in control of this story, bro. Always has been."

He has to be wrong. Sabrina just bared her soul. "What about the security video from the party? How did Sabrina get hold of that?"

"Probably knows someone at Machinus."

"How could she be sure we'd be on camera?"

"She led you to that exact spot, right?" He stands and heads to the bathroom. "Point is, there's something weird going on. And you're starting to look like a prop in someone else's show."

As I toggle back and forth between the photos, my phone rings. It's Brian, which probably means there's bad news, because, well . . . Brian *is* bad news.

"Is your brother there?" he asks. No greeting. No *Hi, Seth!*

"Sure. Why?"

There's a pause. "With all the crap that's been going down—photographs, stories—I hired an investigator to see if there's a pattern. Someone behind it all."

So Gant's not the only conspiracy theorist. I'd laughed at the idea once, but I'm not laughing now.

"My guy looked into that photo of you and Sabrina on the beach. It was sold through an agency, and they don't reveal the identities of their photographers. But that one of you and Annaleigh on Rodeo Drive . . ." His tone shifts. "It was sold by an individual. Someone we know."

I wait for the reveal. Will it be Kris or Sabrina? And why do I still want it to be Kris?

Brian clicks his tongue. "Turns out, our mystery photographer is someone by the name of Gant Crane."

I can't move. Can't breathe. "But . . . there's no way—"

"With all due respect, we're kind of pissed that in return for a free hotel room, your brother's trying to make some money off of us. Makes us wonder what else he's been up to."

The bathroom door is closed. Gant's camera sits on the desk

beside the computer. I switch it on and scroll through the photographs, working back from the most recent. Three photos later, I stop. I recognize the scene: me climbing into Sabrina's Prius just a couple hours ago, looking shady and furtive as if I have something to hide. How would either of us look if this photo got out? What would Annaleigh say if she saw it?

"Did you know he was doing this, Seth?" Brian asks. His tone is gentle, but I don't trust it. It's the voice of Good Cop Brian, and Bad Cop Brian is a whole lot more convincing.

"No," I say.

I keep scrolling through Gant's pictures. I'd almost forgotten about that photo of us on Rodeo Drive. Compared to all the other photos coming out, it was tame and inoffensive. But here are dozens more just like it, all taken from distance with maximum zoom.

"You're going to sort this out," says Brian.

"Yeah," I mumble. Then I hang up, because really, I have no idea *how* to sort it out.

The bathroom door clicks open. Gant steps out and sees the camera in my hands and the look on my face. "What's up?"

"You've been following me. Photographing me."

He shrugs.

"You sold me out!"

"What? I haven't shown them to anyone."

"One of them already appeared in a newspaper, Gant. I notice you've got some of me and Sabrina ready to go too."

"I swear, I never—"

I punch the scroll key on his camera. Locate the photo of Annaleigh and me on Rodeo Drive. Turn the camera so he can see the screen for himself.

"I know how it looks, Seth, but someone else must've been next to me taking pictures as well."

"That's bullshit."

"Well then, maybe someone hacked into my photo library."

"Why didn't you tell me that when the photo came out?"

"Because then you'd want to know why I was following you."

"I still want to know!"

He looks away. "There's money in this, okay? If I can photograph you in secret and get good images, I can film other people too."

I still don't believe he's telling the truth, and he still hasn't apologized. He just stands there, stony faced, no longer my little brother, my rock, but another rogue cell in a fast-spreading cancer.

"You stalked us, Gant. You're like a freaking Peeping Tom."

"Are you serious?" He curls his lip. "Who spent his first night here ogling hundreds of images of Sabrina Layton, huh, Seth? I saw all the links in your search history."

"I'd just met her at a party."

"You met Kris too, right? How many photos of him did you pull up?"

This is crazy. I've done nothing wrong, so why am I on the defensive? "I think it's time you went home," I say.

"I'm not going to leave you."

"I'm not asking!"

He doesn't move. "You going to make me? Drag me past those photographers waiting on the curb? Let them shoot pictures of you stuffing your kid brother in a taxi? How's that going to play out with the fans?"

He knows he's got me. The story of rival siblings is almost as old as star-crossed lovers.

And the end is just as predictable.

30

ANNALEIGH IS TOWEL-DRYING HER WET HAIR. The
hotel bathrobe looks huge on her.

"You're early," she says, letting me into her room. "Where have
you been, anyway? I tried calling this afternoon."

"Just out." I wander around her room, too tense to sit.

"Is that what you're wearing? You know, for the date?" She
makes the last word sound smaller than the others.

"Oh. I . . . I'll change later."

She's not moving at all. Just stands in the middle of the room,
clasping the towel to her chest. "Is everything all right?"

"Yeah," I tell her, but it's obvious that she doesn't believe me.

What am I supposed to say? Annaleigh knows firsthand how
destructive a family member can be, but there's a big difference
between a father who's several states away and a brother who's
just the other side of the ceiling.

"You want to know the worst thing about what my dad did to us?"
she says, filling the silence. "It's that I knew something was wrong and
I never said a word. I just acted like everything was okay." She walks
over to the patio doors, head bowed. "I don't want to be that person
anymore. I want to be honest. And I want you to be honest too."

Annaleigh is backlit by the dusky sky, a shadowy silhouette. The L.A. evening seems to swallow her, *minimize* her, and I want to hold her so much. We've both watched a parent drift away and fought to pull the remaining pieces of our lives back together. I want us to pull together now.

I join her by the doors. We're close. So close.

She swallows. "I need to know you won't hurt me."

"I won't."

"Promise me."

"I promise."

She reaches up and touches my cheek. Her fingertips meander across my chin and onto my lips. She gazes at me, unblinking, as if she's trying to memorize every millimeter of my face.

I touch her too. Run my fingers through her still-wet hair. Feel the delicate curve of her neck, and her smooth, soft skin. She presses her cheek against my hand, breathing faster.

"I never counted on this," she whispers. "On us."

I try to smile, but I'm too nervous. "What about us?" I ask innocently.

"Don't do that. Don't tease. Not now."

She kisses my neck and my jawline. I close my eyes and kiss her right back—her forehead, her nose, her lips. Every part of me is alive and electric. She leans into me, but it's not enough.

I slide my hands beneath the robe, pulling her closer, closer, closer. The robe slides off one shoulder and then the other, landing softly in a heap around her ankles.

Everything seems to be moving faster. I'm desperate to touch every part of her, and to be touched. When she unbuttons my shirt, I cast it aside. Her hands skate over my shoulders and settle against the small of my back, locking me tight against her.

We kiss again, but it's not gentle anymore. I feel like she might slip away at any moment. I can't let that happen.

We stumble to the bed and throw ourselves onto the perfectly made sheets. Our kisses grow desperate as we explore every inch of each other. And when she puts me inside her, the rest of the world vanishes. There's no Gant or Sabrina or Kris anymore. No photographs, and no movie. There's only this moment, and this girl.

Annaleigh is my everything.

I wake to bright sunshine. I'm coiled around Annaleigh so that her feet rest against the tops of my feet and her head nestles under my chin. The soft white sheets only cover our legs.

"Hey, stranger," she says in a sexy drowsy voice. "I thought you were never going to wake up."

It takes me a moment to realize where I am. It's morning, and I'm lying next to a beautiful girl, her lips creased in a smile, raven hair striking against the white pillow. I'm scared and thrilled all at once.

"You realize this is going to make losing you feel really crappy," she says.

"Huh?"

"Well, we wouldn't exactly be star-crossed lovers if we got to live happily ever after."

"Oh. The movie, you mean."

She rolls over to face me, eyes wide open. "What are you saying? That movies aren't real?"

"Afraid not," I say, kissing her. "I'm sorry to be the one to tell you."

She bites a fingernail provocatively. "Well, I must say, this is all quite irregular, Mr. Crane," she announces in an English accent.

"Isn't it, Ms. Ware?"

"I mean, there I was, preparing myself for a lifetime of smoldering glances, and it turns out we don't have to follow the script."

I swallow hard. "No, we don't."

"No, we don't," she agrees, accent slipping. She climbs on top of me. "Not at all."

An hour later, we sit on the bed, facing each other. Annaleigh's wearing my shirt, which is several sizes too large to count as modest on her. There's a tray of room-service crepes beside us, and I'm starving.

"It's weird," she says. "Even with all the stuff that's happened, I'm ready to get back to work." She doesn't flinch as I wipe away a piece of sleep from the corner of her eye. "Plus, tomorrow's New Year's Day, and we get paid, right?"

"Yeah."

"And there's the party tonight. Ryder says it's going be beautiful."

"Which one's that again?"

She smacks me gently on the arm. "New Year's Eve. It's on the itinerary."

"Yeah. I've been distracted."

"Distracted, huh?" She swings her legs off the bed and stands. "Well, we can't have that."

She heads to the bathroom, legs delightfully visible beneath the hem of my shirt. As if she knows I'm watching, she lets the shirt slide off just before she disappears through the door.

"Start without me," she says.

I roll a crepe and take a bite. Unfold today's newspaper and lay it out on the bed. Sabrina, strikingly beautiful in designer shades, graces the front page, her sleek ponytail draped over her left shoulder. Familiar subject and familiar pose, but I'm not certain I have any more idea what's going on behind those shades than I did before I ever met her.

There's a headline too—*Exclusive: Teen Star Is Drug Addict.*

I drop the crepe. Choke on the mouthful I'm eating. I don't want to read on, but I can't *not* read . . . about her breakup with Kris and her spiraling addiction.

With every new sentence the brutal reality hits home—this isn't gossip or speculation.

This is what she told me yesterday.

31

HANDS SHAKING, I PULL THE CELL phone from my pants pocket. I call Sabrina, and go straight to voicemail. I don't leave a message because I feel responsible. The timing can't be a coincidence.

I call Ryder. He picks up right away. "I was about to call you," he says.

"Sabrina—"

"She's okay. Just needs to disconnect while everything blows over."

"Blows over?" I'm stage-whispering so that Annaleigh won't hear me, and the words come out as a continuous hiss.

"This is a shock for all of us, but we have to keep going."

Keep going. How many times have I said that over the past few years? I believed it too, but not anymore.

"Who are you talking to, Seth?" Annaleigh calls from the bathroom.

I catch a glimpse of the newspaper again, and the black-and-white image of Sabrina. "I'll be back in a minute," I shout back.

I don't wait for a response. Just grab my shirt, retrieve the newspaper, and step into the corridor. After everything Annaleigh's been through, hearing about Sabrina is going to completely freak her out. I need to get things straight in my head before we talk.

Ryder's still on the line as I close the door behind me. "Look, you can't beat yourself up about this, Seth."

"Did she say anything? About how this might've gotten out?"

"No." There's a pause. "Why?"

"Because she told me stuff yesterday . . . about being an addict."

"Why would she tell you that?"

"She said she needed to open up."

I wait for the fallout. For questions about what I've been doing since that moment. Who I've seen, and what I've said.

Instead, Ryder sighs. "This isn't something that just happened. It's probably been going on for months. Years, even. Lots of people would've known, and she's been making a lot of enemies recently. She dumped Kris and hooked up with you, so he's probably pissed. Same with her recently fired agent. Rumor has it she's running her mouth to reporters too. Point is, anyone could've done this."

Kris? No. Her agent? Unlikely. But she did speak to a reporter—even told me so.

I want to believe Ryder. But still, the timing . . .

"Where's Sabrina now?" I ask.

"Someplace safe. She'll rejoin us soon enough, but right now she needs to focus on getting help."

Rejoin us. I want to ask what exactly she'll be rejoining. We lost Kris before he even signed on, Annaleigh's still feeling fragile, and Sabrina's out of commission for who knows how long? The whole movie is slipping away.

Conversation over, I hang up and lean against the cool corridor wall. I can't go back into Annaleigh's room. She'll have questions I can't answer.

It's a short journey to my room. I figure Gant will be gone, but he's stuffing his clothes into a duffel bag on my bag.

"You don't need to say anything," he snaps. "I'm leaving."

I toss the newspaper to him. He hesitates a moment, and unfolds it. Looks at the photo and reads the text.

"Another day, another story," he mumbles. "Still think it's all a coincidence?"

I fiddle with the buttons of my shirt. Well, not *my* shirt—the shirt Ryder gave me so that I could become Andrew. Crazy thing is, this shirt is the only thing that separates fictional Andrew from actual Seth, and it's nowhere near enough.

"After you saw me getting into Sabrina's car yesterday, we drove to Griffith Park," I say. "She told me all about being a drug addict. Now the story's out."

"So Sabrina Layton—A-list movie star—dragged you out to a private spot and spilled her guts." He zips the bag closed. "Did anyone see you?"

"No. Well, except for that stalker guy. I emailed you his license plate."

"So there's a witness that you were with her. Very convenient. Makes you the prime suspect for selling her out."

I want to tell him he's out of line if he thinks Sabrina's behind this, but truthfully, I just don't know. There's a long tradition of Hollywood stars going into rehab and emerging more popular than ever. At a time when she's losing the spotlight, is it really such a stretch?

I slump into the desk chair as Gant slings his bag over his shoulder. As usual he has left my laptop open, and the dual images of Sabrina and me—at the beach and at the party—sit side by side on the screen.

"You still think someone was filming us on the beach?" I ask.

"I'm certain of it."

"Then why did he only sell a grainy photo? Why not sell the whole thing?"

Gant mulls this over. "Maybe he couldn't get audio. A movie's only any good if people know what you're saying, right?"

"Then why film us at all?"

He adjusts the bag. The strap stretches his pale blue T-shirt. "Maybe he wasn't thinking . . . just saw an opportunity and took it."

Is Gant talking about the mystery cameraman, or himself?

I close the computer. "I need to tell Ryder and Brian everything. Someone's screwing with this movie. If they don't do something about it soon, there won't be a movie at all."

"Really? Seems to me, even bad publicity is still publicity."

We leave together and ride the elevator in silence. As the doors open, a voice carries clear across the lobby: "Tell me his room number!"

A familiar guy with shoulder-length hair is pounding on the reception desk, and the clerk looks scared. Security guards are closing in. Movie star or not, they won't stand for this.

Kris peers over his shoulder and watches the guards contemptuously. Then he catches sight of me.

He walks toward me, slow at first, and then faster, all twisted features and gritted teeth. "Swear it wasn't you, Seth. Swear it!"

32

KRIS LOOKS RABID, UNHINGED. I'M CERTAIN that he's going to hit me.

"It wasn't me," I say. "I swear, I didn't tell anyone."

All around us people are watching and listening. They've caught a whiff of scandal, and the scent is irresistible.

"Let's go upstairs, Kris."

"No." His voice is low and menacing. "My car. Now."

Reluctantly, I follow. I have to convince Kris that I'm not to blame. Maybe then I'll get some information from him and we'll edge closer to the truth.

This is Gant's chance to leave—I tried to banish him once already—but he falls in line too. Maybe he's afraid that Kris's loyal posse is going to drag me out to a deserted location and beat me up.

He's not the only one.

Kris's Porsche is double-parked outside the hotel. Gant squeezes onto the backseat, legs sprawled across the tan leather, and wrestles the seat belt across himself. In the event of an accident, he'll be screwed. Unfortunately, our driver is probably the most distracted human being I've ever met.

Kris glances at the rearview mirror as he pulls away. "Who are you, anyway?" he asks Gant.

"That's my brother," I say.

"What's he doing here?"

"He's been staying with me."

"Just the two of you?"

"My dad left a couple days ago."

Kris grunts. "You're like the Beverly freaking Hillbillies. One free hotel room, and you invite half the Valley." He watches me from the corner of his eye. "I know you saw Sabrina yesterday. She told me you were going to meet. Said she wanted to talk to you about something." Kris massages the wheel. "I should've done something for her a long time ago. I knew she had a problem."

"It's not your fault."

"Of course it is," he snaps. "Yours too. You walk into our lives like you belong, and a couple days later you think you've got this karmic understanding of Sabrina Layton. You didn't have a damn clue about her then, and you still don't know her now."

I won't argue. He's right, in a way. I liked her, and I wanted her to like me too, but that isn't the same as knowing her.

"Remember the first night we met?" he continues. "You'd just gotten into town. And I was only at that party because Sabrina begged me to come."

"What?"

"Yeah. She calls me up and says she's lonely. By the time I get there, you two are talking, so I stay out of the way until you're done." He sighs. "I knew right away she'd taken something. She wouldn't admit she called me. Maybe she actually forgot. I just wanted to give her a ride home, make sure she didn't drive herself. But then you got involved—went all hero on us."

I grip the armrest. "I didn't know. Why didn't you say something?"

"Why should I have to? You think I owe everyone in L.A. an explanation for why my ex-girlfriend is acting weird? Think none of them would sell the story?" He smacks the wheel so hard I'm sure he's going to break it. "You're lucky I can't think of a single good reason why you would do this, 'cause all signs point to you."

"I just swore, didn't I?" I want to keep him talking. Want to keep the questions coming from my side, and the information from his. "What if she leaked the story herself?"

"Why the hell would she do that?"

"A cry for help."

"That right there shows you don't know the first thing about her. One, Sabrina doesn't want help. Two, she'd be killing her career."

"Going to rehab won't kill her career."

"I'm not talking about rehab. Sabrina's about to flake out of *Whirlwind* for the second time in three months. She has a documented drug problem. Who's going to insure her now?"

I hadn't thought about that—how movies need insurance for stuff like weather delays or injuries to a cast member. An actor who can't be insured is a difficult actor to cast.

I haven't been paying attention to where we are, so it's a surprise to see the coffee shop ahead of us. Kris checks his mirrors, slows down, and idles just outside. He peers through the driver's-side window.

As I unbuckle my seat belt, he pulls away. "I guess today's not a coffee day," he mutters.

I'm confused. "What happened?"

"The barista and me, we've got a code. He knows I like my privacy, so he gives me a sign: Stay, or go. Today was go." Kris turns on the stereo, and promptly turns it off again. "We've got to find out who leaked the drug story. Everything that's been going down, it started when you arrived."

"It wasn't me."

"Then help me find out who it was. I've got friends asking questions too. It won't be long before we know the truth."

My heartbeat is racing. "These friends of yours, did they find out who leaked the story about you and Tamara?"

"No, because I didn't ask them to. I know damn well it was Sabrina, and I don't want anyone else to find out she can be that vindictive." He waves the thought away. "Anyway, start asking Brian and Ryder who else is connected with this project. The way things are going, they're going to want to find out who's screwing everything up too."

"They're already on it," I tell him. "They've got an investigator working for them."

"What?" Gant's voice drags me around. I'd forgotten he was in the car.

"That's what Brian told me last night when he called about . . ." I stop myself in time. If Kris finds out that Gant sold a photograph of Annaleigh and me, he'll assume my brother has been up to other stuff too.

"Told you about *what*?" demands Kris.

199

When I don't answer straightaway, he pulls to the side of the road and stops. Stares at me, waiting.

"They said those photographs of Sabrina and me aren't photos at all," I tell him, using Gant's line. "They're, like, movie stills, or something."

"So what? If someone's been filming you, they're stupid. Paparazzi can sell photos, but no one can secretly film you and release it. Not if they want to make money off it. They'd need you to sign a waiver. Give them permission. And there's no way you'd do that."

Kris rejoins the traffic. I ought to be relieved, but the words *waiver* and *permission* take center stage in my mind. They conjure memories of my audition, and the job offer that followed, and an agreement to be filmed at all times.

At all times.

I'm sweating. My breaths are quick and shallow. "When Ryder offered you a role in the movie, you never got around to signing a contract, did you?"

"What, last week? No. I signed one four months ago, but we blew it up when I left the movie."

"Was the new one going to be the same?"

"I don't know. I pulled out before they sent it through." Kris eyes me suspiciously. "Why are you asking?"

Like a key turning a lock, everything is clicking into place. Only Annaleigh and Sabrina and I signed contracts, and Sabrina fired her agent before he could check it. What if it was slightly different from the earlier version? What if all three of us have agreed to be filmed at all times?

I imagine a gigantic movie set—a beach, say, or Griffith Park. The camera catches the action from afar: Sabrina and me talking, arguing, touching. But like Gant said, a movie without audio is no use at all. If we were really being filmed, our voices would've needed to be recorded from close range on an external microphone. A boom mic, most likely.

But boom mics are obvious. No, it would need to be smaller. Portable. Wireless.

I inhale sharply.

"What?" Kris is watching me. *"What?"*

"The audio." I look back at Gant. From his expression, I can tell he's putting the pieces together too. "I think I know—"

My cell phone rings. The sound is like a punch to the gut, silencing me. I ease it from my pocket with shaking hands. Check the screen, even though I know who's calling.

Brian's voice is quiet but clear. "Time to stop talking, Seth. I'd sure hate for you to say something we can't undo."

33

KRIS DROPS US AT THE FAMILIAR building: small, anonymous, nondescript—the opposite of the large, very public headquarters of Machinus Media Enterprises. Sabrina thought the project was based out of here to ensure privacy. She's probably right too. As long as we're here, Curt Barrett and Machinus can pretend they have no idea what's really going on.

"You should come in," I tell Kris.

"Uh-uh. I'm not exactly welcome right now."

He has no idea how true that is.

He accelerates away as I press the buzzer. Brian answers immediately, looking like someone trying on a smile for the first time. "Seth. Gant. What a pleasant surprise."

I don't know whether to cower or lash out. "You bugged me," I say quietly. Then, propelled by some force deep inside me, I push past him and slam my cell phone on the nearby coffee table, rattling a plastic plant. "You bugged my cell phone!"

Brian glances at Tracie. "Not *your* cell phone. *Ours.*"

I was expecting him to deny it, and his answer throws me off. "This can't be happening," I mumble.

"Very melodramatic. Not exactly *Whirlwind* material, but it might get you some work on daytime soaps." Brian rubs his chin. "Oh, but they don't really exist much anymore, do they? Hmm. Maybe your next community play, then."

Hearing the commotion, Ryder emerges from a room halfway down the corridor. When he sees me, he quickly pulls the door closed behind him, but not before I catch a glimpse of a large monitor in the darkened space.

"What are you doing here?" Ryder asks.

I study his face for signs of concern or remorse, but his expression is neutral. Today is just business as usual. But what kind of business?

"You all work for Machinus," I say. "That's how you got the footage from the party. You've been filming Sabrina and me the whole time."

"Just like your contract stipulated," agrees Tracie.

"But the movie hasn't started shooting yet."

"It started the moment you got here," says Ryder.

I wait for shock to become anger, but I'm too afraid to be angry. How much of the past two weeks do they have on film?

"I'm going to tell Sabrina. How you lied to me. Bugged me."

"You won't get within half a mile of her," says Tracie. "Anyway, she signed the same contract as you."

"She didn't know you'd do this to her."

"Shouldn't have fired her agent, then. He'd have sniffed it out in a heartbeat."

"We're talking about her life here. She's a person, not some character in your movie."

"Actually," says Brian, "she's both."

His words make me think of Annaleigh. "Did *you* leak that stuff about Annaleigh's father?"

"People were bound to find out eventually," he says.

Ryder steps forward. "You're looking at this all wrong, Seth. Yesterday, Sabrina was a drug addict; today she's in rehab, recovering. Annaleigh's dad's been relying on a public defender with the worst track record in Arkansas; now she'll be able to afford to get him proper counsel. You told us your family was cash-strapped; well, not after tomorrow, they won't be. Two weeks ago, no one had a clue who you were; now you and Annaleigh are almost as big as Sabrina and Kris. See what I'm saying? There's a silver lining here—"

"I thought this job was *real*."

"It is real. The most real thing you've ever done."

"But I'm an *actor*."

Brian rolls his eyes. "So are porn stars. And they work a whole lot harder for a lot less money."

He likes that last line, I can tell. I don't think it's spontaneous either. I think he has been waiting for this showdown ever since we met. Like an anti-hero explaining how he pulled off the heist of the century, he looks relaxed, arms folded, secure in the knowledge that his target can't fight back. Or won't.

Brian flicks his head toward the rehearsal room. "We've got things to discuss. Let's at least sit down."

Ryder leads the way. I want to see inside the mysterious room halfway along the corridor, so I let Brian go ahead of me too. As he passes the door, I open it and slip inside.

Three monitors are banked on desks against a wall. Still images of Annaleigh and Sabrina and me fill most of one screen, with a row of smaller images underneath. It looks like editing software, as if Ryder's putting his movie together. Right here, in this tiny room.

I freeze as I take in the pictures of Annaleigh and me on the next screen. These aren't outdoor shots. Instead we're sitting on the bed in her hotel room. The quality is amazing, the images taken from above us as if there are cameras in the ceiling . . . or the light fixtures.

Brian grips my arm. "Rehearsal room's farther along, Seth. I think you're getting turned around."

I shake him loose. "I know where it is."

Gant and I head to one corner of the perfectly ordered room, while Brian, Ryder, and Tracie fan out to the others, conspicuously surrounding us. Like me, they don't sit. If this is an attempt to freak us out, they should stop trying. I'm plenty freaked out already.

"You filmed Annaleigh's hotel room," I say.

I look at each of them in turn, waiting for an apology or denial, but they don't reply. Annaleigh and I opened up to each other in that room. We shared things we never would've said in public. We made love.

I try to block out the images spinning through my mind. I need to focus.

"Why are you doing this?" I ask Ryder. "You've written screenplays, produced and directed shorts. You worked runner on a couple studio films. I looked you up the day I auditioned. You're a real filmmaker."

"Yes, I am. Just like thousands of other real filmmakers, all of us fighting for a chance to make a movie. And when Sabrina and Kris signed on, I felt like I'd finally made it. Good budget, guaranteed distribution. Then they split, and for the next forty-eight hours, that was all anyone talked about." He shakes his head. "They got more publicity for *breaking up* than we generated in months of pre-production. And that's when I realized: People don't care about art, beautiful writing, well-rounded characters. They want scandal. They want to build up stars, make their personal lives public, and then drag them down for the fun of it. So why not make art around that?"

"Like you are."

"Not exactly." Ryder is eerily calm. He's not making excuses. On the contrary, he sounds like he's trying to convert me to a cause. "I've never put words in your mouth, Seth. Or Annaleigh's. The script may be fiction, but the scenario is real: Boy who's struggling to do the right thing, girl who can't escape from her father's shadow. And you've done such a great job of filming—the pool, Rodeo Drive . . . the execution and dialogue has been all you, just like we wanted. *Scripted reality,* remember? You guys have controlled everything. Driven everything."

"You never said you were secretly filming us."

"I couldn't, though, right? This was never about Andrew and Lana. It's about Seth and Annaleigh, unfiltered. I want viewers to see who you really are. The way you talk to each other, look out for each other. Even the way you make love." Ryder sighs. "Look, I know you're confused right now, but you have to believe me, we're making history here. No one forgets the trailblazers. People are talking about you now, and they'll talk even more when the movie comes out."

I can tell from his face, Ryder really believes he's putting me on the front line of cinematic history. He reminds me of a dictator single-mindedly pursuing his vision, blind to the wreckage piling up around him.

"You should be proud, Seth," says Brian. "You're a natural. Take Sabrina, for instance. The reason she was at Curt Barrett's party is because she was on the fence about rejoining the movie in a smaller role. But then you two started flirting—yeah, we have that on camera too, don't worry—and anyone could see the sparks flying. She signed on the next day. Which is great, because when it comes to drama, nothing adds intrigue like a love triangle."

"Except telling everyone she's a drug addict," I snap.

"That's true," says Tracie, nodding sagely. "Although we only found out about the pills because she insisted on sticking around. Sabrina was only in the movie to complicate things between you and Annaleigh, but I guess we underestimated how much she likes you." Tracie smothers a smile. "Oh well. At least she gave us a major publicity push on her way out."

"Listen, Seth," continues Ryder, still upbeat, "I saw you onstage. You had *presence*. But at the end of the show, you couldn't even bow in time with the rest of the cast. Then you told me about the commercial—about how close you'd come—and I realized, we're alike, you and me. We get knocked down, but we keep fighting. That kind of determination, that optimism . . . there's something noble about it, don't you think? And that's the version of Seth Crane I'd like people to see in this movie—talented, aspirational . . . *real*."

It sounds like he's giving me another pep talk, but I'm on high alert now and quickly decipher the underlying threat: As editor, he gets to dictate what version of me people will see.

"So if I play along, you'll make me look good," I say. "And if I don't . . ."

Tracie has heard enough. "You should get on with your work, Ryder. It's going to be a busy day."

Ryder doesn't want to leave—probably still thinks there's a chance he can win me over—but he does as he's told. As soon as he's gone, Tracie slides a small stack of papers across the table.

"I'd like to remind you that you signed a nondisclosure agreement," she says. "Break it, and we'll sue the crap out of you. Play ball, and you get paid tomorrow. Fifty thousand dollars."

"You think I care about that right now?"

"You ought to. If you back out today, the contract is void. Annaleigh's too, if we can't continue. Think she'll forgive you?"

Brian takes out his cell phone and taps the screen. "Just in case you still need convincing . . ."

I try not to look, but then I hear Sabrina's voice coming through the tiny speaker: *"That wasn't a read-through. It was a humiliation. Seth was a fucking mess. If that's all he's got, we're screwed."*

Next is me: *"I don't care about Sabrina right now. For a while there, I honestly thought we were going to get cut. Now we've gotten a second chance, there's no way I'm going down without a fight."*

Sabrina's voice again: *"Why can't you admit you hate me? Just say it!"*

Me: *"I just feel like things would be easier if you weren't around."*

Brian walks over and holds the phone in front of me. The video playing on the small screen was shot right here in the rehearsal room, though I'm the only one in frame. *"You probably feel guilty for letting the Kris and Tamara story get out,"* says Tracie. *"But hey, one fewer cast members means more time for everyone else."* In high-definition, I watch myself accepting money—hundreds of dollars by the look of it. *"You won't tell anyone about this, right?"* Tracie asks. My reply: *"I won't tell anyone. I promise."*

I look up. Tiny cameras dot the rehearsal room ceiling. I never noticed them before. How many other cameras have I failed to notice?

As if in answer, Brian loads new footage onto his cell. The lighting is low, but it's clearly a hotel room—specifically Annaleigh's room, filmed last night. I know because we're both in her bed.

"Ryder thinks we should fade to black," says Brian, turning down the volume. "But I'm not so sure. Seems a shame to waste such great material."

I look away. I can't watch it anymore.

Brian rubs his chin thoughtfully. "I wonder what kind of leading man you're going to be. Are you a sensitive hero, or a guy who takes bribes? Are you the guy who bares his soul to Annaleigh, or the one who baits Sabrina into baring hers? Do we show you making out with Sabrina or making love to Annaleigh . . . or both? 'Cause you ought to be thinking about this stuff. How you come across in this movie affects how everyone else comes across."

"Annaleigh's and Sabrina's secrets are already out there," I remind him.

He glances at the cell phone. "Clearly not all of them. Anyway, who said I was talking about Annaleigh and Sabrina?"

As Brian's eyes shift to Gant, my brother seems to shrink a couple inches. "The waivers," Gant murmurs. "Ryder said they were a formality, in case we appeared in any footage."

"And now you're in plenty," says Brian. "Actually, you and your father have become fascinating characters. He just sits with his laptop, trawling through job listings and checking up on his dwindling bank balance, but you . . . you're a regular little Nancy Drew. Selling photos behind your brother's back—"

"I didn't sell anything!"

"But who'll believe that, huh? I've seen the footage of your argument with Seth from last night, and I'm still not sure. One minute you're browsing through photos you never should've taken, the next Seth is accusing you of selling him out. I think viewers will be disappointed in you, Gant. You come across even colder and more calculating than your brother."

Shock and anger fade away, and now I feel only guilt. Gant swore he didn't sell that photo, and I didn't believe him. Even worse, I gave Brian material to use against us.

"There's still time for a happy ending," says Tracie. "The party tonight is going to be beautiful. Really romantic. The perfect opportunity to show Annaleigh and everyone else what a nice guy you really are. And we'll all be there to make sure that you do." She narrows her eyes. "You do want a happy ending, don't you, Seth?"

Against my will, I nod—an obedient puppy cowed into submission.

"Good boy," says Brian. "You should get back to her now. You ran out on her this morning, and it sounds like she's pretty cut up about it. Oh, and one more thing. That poor little girl isn't as quick on the uptake as you—has no idea what's going on here. I suggest you keep it that way."

"You expect me to believe she didn't read the contract either?" I ask.

"She's a minor. Her parents signed it." He gives the words time to sink in. "Oh yeah, they know exactly what's going on. But she doesn't."

"She deserves to know."

"If Annaleigh quits on us before tomorrow, she'll lose the money, and so will you. And as the whole world knows, her family needs that money to pay for Daddy's lawyer. You think she'll forgive you if her father ends up behind bars? Think she'll be okay that you've been playing her ever since you got here?"

"I haven't played her."

"But that's not how she'll see it, is it? Not when she realizes you took a bribe to stay quiet."

Brian and Tracie file out of the room. Gant follows. I remain a moment longer, taking in the sterile space, empty except for tables and chairs—an office that can be packed up and vacated in a matter of hours. Is that why they're telling me everything? Because our "movie" is nearing its conclusion?

Brian stops beside Gant's duffel bag. "Looks like you're heading home," he says. "I'll give you a ride."

"I'll take a bus," says Gant.

"No, no, no. I insist. It's always a tough moment for an actor, bowing out. The least I can do is make sure it's a safe exit."

Gant heaves his duffel bag over his shoulder. Standing at the door, head bowed, he finally looks his age. He's a sophomore, my *younger* brother, whom I swore to protect that terrible summer three and a half years ago.

I hug him. I honestly don't know if he's going to be a rag doll in my arms, or if he'll push me away. I certainly don't expect him to stare right at me, conveying anger and determination. As clearly as if he were speaking, I understand him: We may have lost this battle, but the war isn't over.

I hold him tight. Maybe this hug is my way of begging forgiveness, or a promise that we'll stick together. Probably both. But it's more than that too, and as I whisper into his ear, I hope that he understands.

Gant turns away and trails Brian through the door. I'm about to follow them when Tracie picks up my cell phone. "Forgetting something, Seth?"

She tosses it to me. I pretend to fumble it. Let it fall to the ground.

Then I stomp it into tiny pieces.

34

BACK INSIDE MY HOTEL ROOM, I head straight for the bedside lamps. Isn't that where they hide spy cameras in the movies?

Nothing.

I check the desk, and the curtain rod, and the TV, but there are no cameras there either. It must amuse Ryder to see me scurrying around, frantically searching every nook and cranny. What will viewers make of my behavior when they see me on the big screen? Will they wonder if I was unaware of what was going on until this moment? Or will they say I'm just acting the role of innocent? Brian's revelations have me caught in a web of second-guessing, and my own mind is doing the spinning.

Someone knocks on the door. I answer it.

"Where have you been?" Annaleigh asks. "I've been calling."

"I . . . I lost my phone."

I try the bathroom, but again, it's clean. No cameras at all.

"Ryder came by," she says, taking my video camera from the nightstand. "He took the memory card from my camera and gave me a new one. When he realized we haven't been filming each other much, he got real pissed. Said we ought to have hours of video by now."

She turns the camera on and films me. I don't speak, though. Don't even move, because it has suddenly hit me how Ryder got rid of the cameras in my room. Tracie sent him away from our meeting because he needed to get on with his *work,* but she wasn't talking about editing. Ryder has been here, clearing away the evidence. I never thought about it before, but he must have a key, otherwise he wouldn't have been able to leave all those clothes in my closet. No wonder he was able to copy Gant's photo from my laptop.

I want to know if Ryder has taken down the cameras from Annaleigh's room too, but it's unlikely. Not while she was still around to see him. In any case, I'm not going to ask her as long as there's a camera pointing at my face.

"Talk to me, Seth," she says. "I can tell something's wrong."

"Nothing's wrong," I say. "Really."

With a deep sigh, Annaleigh puts the camera away and turns on the TV instead. It's a gossip show masquerading as news. There's stock footage of Sabrina and the rehab center she's checked into. The only live pictures are of the photographers lined up at the electric gates, camping out for a long-distance shot of Hollywood's fallen star. And of her parents, still blaming each other for the mess their daughter's life has become; still loving the feel of cameras on their faces, the delusion that they matter long after they've stopped having any influence at all.

Annaleigh's eyes fill with tears. "I didn't know," she says. "I swear, I didn't."

I want to protect her from what's happening, but that's impossible. The only thing I can control is whether to tell her the truth now, or put it off until later. Will she hate me more for perpetuating the lie, or for opening up and making her share it with me? One thing is certain: Annaleigh needs the money even more than I do. Even though he doesn't deserve it, she wants to help her father. Will she forgive me if I sabotage her only chance?

On the TV, the stock footage plays on endless repeat: Sabrina in a sleeveless white gown at the Academy Awards. Her seductive, husky voice as she banters with the red carpet reporters.

Blinking away tears, Annaleigh heads to the bathroom as another person knocks on the door.

"Room service," calls a voice.

I open the door a crack. A waiter stands in the hallway, a large silver tray in his hands. There are two covered plates on it.

"I didn't order anything," I say.

He looks at the ticket. "Says here it's for Annaleigh."

I take the tray and thank him. Go back inside the room and realize that I forgot to tip. By the time I return to the corridor, he's gone.

I place the tray on the bedside table and remove one of the lids. On a spotless white plate is a small Post-it note:

$$\$50,000\text{-}\$500 = \$49,500.$$

I freeze, the silver lid swaying in my fingers. Stealing a shallow breath, I replace the first lid and lift the other.

There's a brand-new cell phone in the middle of the plate.

It begins to ring.

I snatch it up. The line is already dead, but the message is clear: They're always watching.

In the bathroom, Annaleigh shuts off the faucet. I don't know how to explain the tray and the two empty plates, let alone the note and the new phone, so I carry them out to the corridor.

"What did you order?" Annaleigh asks as I close the door.

"Nothing. Waiter got the wrong room."

She glances at the TV. "I'm not hungry anyway."

We lie side by side on the bed. I run my thumb over the tear running down her cheek, and she kisses me. Instead of enjoying it, all I think is how lucky I am that Ryder has cleared the room of cameras, so that at least this moment is ours. Even when I'm not being recorded, Ryder and Brian are still in my head.

We slide under the bedsheets, a barrier between us and the real world, and pull the covers over our heads. In that tiny space I hold her tight against me and we whisper like kids at a sleepover.

At 4:53 I swing my legs over the side of the bed. I don't want to leave Annaleigh, but I have to.

I head to the bathroom to get a drink. I'm only gone a minute, but when I emerge, she's perched at the end of the bed, eyes wide, lips quivering. I follow her gaze toward the TV screen, where the gossip show has found a new and perhaps even more tantalizing target.

Us.

We're two lovebirds caught beside her patio doors. The photo is a little hazy on account of the glass that separates us from the photographer, but in the glow from her bedside lamp, one thing is clear: We're both completely naked.

"Turn it off, Annaleigh."

She turns the sound on instead.

The commentators are running through the full repertoire of facial expressions: surprised, amused, appalled. A woman with big blond hair argues that we're cute, and isn't it good that Seth got away from Sabrina Layton before she pulled him into her sordid world. A ponytailed guy with sleeves of tattoos responds that having sex with a minor is hardly cool, and what must our parents think?

"Please," I beg. "Turn it—"

The TV goes blank, and nothing remains but the sound of our breathing, and yards of empty room between us.

"Why?" she murmurs. "Why is all this happening?"

I don't know what to tell her. Ryder has far more scandalous footage than that.

"Do photographers just hang out there?" she demands. "Do they sleep on sidewalks? In bushes? Or don't they sleep at all?"

I traipse to the patio doors and lean my head against the cool glass. There's no way any photographer could've gotten that shot, not with her room being on the fourth floor. But a camera mounted to the balcony rail would've captured it perfectly.

"How do the paparazzi know which our rooms are, huh?" Her voice is a tortured growl. "Or that we were both there?"

I could answer her questions, but I won't. I won't tell her that Ryder has listened to our nocturnal conversations through Annaleigh's bugged cell phone, and set up enough cameras to capture every money shot. But I won't play along anymore, either.

The clock says 4:58. I'm going to be late.

"We'll get through this," I tell her.

She continues to stare at the blank TV screen. "We just have to keep going, right?" She says the words like she means them. Like this phrase I've been rolling out for the past three-plus years isn't as meaningless as it is unconvincing.

"I should go," I say.

She wraps her arms around herself. "Why?"

"I just have to. But I'll meet you downstairs before the party, I promise. I'm not going to leave you for a single second tonight."

"Even when I go to the bathroom?"

I pretend to think about it. "Yup. Even then."

She chokes out a single laugh, grabs a pillow, and tosses it at me. I take the blow with a smile I don't feel.

"What if my parents don't let me stay?" She slides back along the bed and pulls the sheets up to her chin. "When they see the news, they're going to be pissed. If we're together tonight, we should enjoy every moment, 'cause they'll find a way to screw this up. Trust me. That's all they ever do—screw up my life."

I want to reassure her that we'll have tonight, no matter what. Her parents are counting on tomorrow's payout, and they won't jeopardize it with only a few hours to go. But now that I think of it, she's right. What are the chances that her parents will let us stay together when everything is over? They're about to get what they came for, and they won't want any loose ends.

As for Annaleigh and me, we'll be collateral damage, a sweet story that blossomed fast and will pass away with similar quickness.

Unless I can write us a new ending.

35

I RUN THE FEW BLOCKS TO the coffee shop. Gant's exactly where I told him to be, sitting in the back corner, two lattes waiting on the dark wood table.

The wall-mounted speaker plays soft jazz on a never-ending cycle. I place the phone gently on a shelf beside it, and go through the motions of ordering a coffee. Only, no one's listening to me. Well, no one except Ryder and Brian.

I join my brother at the small circular table across the store.

"Thank you, Gant." The words are hopelessly inadequate. "I wasn't sure you heard me in the office."

"I heard you." He glances at the door, looking anxious. "That Brian is scary. He waited until I got inside our house. Then he drove to the end of the block and hung around for another ten minutes. He wants me out of the picture."

"No wonder. If he's been listening in, he knows you're smart. Did you see Dad?"

"No. He's at work."

At work. Hard to remember now, but watching Dad go to a job interview convinced me more than ever to audition for *Whirlwind.* I thought what he was doing was courageous, and figured

I'd do something courageous too. I don't feel so noble anymore.

Gant tilts his head toward the phone on the shelf. "We'd better hurry. If they can record you even when your phone is off, they can probably get a GPS signal. Either that, or they'll turn the phone on remotely and activate the GPS that way. Hackers do it all the time. Cops too." He sounds completely matter-of-fact. "As long as they can hear you, or you're moving, they'll lay off. Go off the grid and radio silent, like now, and they'll track you down."

"Like the guy in the green Mazda, you mean?"

"Exactly. Whoever he is, I figure he must be working for Brian and Ryder." Gant bites his thumbnail. "Look, they've got us where they want us. The way I see it, you have two choices: Play along and hope they go easy on us, or call a reporter and do a tell-all interview. A story like this'll get printed overnight. By tomorrow everyone will know what's going on."

"Yeah, and they'll blame me for it. Ryder's got video of me taking a bribe, remember? He's also got footage of me saying I want Sabrina gone from the movie. It'll look like I'm the bad guy." I take a sip of coffee. "Chances are, he'll come off looking completely innocent. He might even get to do this thing all over again with a different cast."

"Which is why you've got to tell your side of the story."

"I can't. I signed a nondisclosure agreement. They only told us what's going on because they know we can't repeat any of it. If we do, they'll sue us for everything we've got."

Gant exhales slowly. "All this footage they've got—is it really good enough for movie theaters?"

"Ryder thinks so."

"And the sound? I get that they can do amazing things in post-production, but when the cell phone was in your pocket, the quality's going to be useless."

"It's good enough for blackmailing me, I know that much. That's why we can't afford to get into a fight with them. No, what we need to do is destroy them." I press on before he can interrupt. "I'm thinking we both go to the office and I threaten to stay away from tonight's party—that'll make them take notice. While I keep them busy talking in the rehearsal room, you go to Ryder's editing suite and copy the files."

"No way. First of all, Brian's going to smell something fishy the moment I show up. Second, what are you going to do with the files anyway?"

"Release them on YouTube. No one'll pay to see a movie when most of it's available free."

Gant purses his lips. "You said yourself: The footage shows you fighting with Sabrina, threatening people, taking a bribe—"

"But only if Ryder edits it a certain way. If we could show people the whole of those scenes, they'd know the truth."

Gant rests his elbows on the table, knuckles pressed tight together. "All right, I'll do it. But not now. Later."

"I'm busy later."

"Yeah. And so are Brian and Ryder and Tracie. They said they're going to be watching you at tonight's party, which means I'll have all the time in the world."

"You won't be able to get into the office."

"If I had a key, I could. And the code for the alarm."

"So all you need is a key we don't have and a code we don't

know." I pretend to take inventory. "You want me to ask Ryder or Tracie? Or should I go straight to Brian?"

I wait for Gant to smile too, to reassure me we're in the realm of fantasy here. "You ask Maggie," he says.

"I told you, they fired her. She sold them out."

"You really think Brian would let her walk away? This is a tight ship. Ryder's a trained editor. Brian's the heavy. I'd bet anything that Tracie's a legit attorney, 'cause they need to be sure the contracts are cast iron. So what was Maggie's role?"

"She was an intern. She's at USC film school."

"And I'm on scholarship at Stanford." He takes a gulp of coffee, and wipes his sleeve across his mouth. "Until today, Brian and Ryder had everyone believing in this movie. You and Annaleigh. Sabrina and Kris. Even the movie news sites. How could they manage that if they're the ones selling cast stories and photographs, huh? No, they're using a go-between, and Maggie's perfect—completely out of the limelight."

"You didn't see the way Brian looked at her when she admitted selling the story. It was like he wanted to rip her throat out."

"Maybe she's ready to switch sides, then. Especially if you can make her a better offer than them."

"Like what?"

"I don't know. Whatever it takes, I guess. Look, what's the worst-case scenario? She reports back to Brian and Ryder, who carry on like nothing happened. As long as they need you to show up this evening, they can't mess with you."

I stare at my latte. The foam has congealed. "And what about tomorrow?"

"Tomorrow they're going to do whatever the hell they want." He leans back, his right fist rubbing small circles in his forehead. "You realize, school's starting again in a week. You thought you were going to be here, filming a movie and working with a private tutor. But you're not. So ask yourself: How are people going to look at us if we can't make this right?"

I glance at my watch. We've been here too long already. "Ryder's computers will be password protected."

"So's your laptop, and look how that's worked out for you."

I let the comment slide. I want to tell Gant that I'm worried for him, but he's already made up his mind.

"You got some dark clothing?" I ask.

"I can get some."

"Good. I'll pay Maggie a visit. Let's meet back here in an hour."

"No. Better go someplace else. Where's the nearest park?"

"Top of Rodeo Drive. Beverly Gardens Park."

"Okay." He points at the speaker across the room. "I'm going to need your phone, or they'll track you right to Maggie's apartment."

"If they hear your voice, they'll realize you're still around."

"I'll wrap it up so the microphone won't pick up anything. And I'll keep moving, so they won't bother tracking me." He rolls his eyes. "It's for an hour, Seth. You're going to have to trust me."

If he'd said anything else, I might still argue. But I really do need to trust him. We're on our own now. And the stakes are higher than ever.

36

I TAKE A TAXI TO MAGGIE'S apartment building. Press the buzzer for apartment 17.

The sound of wailing over the intercom tells me she's not alone.

"It's Brian," I say, sounding pissed.

"What?"

"Brian," I repeat, louder.

There's a moment's hesitation. To my surprise, the door clicks open.

I walk inside, my footsteps echoing on the polished black-and-white tiled floor. A plush runner lines the stairs. Her apartment is on the third floor, halfway along. I knock once, hard.

She opens the door, catches a glimpse of me, and tries to close it again. I've already stuck out my foot, though. Arms wrapped around her baby, she can't stop me, from barging in.

She shrinks back. "What do you want?"

"To talk."

"So talk."

"Why did you do it?"

"Uh-uh. You're not here for an explanation. Like it would make any difference anyway." As she pulls her baby closer, I step away from her, hands raised like I'm surrendering. She tilts her head to the side, confused. "They're going to know you're here, Seth."

"No, they're not."

"They hear everything."

"Only if this apartment is bugged. I left my cell phone at home, see?"

She raises an eyebrow. "You're smarter than I gave you credit for. But they'll still find out. Brian finds out everything eventually. He spent years in corporate security. Believes the best form of defense is offense. If I were you, I wouldn't want to find out what that means."

"Like you did? I know you weren't supposed to come clean about selling the Kris and Tamara story." I can tell I'm right because her mouth twitches. "It's the only time I've seen Brian lose it."

She slides carefully into a leather armchair and rocks her baby. The studio apartment is large but empty—no pictures on the walls, or books on the built-in shelves. The stainless steel appliances in the kitchen are way more expensive than the ones we have at home, but they look unused. The four cardboard boxes stacked beside the door suggest that either Maggie hasn't been here long, or she's already planning to leave.

"Why are you doing this, Maggie?"

"Same reason as you. I wanted to work in the movies. Even took a job doing data entry at Machinus, all for a chance to break in."

"Is that how you met Ryder?"

"Yeah. He sold me on the movie—scripted reality, the future of low-budget filmmaking. Brian sold me on the perks—free apartment and good pay. They said a new kind of movie demanded a new kind of publicity. That was my job—to keep the project in the news." She frowns. "They never told me what that really meant, though. How I'd be selling secrets to the media, so that Brian could cut me loose if anyone found out what was going on."

"Why sell secrets at all? Why not save everything for the movie?"

"It's not easy keeping gossip under wraps. Some stuff was bound to leak out, so they figured they might as well profit off it. Plus, it's all free publicity, like a bunch of teaser trailers. Now that audiences know what's been going down, they'll want to see *how* it went down. Trust me, Brian's got it all figured out."

"Then why'd you cross him?"

She bristles. "You know why—you were at the party too."

"Kris told me to apologize to you about that."

"This isn't just about a dress, or Kris, or even me. It's about you and Annaleigh too."

I lean against the sofa, waiting for her to join the dots.

"I thought we were a *team*," she continues. "All of us, in on the plan. But they screwed with you both from the get-go. Your first night here, some guy takes pictures of you and Kris. An hour later, Brian hands me the photos and a story about you . . . even tells me who to sell them to, and for how much money.

"Next thing, they're telling me to sell the story about Kris and Tamara having an affair. Only, I never told them about that, and when you showed up at the office freaking out, I realized you didn't either. Which meant that they must've recorded our conversation." She looks me right in the eye. "I always knew I'd have to fight to get ahead in this business, but not like this. Forget *scripted reality*—this is freaking invasion of privacy. They don't care what happens to you and Annaleigh, and it's pretty clear they've set you up to be the bad guy. That's not *real*. It's just bullying." She nuzzles her baby. "If there's one thing I know for sure, it's that bullying sucks."

"So why didn't you tell someone what was happening?"

"I tried to tell *you*, remember?"

"I mean someone in the press."

"I signed a nondisclosure, same as you. That office was the only place I could admit what I was doing, and get away with it."

Seeing it through her eyes, it must have seemed foolproof. Hearing her confession, who wouldn't step back and take a little time to think things through? But Brian knew my weak spot— with a stack of bills in my hand, and the promise of better days ahead, I cast Maggie as a loose cannon, and trusted Brian more than ever.

"Brian came to see me here later that afternoon," she contin ues. "Told me to pack up and get the hell out. Said the apartment was a perk of the job. I was supposed to have it for three months, and I had nowhere else to go. So like a freaking coward, I said I was sorry and promised to keep selling his damn stories." She holds her baby a little tighter. "I should've realized he was play- ing me again. The landlord stopped by this morning. Turns out, Brian only paid for this place through the end of this month. If he doesn't pony up next month's rent, we get kicked out tomorrow."

I perch on the edge of a coffee table—not because I want to sit, but because I don't want to stand over her. It's time to share my plan, and intimidating Maggie isn't going to bring her around.

"What if you could get money another way?" I ask.

"How?"

"I could do a tell-all interview with you about my life. Nothing off-limits. All the photographs you want. You know how much these stories are worth, and how to sell them. You could start over."

"And you'd do that for me, right?" She turns away. "I'm not stupid, Seth. I can smell a trap."

"Not a trap. A trade."

"For what?"

My knee is bouncing up and down. I clamp it in place with my right hand. "I need to borrow your office key. And I need the alarm key code."

"You're not serious."

"It's only for a few hours. They won't even know I'm there."

"They're *tracking* you."

"I'm telling you, they'll never know." I can tell from her expression that she's still not convinced. "Even if they do find out, you'll still get the interview."

"And what would I do with it? I already told you: I signed a nondisclosure agreement. If I sell a story about the film, they'll come after me."

"So write a story about me instead. You could even get someone else to sell it, so they won't know you're the source. If anyone knows how to pull that off, it's you."

She places her cheek against her baby's head and falls silent.

She's probably wondering whether to relay this conversation to Brian. Telling him about my visit could get her back into his good books.

"You said it yourself, Maggie: They tricked *us*. When the movie comes out, no one is going to believe you and me and Annaleigh weren't in on the whole thing. But *we* know."

She bites her lip. "So when do I get this story of yours?"

"Tomorrow."

"How do I know you'll follow through?"

"You have my word."

"Your word?" She laughs, and her baby stirs.

"What else do you want?"

"I want you to look at us," she says. "I need you to know that if you screw up, it won't just be me you're hurting."

I look at the baby—tiny, rosy-cheeked, and bald except for a tight swirl of soft blond hair. "I promise I won't let you down."

She exhales slowly. "Key's under the coffeepot."

I head to the kitchen and lift the pot. "It's not here."

"Try the countertop."

"Uh-uh."

"Hold on. Let me look." She leans forward and tries to stand, but the chair is low and she's still holding her baby.

"Here. Let me take her."

Maggie pulls her baby closer than before. Then, as I hold out my arms, she passes the child to me. I rest the tiny girl on my forearm and chest. Cradle her head against my neck, her quick breaths warm against my skin.

The key is under an electric kettle. "Two-zero-zero-one is the code," Maggie says. "You have thirty seconds to enter it. Then the alarm starts."

"Does it stop once you enter the code?"

"Yeah. But the security company will still come to check it out." She leaves the key on the counter. "If you set off the alarm, don't stick around to be a hero. Get out and bring me my key. I can't risk us getting hurt over you."

"I'll get out. I promise." I gently pass her baby back. "How do they plan for this to end, Maggie?"

"I don't know. But if they're kicking me out of here in the morning, I'm guessing it'll all be over soon."

"Yeah. Me too."

I take the key from the counter and leave.

Outside, the street is dark and mostly empty. There's a taxi in the distance, so I hail it.

The driver is in the mood for small talk, but I'm too distracted for that. It's not until he mentions the car behind us that I take any notice of him.

"What did you say?" I ask.

"I'm wondering why that guy doesn't pass me," the driver repeats. "He just ran a red."

I spin around. I can't see the car that's following us because of the glare of headlights, but I can make out the first couple letters of the license plate.

It's my stalker again. And this time, the sight of me staring back doesn't deter him at all.

37

I TELL THE TAXI DRIVER TO pull over a block from Beverly Gardens Park. The green Mazda continues a short distance, and stops. My stalker is probably calling Brian right now, letting him know that I just visited Maggie. I can't even warn her.

I hide behind the canopy of a cypress. Fifty yards away a sign spells *Beverly Hills* in golden letters. There's a hum from the traffic on Santa Monica Boulevard across the park.

In the glow from the streetlamp I see the guy emerge: jeans and black hoodie, curly hair sticking out beneath a baseball cap. He heads in my direction, eyes flitting from left to right as though he's the one being pursued.

Someone's running along the gravel path in the middle of the park. I don't want to take my eyes off my pursuer, but the rapid footsteps are growing louder. Too late, it occurs to me that they might be Gant's footsteps.

My brother slows up as he approaches the sign. His hood is down, face visible because he wants me to see him.

What if my pursuer recognizes Gant? He'll report back to Brian and Ryder that my brother is still around. Without the element of surprise, there's no way Gant will be able to break into the office.

Thankfully the guy is focused on tracking me. He's closing in too.

Gant comes to a complete stop and the park falls silent. That's what finally gets the guy's attention. He turns slowly to check out the figure by the Beverly Hills sign. Pulls out his phone and touches the screen, illuminating his face. Gant, the most innocent of several innocent victims, turns toward the light, unaware that he's looking directly into the eyes of our enemy.

Instinct takes over. The guy doesn't see me coming, doesn't even hear me until I'm a yard away. As he turns I throw myself at him, feel the crack of bone against bone, and the wind driven from his lungs as he crashes to the ground. His phone clatters away.

He sweeps his arms across the ground, grasping for his phone. I keep him pinned down, though, and he can't reach it. He grunts with each shallow breath.

"I'm done, you hear me?" I growl. "I'm *done*."

He continues to slap at the ground, fingers inches from his phone. "No, you ain't. Not until he says so."

"You can tell Brian to go to hell!"

"Who's Brian? I ain't heard of no Brian."

"Then who are you talking about?"

When he doesn't answer, I wrench his arm. "Kris," he cries.

My chest tightens. "Kris and I are working together."

"Uh-uh. You working for Kris, but he ain't working for you. Don't trust you. Not since you got in with Sabrina."

"He told you to follow me?"

"No, man. Told me to follow *her*. But she's in rehab now, so I'm on to you instead." He hisses through closed teeth. "And you ain't behaving like you're innocent."

He makes a sharp movement, but I jam my knee into the base of his spine. His cry carries across the park.

"How did you text me? Kris didn't even know my number."

"Sure he did. That producer guy gave him all your numbers, soon as they started talking."

"So, what—you were trying to scare me?"

"No man. I was trying to wake you up. Kris said you're like a racing dog with blinders on—soon as you spot a rabbit, you don't got room for nothing else. Think about it: You arrive, and things start getting weird. Sabrina sees you yesterday, and now she's on the front page. If you ain't the problem, you sure as hell know who is."

A couple is heading toward us, drawn by his cry and our shadowy outlines. Two women. One pulls a cell phone from her pocket.

I've got more questions, but I'm not sticking around for the cops to arrive. My guess is that this guy won't either. So I push off him and sprint for the shadows. Rejoin the gravel path beyond the sign. Keep running in the direction Gant must have gone.

Several yards ahead of me, Gant slides out from behind a tree. "What going on?" he whispers furiously.

"Forget about it. That guy won't bother us anymore."

"Yeah, but Brian and Ryder might." Gant taps his pants pocket lightly to remind me about the cell phone. "Don't worry. It's wrapped up real tight. But we'd better get moving."

We walk briskly along the path together. I retrieve Maggie's key from my pocket and hand it to him. "The alarm code is two-zero-zero-one," I say, voice low.

"*Two Thousand and One: A Space Odyssey*. Way to ruin the movie for me." He grunts. "You sure we can trust her?"

I picture Maggie holding her baby, the look in her eyes as she reminded me of my promise. "Yeah."

The lights of the Beverly Hills business district cut through the trees, beckoning us back to the madness. We keep a quick pace—important to give Brian a moving target—but I'm cold in the aftermath of the fight.

"What's your plan?" I ask.

"I'm going to wait till after ten. No way anyone's going to leave a New Year's Eve party that close to midnight. Once I'm inside the office, I'll do whatever I have to do." He pulls a black hat from a carrier bag. "It's a designer label," he says. "Got to look my best when I'm breaking in."

He wants me to smile, but I'm too worried for that. "Here," I say, pulling bills from my wallet. "Get something to eat. I'd tell you to save some for a taxi, but you probably don't want to take a taxi from the scene of a burglary."

"Probably not."

"Listen. Please take—"

"Care. Yeah, I know." He stuffs his free hand in his pocket. "If there's a car parked there, I bail. If anything feels weird, I bail. If a butterfly flaps its wings in China, I bail."

"I'm serious, Gant."

He takes out my phone and hands it to me. It's wrapped in a dozen napkins, and feels a lot heavier than it actually is. "I know you are," he whispers. "And I'd still prefer to break into an empty office building than deal with whatever they've got in store for you tonight."

38

I PUT ON A WHITE SHIRT and blue blazer. The clothes aren't mine, but neither is this life. Seth Crane wears jeans and acts in plays, and maybe it's not the most extravagant lifestyle, but at least it's real. It's also a whole lot better than whatever Annaleigh is trying to escape.

I meet her in the lobby. She's sitting bolt upright in a cream-colored armchair, hands resting on her knees, looking pensive. As she sees me, her expression brightens, the kind of spontaneous reaction that can't be feigned.

She slides off the chair and approaches me. She's wearing a light blue dress that accents her eyes, and high heels that make her legs seem endless. Dramatic black mascara is softened by a hint of blush on her cheekbones. I pull her toward me. Her dress is soft beneath my fingers.

We leave hand in hand. Hotel employees hold photographers back as we climb into a limo. A large tinted panel separates us from the driver to give the illusion of maximum privacy, but I'm not fooled. There'll be a camera here too.

As we pull away from the curb, Annaleigh leans her head

against my shoulder. Her hand drifts across my blazer and up to my face. She wants me to kiss her again, and I want to kiss her too, but not here. Not like this.

She settles for holding my hand. "I've made a decision," she says. "I'm not going to let my parents mess this up for us."

She looks so serious, like she honestly believes she can control this situation. Is this how I appeared to Kris when he accused me of being naive?

"They can still take you away," I reply.

"Uh-uh. I called Mom. Told her, if she breaks us up, Dad won't get a penny from me."

Annaleigh leans back in the seat, wallowing in the beauty of her logic. Only, her parents are going to get their hands on that money no matter what. More, probably.

It's heartbreaking to see her smile and know that the one I return is a lie. Our movie is about to wrap. We are, it turns out, real-life star-crossed lovers, staring at the final curtain when we should be celebrating our moment of triumph.

The party is in Hollywood, in a place that resembles a European castle. Even the manicured vines suffocating the white walls look painted on. It's Jane Austen meets Disney, a building disguised as a movie set.

The limo door is still closed when the camera flashes start. Not just a few either, but a blinding assault. Evidently America has seen the photo of us and realized that we had sex. It makes our story even more irresistible.

Annaleigh squeezes my knee. "I'm ready to show America the most handsome boy in Hollywood. And you should know better than to keep your date waiting."

We press through the gaggle of photographers and into the building. A server meets us at the door and hands us drinks— some fruity punch that makes me feel like I'm twelve. I gulp it down and hand the empty glass back to her.

Annaleigh follows my lead. Even forces out a belch. "Strong stuff," she says.

"It should be. Made from one hundred percent concentrate."

"What it is to be rich and famous."

We move from the lobby to the main hall, where a live DJ provides thumping music. Lights rotate above us, bright and disorientating. Nearby couples, talking loudly, are having fun. Several of the teens seem familiar from the party at Machinus, and I don't think it's a coincidence. Maybe they've been paid to be here, extras in a drama more convoluted than they can possibly imagine.

As Annaleigh pulls me in for a kiss, a flash goes off just in front of us.

"Can you do that again?" asks the photographer, a woman with spiked blond hair. "I was late on the shot."

Annaleigh frowns. "Uh, no, thank you."

The woman stops us as we turn away. "I'm Kira," she says. "From the magazine. We're running that feature about your relationship—life imitating art. I'm shadowing you, remember?"

Annaleigh grips my hand tighter, an anxious expression darkening her face. I rub my thumb across the back of her hand to soothe her. I have no idea if Kira works for a magazine and if there's a feature. Doesn't matter. Chances are, this is just the beginning of the evening's surprises, and Brian and Ryder need to see that we're playing along.

Kira raises the camera again, but Annaleigh covers her eyes. Kira gives her a moment to reconsider this move, and leans closer so that the couples eavesdropping only a few yards away won't hear. "I'm sorry you didn't know I'll be with you tonight, but I will be photographing you, and I will be talking to you, and I do expect you to answer my questions."

"No comment," replies Annaleigh.

Kira bristles, but recovers her poise with a deep breath. "Seems like you're buying into your own hype already. Think you own Hollywood." She runs her tongue across bright white teeth. "Make no mistake, though—tonight, I own you."

Kira raises the camera and snaps a dozen photos in rapid succession. She works smoothly and efficiently, which makes me think she's a real photographer. But her words remind me of Brian. If she's here to babysit us and keep us in line, where the hell are Brian and Ryder?

"You look tense, Seth," Kira remarks. She pulls out a tiny recording device. "It must be hard to comprehend everything that's happened to you. From community theater to a motion picture. Rags to riches."

It's an invitation to open up, but she's not getting that from me. She can have all the photos she wants, but she can't make me talk.

Annaleigh pulls me onto the dance floor and wraps her arms

around me. I can't focus, though. My eyes dart around, searching for movie cameras. They must be here somewhere, forever focused on us, capturing every second.

"Hey." Annaleigh cups my chin. "I'm sick of being watched all the time. If that's the way it is, so be it. But I'm going to be me tonight. And I want you to be *you*." She moves so that we're cheek to cheek. Her breath is warm against my ear, voice just the slightest bit husky. "I like being with you, Seth, and I don't care who knows it."

We kiss. I run my hand over the bare skin of her neck and rest my thumb against her cheek. When I close my eyes, the camera flash pulses through my eyelids. I don't want to think of these photos, or the movie cameras filming in secret somewhere. I just want to enjoy the feeling of being with her, and kissing her, because I'm so afraid it can't last.

Finally, we ease apart. Annaleigh smiles sheepishly. "I think Kira got her money's worth."

"I'm kind of hoping the camera wasn't working. It'd be nice to do another take."

"Party's over at one, right? Less than four hours to go."

"Works for me." I feel myself reddening. "By the way, you might want to fix your lip gloss. I think I kind of messed it up."

"Five minutes with you and I'm a hot mess." She taps me on the nose with her finger. "I'll be right back."

She takes off for the women's restroom. Kira follows her, snapping photos the whole way. I make my way toward the nearest server. A few steps later, someone grabs my shoulder.

"Seth!" booms Brian. His hand is like an anchor. "Come and have a chat."

He leads me toward a booth in the far corner. It's not hard to guess why he chose this table to spy on us.

"Sorry we're late," says Tracie. "We didn't want to steal your spotlight."

"This is your night," agrees Brian. "Just you and Annaleigh. The gossip sites say she's really into you."

My hands are fists under the table. "You shouldn't have put out that photo of us."

"And you should remember how many more we have lined up. And how much footage we have of you and Annaleigh from last night. You want Ryder to edit this stuff tastefully, right?"

"You're a pervert."

"Uh-uh. I hardly looked at any of it. It's the people who buy the magazines that are messed up." Brian takes a sip of his drink. "Come on, you know the drill: No market, no sale. We're all victims of capitalism, really."

"Sure we are."

I try to stand, but he digs his fingers into my quad. Pain flares across my leg. "I don't trust you, Seth."

"I wonder why."

"You're not going to say something stupid in front of Anna leigh, are you? Try to bring us all down? 'Cause I've got to tell you, she looks radiant tonight. You ought to enjoy her while you can."

My phone starts vibrating. Not a surprise under usual circumstances, but this is different. Annaleigh is here at the party, and so are Brian and Ryder and Tracie. The only other people who might call me are Kris or Gant. Either way, it'll spell trouble.

I slide the phone from my pocket and glance at the screen. I've already prepared a nonchalant expression so they won't know anything's up. But I can't keep up the illusion.

It's Sabrina.

39

"WHO'S CALLING YOU, SETH?" TRACIE ASKS.

"Annaleigh," I answer quickly.

"Why would Annaleigh call you from the restroom?"

I slide out of the booth. "So she can speak to me without Kira and the whole world hearing."

Tracie returns an icy smile. "That's ironic. 'Cause some of the world will definitely be listening to this call later tonight."

I walk to the bar, but don't take the call until I'm sure I'm not being followed. Even then, I glance back to check that Brian and company aren't eavesdropping on another device. They're not, but Tracie isn't kidding when she says they'll be listening to every word later on. I have to keep this brief.

"Are you okay, Sabrina?"

"Did you tell anyone?" she asks.

There isn't time to pretend I don't understand. "No. I swear I didn't."

She sighs. "I believe you. Kris was on the news earlier. Says I can finally get help now. I think he's the one who did this."

"Why, though?"

"Gen must've told him everything."

"*Gen?* What are you talking about?"

"I need to see you." Her voice is so small that I can hardly hear her. "I left the center."

"What?" The room seems to shift around me—too much noise and activity. "Why?"

"It was claustrophobic. I need space."

Brian and the others are still seated at the booth, but their eyes are fixed on me. Sabrina's confiding in me again, and yet again, Brian's going to discover everything she says.

"Hang up," I say. "This phone's flaking out. I'll call you right back from a different one."

There are dozens of people milling about. Like well-behaved extras on a movie set, they don't interact with me, but they can't resist stealing glances. I move out of Brian's line of sight, and catch the eye of a young woman.

"My cell phone just died," I tell her, "and I've got to make a call."

"Okay." She hands hers over without hesitation. It's pretty beaten up.

"This is *your* phone, right?"

She looks at me like I'm crazy. "Yeah."

"Good."

Sabrina's number is still branded in my memory. I don't think I'll ever forget it. I make the call and she answers immediately.

"How did you get out of the center?" I ask.

"It's not a prison."

"They let you go?"

A hesitation. "I climbed a wall at the back." Her voice cracks. "I don't know what to do."

So much for Kris hoping she'd get help. "Where are you?"

For a few seconds, I only hear her ragged breaths. Then: "Intersection of Laurel Canyon and Hollywood Boulevard."

She's at least a twenty minutes' drive away. My mind races through different scenarios, but there's only one that makes sense. "You've got to go back."

"I can't. There's paparazzi at the gates."

"Then go home."

"You're not listening, Seth. They're *everywhere*."

The woman who lent me her phone is hovering, eavesdropping. Brian will be wondering why I'm turned away from his booth. I need to wrap things up.

"Just give me a couple minutes," I say. "I'll call Kris."

"No!" Her voice changes—focused and furious. "He's the reason I'm here."

"I don't think he leaked that story about you—"

"Why not? He's the reason for everything else. You don't have a clue what's really going on, so don't you dare call him." Like she's flicking a switch, her voice softens again. "I can handle this. You believe me, right?"

Annaleigh emerges from the restroom, lip gloss perfect. She has her life in order, even as her parents conspire to ruin it for her. From their booth in the corner, Brian and company won't be able to see her yet, but soon they will, and they'll notice she's not on her phone.

I try to get her attention. "Look, Sabrina, things are real complicated—"

"Forget it," she snaps. "I'll call Ryder."

"No!" I practically shout the word, and Annaleigh's head whips around. She shoots me a quizzical look. "Don't call him, Sabrina. Please."

"Then help me. I don't think I should be alone right now."

Annaleigh joins me. I can't tell if she heard me say Sabrina's name, but she knows something is wrong. She glances over her shoulder as Kira emerges from the restroom. It feels like everyone is closing in on us.

It's past nine thirty. I don't want to leave, but I'm scared for Sabrina. If anything were to happen to her, I couldn't forgive myself. Given the state she's in, I have a terrible feeling that something will happen. And soon.

"I'll come get you," I say.

"Thank you," says Sabrina, more breath than word.

I hand the girl's phone back and thank her. The party is in full swing now. People are dancing and laughing, but not Annaleigh. She gazes at me, all crystalline eyes and worried brows, waiting for me to explain what's going on.

I lean close and keep my voice low. Our phones are still recording us, even though she doesn't know it. "Sabrina checked herself out of rehab."

Annaleigh seems to deflate. "Why would she do that? Should we call the police?"

"No. She hasn't done anything wrong. I just want to make sure she gets home safe."

"You're not responsible for her."

I can't possibly explain how wrong she is about that. "Who else does she have? Kris? Her parents? The agent she just fired?"

"You can't leave me here. What about Kira?"

"I won't be gone long. An hour, tops. Kira can get all the shots she wants then."

Annaleigh nods, but she looks crestfallen. As if to remind me what I'll be missing, she runs her fingers across my cheek and pulls me in for another long, deep kiss. Her heartbeat races beneath the folds of her thin blue dress.

"Call me, okay?" she says. "The moment you get her home. Just so I know everything's all right."

I'm not sure if she means everything with Sabrina, or with me. Or if she's still worried there's more going on here than there appears to be. Doesn't matter—there's no way I'm taking my cell phone on this trip. Brian won't be listening to any more of my conversations.

"Battery's flaking out," I say, patting my pocket, "That's why I needed to borrow that girl's phone."

Annaleigh reaches into her fabric clutch purse and pulls out her phone. "Here, then. I'll swap you."

"How will I call you if I have your phone?"

"On this." She retrieves her old phone, with tiny cracked screen and unreadable keys. "I only carry it in case my mom calls, but it still has some charge."

I steal a glance across the room. Kira's looking for us. Ryder is heading for the bar, and I don't think he's after another drink.

I swap my phone for her old one that Brian can't track. "I'll use this."

She flicks a piece of dust from the lapel of my blazer. "I'm sorry. I know she needs your help, but it's hard not to feel jealous. She's still Sabrina Layton, you know?"

I can almost feel Ryder getting closer, but I kiss her anyway. "It's only you, Annaleigh."

"I'll cover for you. Just hurry."

I check on Ryder. He's only ten yards away. For a couple seconds, we stare at each other. Then, as if he has seen exactly how this is going to play out, he raises a hand to summon help.

I spin around and run. Ahead, a corridor leads to the restrooms. A red exit sign glows above double doors at the end.

"Seth." Brian's growl carries over the music.

I blunder through the double doors. Ignore the surprised looks of the kitchen staff, smoking outside. I'm at the back of the building, well away from the paparazzi.

"Seth!"

There's an alleyway to my left. Beyond it, traffic crisscrosses at low speed. With Brian's heavy footsteps drawing near, I break into a sprint.

At the street, cars trundle by in stop-and-start slow motion. Brian hasn't given up chasing, so I run along the sidewalk, squinting at the bright car lights. There's a taxi about fifty yards ahead of me, on the other side.

I weave through traffic. Brakes squeal and car horns fill the air, but I keep going until I'm within shouting distance of the taxi.

The driver signals to rejoin the traffic. As the taxi pulls away from the curb, I rap my knuckles against the trunk.

The car stops suddenly. I yank the back door open and slam it shut behind me.

"Go!" I shout.

The driver follows my eyes across the street, where Brian is waiting to cross. "Got you some kind of problem?"

Brian steps into the gap between two cars.

"My dad doesn't like my girlfriend. But it's New Year's Eve, and I want to spend it with her, not him, you know?"

The driver chuckles. "He don't look old enough to be your dad."

Brian's ten yards away. "Yeah, well . . . back in the day, he sneaked out with his girlfriend on New Year's Eve. I'm the result."

"Amen to—"

Brian slams his palms against the window next to me. I slide across the seat, hands raised defensively, helpless as he yanks the door handle.

40

BRIAN WRENCHES THE HANDLE OVER AND over, but the doors are locked. As if he hasn't even noticed the crazy guy beside us, the driver calmly pulls into traffic.

Brian chases us for a few yards, but gives up as we accelerate. Whatever he's shouting is drowned out by jazz from the car stereo. The music is frenetic and complicated, a perfect soundtrack for my life.

"So where are we heading?" the driver asks.

"Laurel Canyon and Hollywood Boulevard." I press myself against the backseat, face turned slightly away from the mirror. "Please."

"Sure thing, boss."

For twenty minutes, Hollywood spins by, a blur of Christmas lights and New Year's Eve energy. "Which building you want, man?" the driver asks, pulling over.

"I don't know." I hand him a twenty. "Keep the meter running, okay? I'll be right back."

I can't see Sabrina. The driver isn't going to wait forever, so I run down the street, peering through gaps in bushes. I'm almost past an alleyway when I notice a stream of smoke curling up from behind a dumpster.

"Sabrina?"

She peers around it. Slowly, awkwardly, she pulls to a stand. She's wearing jeans and a gray hoodie. Her hair is dragged back in a lank ponytail. She drops her cigarette and stumbles toward me.

"What are you doing here?" I ask.

She leans into me. Presses her face against the nape of my neck. "I thought I heard them following me. Photographers."

There's no one around.

"Please take me home," she says.

I walk her to the taxi. It's not especially cold, but as she slides onto the backseat, she's shaking.

"Where we heading now?" asks the driver.

"Pico and Century Park," says Sabrina. She pulls up her knees and hugs them. Her teeth chatter.

"Can you crank up the heat?" I ask.

The driver turns a dial.

"You're so sweet, Seth." Sabrina's eyes well with tears. "But it's not about the cold."

As her meaning becomes clear, it's impossible not to think back to our first meeting at Curt's house—how she seemed so alive, so blissfully in control. I flattered myself that her mood had something to do with me, but it was all about the drugs. I was just a foil, a character that enabled her to play the most alluring version of herself.

Maybe the realization should make me feel sad, but it doesn't.

I can be more than a foil now. I can get her home safely. If Sabrina can't rely on herself anymore, she can count on me.

I shuffle along the seat and let her lean against me. She holds me so tightly that she almost crushes me. She doesn't stop shaking, though.

A quarter hour later, we pull up in a district of apartment buildings. I give the driver another twenty and he tips his head in thanks.

As the taxi pulls away, Sabrina points down the adjacent street. "It's a block that way," she says. "I wasn't sure if the driver recognized us, so I didn't give the correct address."

We're nowhere near the beach or the hills. The clean, orderly street of modern apartment buildings seems more suited to go-getting professionals than a young actress. "I didn't picture you living here."

"It's only a half mile from my agent's office," she says, like this explains everything. "Ex-agent's office, I mean. Being near him made it smoother when I petitioned for emancipation. The judge liked knowing there was someone close by to watch out for me."

We stop beside a tower block with smooth concrete walls and chrome accents around the doors. Sabrina buzzes in. The marble-clad lobby is spacious. A water feature against the far wall tinkles therapeutically.

"Ms. Layton?" The doorman's greeting turns into a question at the last moment. He has seen the news too, and knows she's supposed to be in rehab.

"Hi, Neil," she says, still clinging to me.

He's only mid-twenties, but the wary look he gives me seems almost paternal. It might've annoyed me once, but now it's a relief to know there's someone else looking out for her.

We take the elevator to the ninth floor. She jams her keys into an apartment door and slips inside.

Before she turns the lights on, Sabrina closes every blind.

"I can't help it," she says. "I feel like they're watching me all the time. Every moment, just looking."

Yesterday I would've called her paranoid. Now anything seems possible, even on the ninth floor of an apartment building.

"Has Ryder ever been here?" I ask. "Or Brian? Anyone to do with the movie."

"No. Why?"

"I just wondered."

The apartment is surprisingly small. The kitchen and living room are joined, bathroom and bedroom partially visible through doors at the end.

"Sorry about the mess," she says. "Kitchen's clean, though, if you want something to eat. I always keep the kitchen clean."

As Sabrina goes to her bedroom, I run the kitchen faucet and splash my face. The clock on the microwave reads 10:38.

I wander through the living room, footsteps silent on thick-pile carpet. The walls are covered in framed movie posters—not Sabrina's films either, but classics: *Casablanca, Double Indemnity, Vertigo*. A cream-colored sofa faces a state-of-the-art home theater system.

Sabrina doesn't even look around as I enter her bedroom, just remains seated on the edge of her double bed, cradling a small prescription pill bottle. She uncaps it carefully, almost reverentially. Then she catches my reflection in a mirror and freezes.

"What are you doing, Sabrina?"

"Nothing."

It's my cue to leave. To stop asking questions when the answers are all too obvious. She's making it easy for me, really.

Instead I lunge for the bottle and snatch it away.

"Give it back," she shrieks.

"I'm calling the center."

Fury morphs into derisive laughter. "You can go home now. You've done your good deed for the day."

"I'm not going anywhere."

"I wasn't asking."

"Are you going to make me?" I wave the bottle. "You going to call the police?"

She flails at the bottle, consumed by something much stronger than anger. When she can't reach it, she hits me. Each blow stings, but I don't fight back and I don't give in. A few seconds later, breathless and bright red, she crumples on the bed, sobbing.

I tell myself it's drugs doing this to her, not me. But so what? She looks like a trapped animal, instincts screaming that worse is still to come. And I hold everything that she wants in my right hand. Her world—at least, the part of it she cares about the most—can be confined to a plastic bottle a couple inches tall.

I stuff it in my blazer pocket and sit down beside her. I don't know whether to hug her, or simply to leave her alone. I don't know if she's spent, or if she'll summon a second wind.

I don't know her at all.

But she called me. Not Kris. Not Genevieve. Not her parents, or her ex-agent.

Me.

"I think you called because you knew what'd happen when you got home." I let the words hang there for a moment, a cautious opening. "I think you wanted me here so I could stop you."

The sound of her crying grows quieter, but she won't look at me. Maybe she knows on some deep level that I'm not the problem here. Or perhaps she just doesn't want me to see how much she loathes me— -that whatever she was thinking when she made the call earlier, now she'd like nothing more than for me to get the hell out of her apartment and let her take whatever she wants.

She reaches under her ruffled pillow and pulls out a long cotton T-shirt. There's a faded image of Kermit the Frog on the front. She straightens it out on her lap and sits there, staring at Kermit.

The phone in my pocket rings, a tone I don't recognize. The cracked screen identifies Annaleigh as the caller. I step out of the bedroom and pull the door closed behind me.

"I'm sorry, Annaleigh," I whisper. "I'm just about to leave."

Silence. The microwave clock reads 10:44.

"I just want to make sure she's safe," I explain.

More silence, only this time there's breathing too—heavy, ominous.

Finally, a voice. But it's not Annaleigh's. "You're a tricky little fucker, aren't you, Seth?"

41

BRIAN'S VOICE CARRIES CLEAR OVER THE line, taunting me. "You really screwed up."

"Where's Annaleigh?"

"Waiting for her date. Know where he is?"

"Like I'd tell you."

I check that Sabrina's bedroom door is still closed, and sit on the kitchen floor, back to the cupboards, legs out in front of me. I can't afford to be overheard.

"Annaleigh didn't want to give me this number," mutters Brian. "But I was persuasive. She finally told me she'd given you her old phone. Said something about your battery flaking out. I've got your phone right here and it seems the battery's just fine. Want to tell me what you're up to?"

"No."

"Hmm. That's too bad. Funny thing is, I figured I knew where you'd gone. Especially after your visit to Maggie this evening."

He lets the words sink in. There's no mistaking what this news means, but I can't believe it. When I looked Maggie in the eyes just a few hours ago, she was telling me the truth. I would've bet anything on it. *Did* bet everything on it.

"I've got to tell you, Seth—I don't think you're Maggie's favorite person anymore. Not after you led us right to her apartment. Which reminds me, thanks for taking that photo of the license plate. We've been following the green Mazda since this morning. And, well . . . that guy's been following you, of course." Brian chuckles. "But don't worry, one visit from me and Maggie realized she's safer on Team Brian. She won't be needing that tell-all interview from you, either."

I want to throw up.

"Yeah, she told me all about your plan. So when you disappeared this evening, I figured I'd head out too—beat you to the punch. But do you know who came waltzing through the office door just now? I'll give you a clue: It wasn't you." He laughs, loud and humorless. "You and Gant are quite the operation."

"Where is he?"

"Right here. And now I've got a difficult decision. Call the police and draw unwanted attention to our project, or let him go."

"Sounds like you don't have a choice at all."

"Oh, but I do. He was caught breaking and entering."

"He has a key."

"Which Maggie gave to *you*, not him. A small point, but our lawyer says it's significant."

I ball my hand into a fist and punch the ground. "You really think anyone would believe he was breaking in?"

"Absolutely. He was having second thoughts about his role in the movie. Figured he'd delete all our footage. He was probably planning to destroy our hardware too. The irony is that his own father signed him up for all this, and we've got a waiver to prove it." He whistles. "Such a sick, twisted family you are."

"Let him go, Brian!"

A door closes behind me. I peer around the cabinets to see if Sabrina has joined me, but the living room is empty.

"You'd better calm down," he says. "I get to decide how this plays out, not you. Maybe I'll tell Ryder to film Gant getting arrested. It'd be a perfect climax to the parental neglect subplot—Dad abandons sons in hotel room; younger son turns to crime. Audiences love that shit."

I close my eyes. "What do you want me to do?"

"I want you to get back to Annaleigh."

"Why? You're just going to break us up. Even if you don't, her parents will."

"You're such a disappointment, Seth. Ryder really thought you'd see the bigger picture, embrace the idea of a new kind of movie. Me, I just figured you'd be smart enough to realize that fifty grand and fame were a pretty good start for a kid in Hollywood. But all you do is whine." He sighs. "You're not even here fighting for Annaleigh. The way I see it, we won't have to break you two up at all. If she's got any sense, she'll dump you herself."

"Maybe she will."

"Or maybe you'll get back here and be your charming self, and we'll forget about this unfortunate situation with Gant."

"You swear it?"

"Yes. Do *you*?"

I pause, but it's mostly for effect. We both know what I'm going to say. "Yeah."

"Good boy." There's a delay, and a faint murmuring as if he's covered the mouthpiece and is giving instructions to someone. Then he's back. "Get your ass here now, you hear me? If you're not around at midnight, we're going to have a real falling-out, you and me."

I hang up. I'm relieved that Annaleigh kept Sabrina out of this, but I wish she hadn't told Brian about us switching phones. Never mind that he can't track me or eavesdrop. If he has this number, he'll probably find a way to locate me. I turn the phone off and slip it inside my trouser pocket.

I return to an empty bedroom. "Sabrina?" .

"I'm in the bathroom. Changing." Her voice comes from behind another door. "How's Annaleigh? She must be waiting for you."

"Yeah."

"You should go, then. Thanks for helping me."

Her tone is all wrong—too conciliatory.

I scan the room. Her clothes lie strewn across the bed. The Kermit T-shirt is gone. "You've already changed."

A hesitation. "I'm peeing."

I try the handle, but it's locked. I run around and try the other bathroom door, the one from the living room. That's locked too.

"Open the door, Sabrina."

"I'm on the toilet."

"Open the door!"

She opens it. "What's the matter?" She flushes the toilet. Turns on the faucet.

I watch her in the mirror. She has undone the ponytail so that hair drapes across her face. She stares at her hands, lathering soap quickly, rhythmically.

"Look at me, Sabrina." More lathering. "Please."

She rinses her hands, shoves the faucet off, and glares at me. "Happy now?"

She opens the medicine cabinet above the sink as if she's looking for something. But she just wants an object between us, something to stop me from watching her.

"What did you take?"

"Nothing." She sorts through the cosmetics in the cabinet, fingers skipping from vial to compact. But she doesn't need makeup. She doesn't need anything at all anymore. "You should go. Annaleigh's waiting."

I try to close the cabinet door, but she bats my hand away.

"I said go!" She spins around, face flushed, eyelids twitching.

"I'm calling the center."

"Go ahead. They can't make me go back."

I feel lost. It seems crazy now, but when I found Sabrina behind the dumpster I cast myself in the flattering role of knight in shining armor. But she's shattered the illusion, and returned me to my rightful place in the audience. I'm a spectator, nothing more.

"Please, Sabrina. Just . . . *please*." The last word comes out quiet and tired. I don't know what to ask for anymore. I just want something different for her.

We stare at each other. For several seconds she doesn't move, or make excuses. She simply lets me witness the version of Sabrina Layton that no one is supposed to see: high on drugs, dirty hair, no makeup.

I'm the one who looks away first.

"You're sweet, Seth, but you can be really boring." She runs her fingers along the neck of my shirt. "I should've called Kris."

Adrenaline courses through me. "But you didn't. Because he would've known you'd go looking for drugs. Wouldn't have left you alone for a moment. Wouldn't have been so . . ." *Easy,* I want to say. But the word in my mind is Kris's: *naive.*

There's no use in calling the rehab center. They won't come for her. Even if they do, the first step to recovery is admitting you have a problem. Sabrina isn't ready for that. Her other relationships may have disintegrated, but not this one. This she values above everything.

It's not difficult to walk out of her apartment. Gant and Annaleigh need me, and Sabrina wants me gone. But as I press the call button for the elevator and pace back and forth along the gray industrial carpet, I still wish I could do more. If only there was someone I could call. Someone who cares for Sabrina as much as I do. Someone like . . . Kris.

I take out the phone, but his number isn't on it. So I ride the elevator to the lobby and approach the doorman. He's reading a thick book, like he doesn't anticipate having much to do, even on New Year's Eve.

"Do you have Kris Ellis's number?" I ask. "I want to call him."

His expression hardens. "You better not bring him here."

"Why not?"

The guy snaps his book shut. "Ms. Layton was absolutely clear. If he tries to get in, we're to stop him. Call the police, if necessary."

His words silence me. Is this why Kris was having Sabrina tailed? Because she wouldn't see him anymore?

So many clues, yet the picture is as hazy as before. Sabrina was determined to get high, so why call me at all? Why not hail a cab and come home alone? Unless there's another reason she wanted someone to watch her. Someone to protect her from—*what?* What could be more destructive than the pills scattered about her apartment?

That's when it hits me. There's something far more destructive than getting high.

And far more permanent.

42

I SPRINT BACK INTO THE WAITING elevator and jam the button for the ninth floor. Pound along the corridor and bang on Sabrina's door.

I'm so convinced that something terrible is happening that it's a shock when she opens the door. Tears trace lines down her cheeks. Her movements are labored, head lolling from side to side. But it's the eyes that really get me, her constricted pupils like dark pinpricks submerged beneath an ocean of brown. I'm not looking at Sabrina Layton. I'm looking at the shadows of her personality left behind as drugs work over every molecule in her body.

She hugs me. "You shouldn't be here," she whispers into my hair.

My fingertips rest on the bumps of her spine. She feels fragile in my arms, as breakable as glass. "I need to know you're going to be okay," I tell her.

"Annaleigh," she croaks, leaning back. "She seems like a good person. You deserve that."

Sabrina is giving me permission to leave again, but I can't. I kick the door closed behind me.

I follow her as she weaves toward the bedroom. The Kermit

T-shirt barely reaches her legs and pulls tight against her breasts. It leaves little to the imagination, but there's nothing remotely sexy about the way she's squeezed into the garment.

That's when I realize it's not a T-shirt at all. It's a little girl's nightgown. Something she may have worn a decade ago, back when everything was different.

She slides onto the bed and hugs a pillow. "I hate being alone," she says.

"I'm here."

"You know what I mean."

Yes, I do. "People love you, Sabrina." I try to sound positive. "You've got more fans than any young actor in Hollywood."

"Right. Mustn't forget the fans—all that hollow, unquestioning love. So easy to adore someone you never have to understand, isn't it?" She rests her chin on the pillow.

"Tell me about Kris."

Hearing the name seems to sap her remaining energy. Or maybe it's the pills, fogging her mind.

"I think he still loves you, Sabrina. And I think you love him too."

She doesn't say anything for several seconds. Then: "Doesn't matter."

"How can it not matter?"

"Because . . . he got me pregnant."

Silence. We're exactly as we were a moment ago, but everything has changed. Not only because of this news, but because I can tell that she's talking in the past tense.

"What happened?"

"I lost the baby." Her voice catches. Tears fall so fast and hard she can't choke them away.

I sit on the edge of her bed. "Does he know?"

"No."

"Does *anyone?*"

"Genevieve. She made me take the pregnancy test. Told me I had to get clean. Spelled out the risks, like I didn't know. But I couldn't stop. Or maybe I just didn't want to." She covers her face with her long, slender arms. "That's what Gen thinks, anyway. Thinks I kept going deliberately because I didn't want to have Kris's baby."

Sabrina's face is still covered, but under the recessed spotlights that pepper her bedroom ceiling, I finally see her three personas for what they are: the real Sabrina, and the masks she hides behind.

The clock on the bedside table reads 11:07. I need to check on Gant. Need to get back to Annaleigh, impossibly beautiful in her pale blue gown. Need to let Kira take photos and Ryder take film, and pretend that everything is okay when nothing is okay.

But I won't leave Sabrina like this. She'll be asleep soon. Until then, I'll stay to show her that I care. Friendship is a form of love too, and I might be Sabrina's last friend.

I creep into the bathroom and close the door. Turn on the cell phone and call Annaleigh.

She picks up immediately. "Are you still with Sabrina?"

I rest my forehead against the cool tile wall and close my eyes. If Brian's tapping into this conversation through her new phone, he'll know where I am now.

She interprets my silence as a *yes*. "Brian and Ryder left just after you. They were pissed. Why aren't you back yet?"

For a moment, I fantasize about coming clean and telling her everything. How it's partly my fault that Sabrina's drug addiction went viral, and that when she finds out, the only thing stopping her from hating me will be this evening, when I stayed with her and helped her through the worst of it.

Instead I say, "I'll be back soon. I so want to be with you right now."

"Yeah. Well, I hope you can still say that the next time I see you."

Then Annaleigh waits for me to hang up, so I'll know she's just angry, not that she really means it.

I turn off the phone again.

Sabrina is curled up, fetal style, lighting a cigarette. "You should get back to Annaleigh," she says.

"I will. Soon."

"Do you think she'll forgive me?"

"There's nothing to forgive."

Her hair is draped across a pillow, revealing the nape of her neck. Her tanned skin glows in the amber light from her bedside lamp. I'm not the type to pray, but in this moment I do: that she'll accept help; that she'll be able to quit drugs; that she'll still call me her friend during rehab.

I know the last one is the most unlikely of all.

She pulls on the cigarette. "Will you hold me, Seth?"

I toss my blazer on the floor and lie down next to her. Lay my arm across her thin shoulders. She doesn't ask for more, and

I wouldn't do anything if she did. I just want to stay with her awhile, so she'll know that trust and love exist, even in the capital of make-believe.

"Happy New Year," she says finally.

"Yeah," I say. "Happy New Year."

43

I WAKE TO BRIGHT LIGHT—LOS ANGELES, still pretending that winter is a myth perpetuated by the rest of America. I don't understand where I am. Or why Sabrina is beside me, fast asleep.

My mind snaps back to the previous evening. Me comforting Sabrina, reassuring her that she's not alone and that someone still cares. I just wanted to see her fall asleep. I never meant to fall asleep as well.

The clock reads 8:10 a.m.

Shit.

I reach for Annaleigh's old cell phone. Turn it on and discover messages.

Lots of messages.

Before I can listen to them, Sabrina stirs. She stuffs a pillow against the headboard and drags herself into a seated position, long legs stretched out in front of her. She looks rough—no makeup, greasy hair. But most of all, it's the eyes that scare me: dull and empty, waiting for an infusion of energy . . . or something else.

Maybe every day begins like this.

We haven't made eye contact yet, but something about the way I'm looking at her makes her sigh. She swings her legs over the side of the bed. "You don't need to stay," she says.

"Huh?"

"I know how I look."

"No. I just never meant to fall asleep. I need to check on my brother. And Annaleigh."

"Then go," she says, walking to the bathroom.

"Not until you're back at the center."

"I can take myself."

"I want to go with you."

She stops in the doorway. "Actually, I'd prefer it if you didn't." She runs a finger along the wooden door frame. As she watches its steady descent, her hair falls across her face. It doesn't seem accidental. "There's nothing attractive about seeing someone check into rehab."

"Attractive?" The word makes me angry. It's like we're measuring our friendship in different currencies. "I'm going because I want to see you get well. And I know it's scary for you, but I'm proud of you for doing it."

Her face tightens, eyes squeezed shut. "Don't say that yet. Be proud of me in a couple weeks, okay? By then, I might be proud of me too."

"Okay."

"Now go see Annaleigh."

Still I hesitate. "You promise you won't take anything?"

She doesn't pretend to be offended. "I promise. It's New Year's Day, right? The perfect time for a resolution."

✳ ✳ ✳

Different doorman—larger, older—but he obviously got a status report from his predecessor. As I leave the elevator he ushers me toward a rear exit, away from the photographer loitering beside the main doors. He tells me to head a block east before hailing a cab.

I run along the street until I see a taxi. Tell the driver Wilshire and Rodeo instead of the hotel name. I guess I'm becoming paranoid too.

On the way, I listen to the messages. The first is from Brian. He doesn't bother threatening me with retribution for not returning to the party—I know perfectly well there'll be a price to pay. Annaleigh's messages are even worse, though. She doesn't sound angry, just resigned, like she knew I'd stay with Sabrina from the moment I left the party. Her third and final call was at four a.m. She didn't bother to leave a message.

There are no messages from Gant. Maybe it's because I'm using Annaleigh's old cell phone, and he doesn't have the number. Or maybe Brian called the cops after all.

I run along the corridor to my room. Gant is there, sitting bolt upright at the desk. His eyes are fixed on a blank sheet of paper. From the way he turns his head slowly, I'm afraid that he's hurt.

I approach him like a hunter tracking skittish prey. "Are you okay?"

"I called you. As soon as I got back here, I called you. But your phone was right there." He points to the bedside table. Someone must have brought my phone to the room. Brian presumably. Or Ryder.

270

I place the phone inside the empty minibar so we won't be overheard. "I'm sorry, Gant."

"Where have you been?"

"With Sabrina. Something bad happened."

"Oh yeah? Don't tell me you spent the night with her."

"I . . . I fell asleep."

He digs deep for a smile. He knows I must be screwing with him. Except that I'm not. And pretty soon, he realizes it too.

"You *fell asleep*?"

"Sabrina needed help and—"

He jumps up and tackles me. Sends me crashing against the bed. I've got a few pounds on him, but not the will to fight. He brings his fist up. I know what's coming, and in a strange way, I welcome it.

As suddenly as he attacked, Gant stops. I can almost see his brain working, analyzing the situation and concluding that this is not the way to go. He rolls away and punches the mattress instead. Slides off the bed and crumples to the floor, arms wrapped around his legs, forehead resting on his knees.

"Someone just called from reception," he mumbles. "Checkout's twelve o'clock."

I figured today was the endgame, but I'm still surprised Brian's kicking me out already. How can Ryder produce a satisfying ending for his movie when so much is unresolved? Sure, Annaleigh probably won't speak to me ever again, but if they don't capture our breakup on film, viewers will never know what played out between us.

Gant faces me. "You have to warn Annaleigh. Whatever they're planning, she's in the middle of it."

My cell phone rings, muted inside the minibar. Gant stares at me, in limbo until I decide whether or not to answer it.

I let it go to voicemail, but Brian has made his point yet again: He can always get to us.

I pull some of the remaining bills from my wallet. "You should go home."

"No."

"You need money for a cab."

"I said *no*. They took me on too, not just you. Ryder's going to make whatever the hell kind of movie he wants, and millions of people will see it. No matter what, I want them to see us fighting to the end."

The end. Isn't this the end, right here? Or does that come when Brian and Ryder and Tracie show up at noon to make sure I've checked out? I can picture the scene: Tracie, arms folded, explaining that I blew it last night, and that they owe me nothing; Ryder, genuinely disappointed that I couldn't share his vision; Brian, all smiles, running through the countless ways he's outwitted me. He'll enjoy twisting the knife he inserted weeks ago.

"What happened last night?" I ask.

"After Brian called you, he took me to the party. It was so weird—all these teens were acting like everything's cool, and Brian's getting more and more pissed. I think that whole thing was laid on for some kind of showdown. I hate you for not showing up, but it might've been your best play."

"How did you get away?"

"I waited until Brian and Ryder were talking to Annaleigh, and made a run for it. I've been waiting all night for them to knock on the door."

"You should've gone home."

"I was worried about you. I'm still worried. Which is why I'm not leaving."

I rub my temples. "Do you have a way to record a conversation?"

"No. Why?"

"Brian and Ryder will want to see me before checkout. I'm sure of it. If we can record them, maybe we can make *them* the story, instead of just us. It might even turn people against the movie."

Hoping that Brian accidentally implicates himself isn't Gant's style—too passive—but he must be out of ideas, because he finally takes the bills from my hand.

"I'll be back at eleven," he says. "Make sure you're here."

He doesn't look at me as he leaves.

I retrieve the cell phone from the minibar and head out too. I owe Annaleigh an explanation. Chances are, she's going to break up with me, no matter what I say. I'll bet Ryder has cameras set up to capture all of it.

I knock on Annaleigh's door, but there's no answer. I call her, and go to voicemail. Finally, I go to the only place I can think of.

She's alone in the gym, welcoming New Year by pounding eight-minute miles on a treadmill.

I need a moment to think. To gather myself. To make sure that whatever's about to happen doesn't play out like a made-for-TV special. Maybe I don't deserve Annaleigh, but Ryder doesn't deserve good footage of our breakup either.

As I wait, I check the voicemails from my phone. The first is from the middle of the night—Gant telling me in a petrified voice that he's back in the hotel. The call is short, probably because he realized my phone was in the room too. The other message is from Sabrina, only a few minutes old: "Uh, Kris left a message. He did some asking around about that story on me and . . . look, I need to talk to you." Her voice sounds muffled, hesitant. "Call me, okay?"

I never doubted Kris when he promised to get to the bottom of things. But I didn't realize he'd work so fast, either.

44

I NEED TO TALK TO SABRINA, but face-to-face, not over a phone. I can't kid myself that she'll trust me, but as long as I'm with her, I can still get her back to rehab.

When I look up, Annaleigh stands astride the treadmill, watching me.

She starts running again as I approach her. She's sweating like crazy.

"I'm sorry," I say. Then louder: "I'm sorry!"

She places her feet on the frame. The rubber track spins by. "I don't believe you."

"Nothing happened, I swear. I just wanted to make sure Sabrina was okay."

"Who were you talking to, just now?" she asks, glancing at my phone.

"It was a voicemail."

"From Sabrina?" She jams the stop button and climbs off. Grabs a towel and runs it across her face. But it's tears she's wiping away, not sweat. "They told me to check out by noon. My mom's coming to get me. The movie's over, Seth. All because you walked away."

I'm enough of an actor to register shock, but in the back of my mind, I'm trying to remember a time when it still felt real.

"I never meant to stay with her, Annaleigh."

"Oh, please. You knew how much I needed this, and you killed it for me. People like me don't get a second chance. I always knew my parents might ruin this for me, but not you."

"It was a mistake!"

"Yeah. It *was* a mistake. You've been playing both of us the whole time, and I'm done now." She takes her phone from the treadmill and heads for the door.

I follow her into the empty corridor. "You know it's you I want."

She turns to face me. I can see the conflict playing out in her sharp blue eyes—how she wants to trust me, even though I've given her every reason to doubt. "You stink of cigarettes."

"Sabrina was smoking."

"Figures. Did you at least get her back to the center?"

"No. I wanted to see you."

Her expression softens. "So you're with me now? For good?"

"I . . . I said I'd go back and take her."

"Oh, for— Why can't she just take herself?" Annaleigh purses her lips and looks away. "Forget I said that. You're being a good friend, and God knows, she needs one." She drapes the towel across her shoulders. "I'm never going to see you again, am I?"

It's a genuine question, and I wish I knew the answer. Her mom may take her away before I can return. Even so, there's a message behind the question: In spite of everything, she still wants me.

Annaleigh takes my hand. "Come with me," she whispers.

I really want to follow, but I won't go to her room. Not if there's a chance that Ryder's cameras are still in place, filming everything we do. And not while Sabrina is waiting for me, wrestling with the idea that I'm behind the drug story.

I pull Annaleigh toward me and we kiss. Her lips are warm. I can feel her coming around, trusting that what we have is real. There are no cameras here, and no movie. This is just for us.

The phone in my left pocket rings. Annaleigh pulls back suddenly. She probably thinks it's Sabrina calling, but this isn't Sabrina's number.

"It's your old phone," I say, handing it to her. "You take the call."

She seems surprised that I still have it. "Hello? . . . Hello?" She waits a few more seconds and hangs up. "That was bad timing."

"Yeah. It was."

She faces me again, all messy hair and flushed skin and irresistible eyes. "Go to Sabrina, and come straight back. I won't open my door for anyone else." She holds out the phone. "Do you still need this?"

"No." I pull my cell from the other pocket. "Mine's good again."

She studies the two phones—one brand-new, one barely functional—each reflecting a different stage of our lives. "I wonder if they'll make us give them back," she says.

"I don't care if they do."

"Maybe your old one still works great, then. But Brian says mine's on borrowed time." She rubs at a crack across the screen. "He fixed it for me once already."

Before I can process this, my phone rings. Caller unknown, but it's going to be Brian. I know from the timing of it, and from the way he hung up when Annaleigh answered her phone just now.

"Hello, Seth," he says. "You two done making up now? Or did I call at a bad time?"

I don't say anything. I need to listen. I need to think.

"No answer, huh? Well, that's rude. And I thought you'd made so much progress. I mean, the way you talked to Sabrina last night . . . that was really thoughtful." His voice is measured, unemotional. "Happy New Year."

Maybe he chose the words by accident, but no—he knows that's what she said to me before we fell asleep. Which means that he must have bugged Annaleigh's old phone too. In which case, he knows everything else that Sabrina told me.

Everything.

Annaleigh looks scared, watching me. I'm scared too.

"Brian, look," I say, "let's talk about this."

"No. Let's *not.* You brought this on yourself. It's like Gant told you: That party was everything. Do you have any idea how much planning went into it? All we needed was one final perfect moment—a kiss as the clock strikes midnight—something to make audiences swoon. Then Annaleigh's mean, vindictive mother comes in and tears you apart. Both of you would have come off looking like victims. You would have seemed noble and tragic. But not anymore. Now you go down hard and ugly. Now you get to be the bad guy."

"I'm sorry. Please, just tell me what to do."

The line goes dead.

45

I RUN THROUGH THE HOTEL LOBBY. One of the porters is wheeling suitcases inside, but holds the door as he sees me approach. I'm only ten yards away when two figures converge on me.

"Checkout time," says Brian. "You're not going anywhere."

I slow my steps, and Brian and Ryder relax momentarily. It's all I need. Four strides later I slip past the grabbing hands and sprint through the doors, yelling for a taxi.

Ahead of me, a car door opens. I dive inside and slam it shut. The driver doesn't wait for instructions before pulling away.

I stare out the rear window. Brian and Ryder are catching a taxi too. Do they already know where I'm going? Or will I be giving them even more information they can use against me?

"Pico and Century Park," I say, breathless. "And can you lose that taxi behind us?"

The driver's an old guy. Scary thin. He eases a toothpick from his mouth and catches my eye in the rearview mirror. "What do you think this is, son? A movie?"

I take a twenty from my wallet and toss it onto the passenger seat. "Double if you lose them."

He glances at the bill, sighs, and pulls to the side of the road. The other taxi slots in behind us. The doors open. Brian and Ryder climb out.

I try to open my door, but it's locked. I'm trapped. Did Brian plan this too?

Ryder raps the window twice. "Come on, Seth. Time to go home."

The driver keeps his eyes fixed on the traffic signal ahead of us. It's almost like he hasn't noticed the two guys banging on the windows, trying to get at me.

"Is your seat belt on?" he mutters.

"What?"

He floors the gas. We careen into the street and plow through a yellow light. Behind us, Brian and Ryder are rushing back to their taxi, but there's no way they'll catch us now.

The old guy exhales slowly and stretches his right hand backward, palm open. "You can put the other twenty right there, son."

I give him the second bill, and another as we reach the Pico–Century Park intersection.

I get out and run. Near the end of the block, my phone chimes. It's a text message from Brian—a link to a news story. Before I can click on it, I turn the corner and stop dead.

TV vans are gathering in front of Sabrina's apartment building. Photographers jostle for position beside the main doors. This isn't about a drug revelation. This response is reserved for the really big news. The kind that won't fade over time.

I've dealt Brian his ace card. Now he's playing it.

A dozen paparazzi turn toward me as I approach. Cameras flash, fast as strobe lights. I'm bumped from every direction. I want to hide my face, but I'm only wearing a shirt. I don't even remember taking off my blazer.

Safe behind the locked glass doors, two doormen watch it all unfold. When I get within a couple yards they drag me inside while keeping the paparazzi at bay.

"What's happening?" asks the doorman I saw earlier. "There's this story—"

"Has Sabrina left the building?"

"No. Why?"

I don't answer. Just take the elevator to the ninth floor and pound on Sabrina's door. There's no answer, so I keep going, louder and louder.

The phone rings in my pocket: Annaleigh, or possibly Brian. Doesn't matter. I'm desperate now—a coiled spring craving release. I kick the door.

A neighbor ventures into the corridor. I scream at him to back the hell away. He hurries inside his apartment, probably to call security.

I don't care. And I don't stop.

The frame gives before the lock. It splinters open in an explosion of wood, and the door swings wide. Everything inside looks exactly the same as it did two hours ago. But the stillness feels horribly, frighteningly wrong.

I shout Sabrina's name. Blunder through the living room and into her bedroom.

She's lying on her back in bed, seizing. Crooked legs and sweaty mannequin face. Eyes open but seeing nothing. A sick caricature of the girl formerly known as Sabrina Layton.

I run to her. Hold her down to keep her from falling off the bed and hurting herself. Throw up in my mouth and spit bile onto the floor. Call 911 and try to find words. Hold Sabrina and follow the dispatcher as she guides me through the insanity of what I've stumbled into.

The dislocated voice on the phone offers nothing but encouragement as I try to breathe life through Sabrina's blue lips. With the seizures over, she's deathly still, locked inside that body where all the tears in the world can't reach her. Between breaths I yell at her. I swear at her over and over, until one of the doormen drags me away and the neighbor takes over for me.

I watch the scene play out as if I'm not even there. My brain is somewhere far away, trying desperately to create a new scenario in which I'm not responsible. But my heart tells a different story.

Now you get to be the bad guy.

I am the bad guy.

I let this happen.

I close my eyes and pray that Sabrina will live. That she'll return from wherever her brain has retreated. That one day, she'll forgive me.

The EMTs arrive and the scene grows simultaneously busier and more orderly. They have a calm about them. Their consciences are clean. A woman even crouches down beside me on the floor as the others cart Sabrina's unconscious body to the elevator. She asks me if I'm okay. If I need anything.

I don't answer, but what I really want to say is: *I need not to be me anymore.*

I don't know how long I stay on Sabrina's bedroom floor. The police arrive and ask me questions—not because of the overdose, but because the neighbor called them about a disturbance. Breaking and entering. I tell them the truth. That I stayed overnight after Sabrina checked herself out of rehab. That I returned this morning to take her back to the center. That one of the doormen mentioned a breaking story, and I was afraid of how it might affect her, so I smashed the door down.

A woman asks me if there are any other drugs in the apartment. I look around the room, wondering if Sabrina kept stashes everywhere. Instead I see my blazer. I must've left it behind in my haste to leave. Thoughtful Sabrina hung it from the back of her door—didn't want it getting creased as she overdosed.

The pill bottle I stuffed inside the pocket is empty.

The doormen, on high alert now, escort me out the back of the building. There isn't a taxi around, but no matter. I need to run. To gasp for air. To hurt.

I'm only vaguely aware of the streets as I pound out block after block, but I must know where I'm going. How else would I end up at the office building?

I beat at the door until my knuckles bleed.

No one answers.

I stalk around the building and peer in through the windows. Every room is empty. Brian and Ryder and Tracie have pulled out.

Cleaned up so thoroughly there'll be no trail, no hint of what went on here for a couple twisted weeks in late December.

I slump beside the main door. Pull my knees up and hold on tight as I shudder. I'm drenched in sweat and tears. The pain I longed for is here, but it's not enough. It can't make me forget.

The phone chimes. I pull it out and read: *Checkout time is 12PM. You overstay, you pay.*

I'm up and running again. I know where I'll find them.

46

BRIAN, RYDER, AND TRACIE ARE INSIDE my room, lounging on the sofa and armchair. Gant is there too, looking nervous as hell.

"Join us, Seth." Brian waves a slip of paper through the air. "We come bearing gifts."

So here it is: my long-awaited payout. I've earned that money too—through blood and tears, both mine and others'.

"It's not the full amount, of course," says Tracie, "but technically we owe you nothing. Last night's party was a contractual obligation."

Seeing the check makes me sick. I would sacrifice anything to make Brian feel the pain I feel. The pain that Sabrina's feeling still.

Unless she's dead.

"I must say, I'm not so happy to see your brother here, though," continues Brian. "I enjoyed our first meeting at the office, Gant. Enough that I took you home—tried to keep you out of this. Then you broke into our office, and I *still* let you off the hook." Brian clicks his tongue. "There's a saying: Once is happenstance. Twice is coincidence. The third time, it's enemy action. Now, give me the recorder."

Gant tries to hide his surprise, but it's obvious that Brian knows everything.

"As Seth will confirm," says Brian, sounding bored, "we heard your conversation this morning. Through another phone, to be specific. Which is how we know you just bought a recording device. And I can promise you this conversation won't get interesting until you hand it over."

Gant knows he's beaten. He pulls the recorder from his pocket and tosses it onto the floor.

"Good." Brian rolls up the sleeves of his shirt, revealing powerful, tanned forearms. "Now get the hell out of here."

Gant checks with me before moving. "I'll see you in the lobby," I tell him.

He crosses the room and slams the door shut behind him.

I edge closer to Brian. "Sabrina overdosed."

Ryder and Tracie look away. Even Brian hesitates. "Why did you leave the party last night, Seth?" he asks.

"She needed help."

"No. She needed to get back to rehab. Which you could've made happen. Hell, *we* could've made it happen."

"Sure. And how would that have played out in your movie?"

"A lot better than it did in real life."

I lunge at him. Tackle him with both arms and take him down. His head connects with the coffee table and he gasps as the corner slices neatly across his temple. I get in two good punches before he silences me with a jab to the gut. He doesn't stop either, but volleys punches to my upper arms and legs as his blood drips onto my white shirt. He doesn't touch my face, though. No one will see what happened here.

As Ryder drags him away, Brian glares at me, all gritted teeth and rapid breaths. Blood runs down his left side. Tracie leads him to the bathroom to clean up.

I drag myself to a seated position. "How did you know?" I ask Ryder. "That all this would happen?"

He rubs his goatee. "We didn't. We just set the scene. *You* made it happen."

"But the stuff about Sabrina . . ."

"All we knew was that she and Kris broke up, and no one was saying why. Sure, we hoped the truth might come out during filming, but we weren't counting on it."

Brian appears in the bathroom doorway, a cloth pressed tight against the side of his head. "Sabrina was in this thing to draw attention to you and Annaleigh. To add a little drama. That's all. This was supposed to be a movie about star-crossed lovers, not a fallen star."

"Then why tell everyone about the miscarriage?"

"Because you left us no choice. After you bailed last night, we needed to end the movie somehow."

"It's not over yet. Not as long as Annaleigh and I are still together."

Laughter rings out from the bathroom, and Tracie joins us. "You really think an audience needs to see Annaleigh dump you? You ditched her last night. Went off with Sabrina in private, and lured her into confiding her deepest, darkest secrets, even though you knew we were recording you. Now every newspaper in America is linking you to an attempted suicide. You're toxic. Who *wouldn't* dump you?"

They've been right about everything else, so why not this? Perhaps they're counting on me telling Annaleigh the truth, so that things will end at precisely the appointed hour.

Tracie picks up the check and puts it back on the coffee table beside me. "I wonder if anyone'll believe you'd do so much damage for just fifty grand."

I don't look at the check. I just feel the emptiness of everything—money, trust, hope. Or maybe not *everything*. Because in the room directly under mine, Annaleigh might still be waiting.

Brian runs a finger over his wound. Inspects the bloody fingertip. "Just so you know: You signed a nondisclosure agreement. If you talk to anyone about this movie, we'll come after you. So do yourself a favor. Go home and make like a hermit for a few months. We'll be sure to let you know when you're on TV."

Ryder's head whips around. Tracie glances from one man to the other. I get the feeling Brian wasn't supposed to say that last part. Either that, or this is yet another choreographed response designed to screw with my head.

It doesn't matter. I know what my next move has to be. I need to come clean to Annaleigh, and risk everything on the truth. If I can't do that, I don't deserve her.

I don't deserve anything at all.

47

BRIAN KNOWS HOW TO HIT. I grit my teeth and concentrate on walking normally, just so he won't have the pleasure of knowing how badly he hurt me.

They follow me as I leave, my three dark shadows. Escort me into the elevator and tell me we'll wait for Annaleigh in the lobby.

Brian baits me with comments, but I don't reply. Words are the only things I can still control, so I shut him out and think about how to explain everything to Annaleigh. As my prepared speech takes shape, I'm certain that it'll be the last time we see each other.

The doors open to the lobby. In the elevator's reflective metal interior, I watch the three of them file out. Then I spin around and press the *door close* button.

Ryder's the first to realize what's happening. As he runs toward me, I throw my bag at him and he tumbles backward. Brian's right there too—at least until Gant flashes into view and blindsides him with a tackle.

The doors close, shutting out the chaos.

I get off on the fourth floor. Hobble along the corridor and bang on Annaleigh's door. "Who is it?" she calls.

"Me."

She opens the door immediately. Closes and locks it behind me. Applies the security chain for good measure.

"Sabrina," she says. She glances at the blank TV screen and back to me. Wipes tears from her eyes. "I saw the news. Were you there?"

"Yeah."

"Is she . . . okay?"

"I don't know."

She pulls me into a tight hug that makes me gasp. I bury my face in her hair and savor her familiar scent. I just want a few more seconds—time to breathe in her perfection before I lose her forever.

"I should've done more," she says. "Reached out to her. If only I'd known what she was going through . . . but she was a star, you know? Who am I?"

I shake my head. "This is my fault. I knew things were messed up, and I'm the reason it's all out there now."

She leans back and places her palms flat against my cheeks. "No, Seth. You didn't make her an addict, and you didn't get her pregnant."

I open my mouth, but it's dry. I need to hurry, say what I have to say before Brian bursts through the door and takes matters out of my hands. Gant won't be able to hold him back forever. But I don't want this to end. Why does everything good have to end?

"That's not the point," I say. "The drug story got out because *I* was being recorded."

She narrows her eyes. "What do you mean, recorded?"

"My conversations. Every freakin' word."

"Not the ones with me, though."

I take a deep breath and nod. She steps back suddenly.

"Look, Annaleigh, I never meant to hurt anyone—"

"Sabrina's in intensive care. She might *die*." She stares at me with wide, wild eyes. "You're even worse than my father. You're a monster!"

"Please, just listen—"

"Get the hell away from me. Go. You're toxic."

She's right. I *am* toxic. But something about that word keeps me rooted to the spot. Tracie said I was toxic too. I almost expect to find her in here now, watching with Brian and Ryder.

I take in the familiar objects around the room. But that's not all I see. There are smaller objects hiding in plain sight too—a tiny camera peeking around the TV, another tilted upward from behind the sofa, and a third angled toward me from the darkened bathroom doorway.

"Get out," screams Annaleigh. "Get out! Get out! Get out!"

She bends over, hands on her knees like a runner after a long workout.

"Why are there cameras in here, Annaleigh?"

Slowly, she straightens. I expect to see a look of fury or desolation, but as she blinks away tears, she begins to laugh. "Geez, Seth. You can't do anything right, can you? The way you keep ruining these final scenes, it's like you've got a crush on me or something."

I hear the words, but I don't believe them. They're not Annaleigh's words. Can't be.

"Oh, what? You're going to pretend to be surprised? Well,

don't bother. Brian stopped by an hour ago—told me you were in on the plan the whole time, same as me." She mistakes my shock for embarrassment. "Yeah, I was speechless too. I've spent two weeks worrying the truth would slip out. That I'd say one stupid word and everything would come crashing down. You have no idea how hard it's been for me to watch shit happening to you. And all along, you *knew*."

I shake my head. "No, I didn't. You didn't, either."

"What, you think you're the only one who can act? I was there when my mom signed the contract. It was me who told Brian to expose my dad in the newspaper."

"But you were . . ." *Distraught. Inconsolable.* But of course she was, because that's what the part required.

What did Sabrina say? *Timing's a little off, but the instincts are good.* I blasted her for that.

I grip my hair. "No. This isn't happening."

"Why did you have to take things so far with Sabrina, huh? Why couldn't you just leave her alone?"

"I never meant for that stuff about her to get out. That's why I took your old cell phone when I went to see her last night."

"You knew you were being recorded all the time. You just said so yourself!" She huffs. "Look, I warned you not to leave the party. That was the climax of the whole movie—all those extras, and camera setups. My mom on standby outside, ready to kill our dreams as the clock strikes midnight. But I let you go because I was worried about Sabrina. I *cared,* which is a hell of a lot more than you can say."

"I didn't know—"

"Just stop it, okay?" She jams her palms against my chest, fresh hits on top of still-forming bruises. "I fell for you. I slept with you. I *fought* for you. Ryder and Brian wanted you to be the bad guy, but I said no. I really figured that once filming was over, I could put everything behind me. I thought we could make things work, you and me."

"So did I."

"Then why did you run off and sleep with Sabrina?"

"I didn't sleep with her."

"That's exactly what you did."

"I'm the innocent one here, not you!"

"The hell you are. I've lived a lie, sure. But the things you've done . . ." She looks up at me with icy blue eyes. "You make me sick."

I take a step back and lean against the wall. The cameras follow me remotely. I feel tired and angry, but more than anything, I feel empty.

"They're filming all of this, aren't they?" I ask.

"Of course they are. Ryder said the footage from the fitness center this morning wasn't good enough. I was pissed when he told me that, but now I'm glad. Once everyone hears you come clean, they'll know why I have to leave."

Annaleigh grabs the handle of her case and heads for the door.

"You're wrong about me," I say. "You are so wrong, and one day, you're going to know it."

She lifts her case and clatters it against the floor. For a moment I think she's going to yell at me again, but she just shakes her head. "You're a decent actor, Seth, but take it from me—this is not your most convincing performance."

As she opens the door, I expect to find Brian and Ryder outside, eavesdropping. But of course they're not there. They set this up too: telling me not to confide in Annaleigh; telling Annaleigh I was in the dark, then shifting course. They knew this meeting had to happen, and that by the end of it, their story would reach its conclusion in real life, as it has in the movie.

We're star-crossed lovers, after all. Didn't they make that clear the very first time we met?

48

GANT IS WAITING FOR ME IN the lobby. He leads me out of the hotel and toward a taxi. Fights off the paparazzi when they swoop in for one last money shot, like he's my personal bodyguard.

He gives the taxi driver our home address. No bluffing, no trickery—just the address in Van Nuys. The driver makes a half-hearted attempt at small talk, but Gant's short answers discourage him. We tumble into silence.

I follow the taxi's turns. West on Wilshire. A shortcut through the Los Angeles Country Club, and past Westwood. Join the 405 North and pass the Getty Museum tucked high up on a hill to the left. We're surrounded by hills here, and I could almost believe we're in the middle of a vast natural park. But each hill is hiding something—a neighborhood, a reservoir, a secret—and I can't see beyond any of them.

Appear to show everything, but always control the view.

We emerge to the flatness of the Valley. Streets in grids, houses in rows, and nowhere to hide. I welcome it, and I loathe it. But above all, I need it.

Dad sees us pull up and comes out to meet us. There are a

couple news trucks outside our house, but not as many as there will be. I need to apologize to my father, but not with TV cameras capturing the whole scene. Some things should remain private.

Dad pays the driver and retrieves my bag. A reporter from the local cable news station barks questions, but the words are just white noise. As I walk inside, legs leaden, mind numb, my father speaks for me.

I take a seat at the kitchen table. It's odd to be back in the Valley, scene of my triumphant turn as Romeo. I'm center stage again now too, and like Romeo staring at his lifeless Juliet, I see only what I've lost. No wonder Romeo drank the poison.

Gant pours two glasses of orange juice and hands me an energy bar.

"We need to eat," he says.

He takes the seat across from me. I nibble the bar, but it doesn't sit right.

"I was sure Brian was going to beat the crap out of me," Gant says. "But the moment the elevator doors closed, they all started smiling. They didn't even go after you." He takes a bite of his bar and chews it. "Annaleigh knew, didn't she?"

I nod.

The sound of the door closing startles me. Dad appears in the kitchen. "What is ha . . . happening?" he asks Gant.

For most of an hour, Gant explains everything, while I ride shotgun in his crazy story and think how unrealistic it all sounds. How could anyone be as stupid as this Seth Crane character? Audiences will find it hard to relate to him, I think. No one likes a patsy.

When Gant finishes, Dad steps over to the counter and thumbs through some pages—the waivers, I guess. I think it might be the first time he has ever truly read them. He grips the skin around his mouth and stretches it. As he reaches the final page, he closes his eyes.

"I'm so s-sorry," he says.

"It's my fault," I tell him.

"No. I . . . I should've read it."

"And I should've told you both that something weird was going on."

Gant ends the discussion by placing Brian's crumpled check on the table. He flattens it out carefully. "Tracie gave me this before they left."

I shake my head.

"They screwed us over, Seth. Don't let them keep their money too."

I brush the check onto the floor. I don't want to hear about how it could change our lives. If we profit from this, I'm no better than Brian.

Gant folds his arms on the table and rests his chin on them. Peers up at me with heavy eyes. "What do you want to do?"

"I want to make things right."

"We need to f-focus on us," says Dad.

"Dad's right," says Gant. "We need to keep a low profile until we know exactly what's happening."

"Hide out, you mean." I pick at the energy bar. "That's what Brian told me to do—go into hibernation for a few months."

"What happens in a few months?" asks Gant.

"The movie comes out."

As soon as I say it, I realize that's ridiculous. There's no way Ryder can get a final cut ready for theatrical release in just a few months. The footage is still raw, the sound even weaker.

I pull out my laptop and check on the movie's status. It's still listed as *in production*.

"W-what is it, son?" Dad asks, peering at the screen.

"Something doesn't add up," I say. "They need this movie out soon, before everyone forgets about it. But theatrical releases are scheduled months in advance. How else are they going to—"

I look at the screen again. My name is there, along with Annaleigh's and Sabrina's—a close-knit cast of three. Ryder is listed as director, and Curt Barrett as executive producer. Brian's name is conspicuously absent.

I search for *Curt Barrett* and *Machinus Media Enterprises,* and scan the news feed. The first result is a press release from this morning: *Machinus unveils plans for cutting-edge pay-per-view drama.*

I only read the first few lines, but it's enough. For the price of a movie ticket, people will be able to download the feature-length release. Details are closely guarded, but it will change the face of moviemaking.

I can guess who the stars will be.

I turn the laptop around. From the look on their faces, I know that Gant and Dad are thinking the same thing as me. It won't matter that the images and audio aren't cinema quality, because no one will be seeing this in theaters. They'll be watching Sabrina and Annaleigh and me on their TVs, tablets, laptops, and phones, and any shortcomings in the footage will be amply compensated by the drama.

"You n-need to . . . to sleep," Dad tells us both.

Gant yawns as if in agreement, but I'm wide-awake now. I have a deadline, and a few months is long enough to tell a different story. A *true* story.

"W-what are you d-doing?" asks Dad as I pull the laptop around.

"Writing," I tell him.

I launch a blank document and give it a title: *Imposter*.

EPILOGUE

I WRITE BY DAY, WHEN LIGHT filters through the blinds, energizing the reporters keeping vigil outside our house. And I write at night, when they retreat to their vans and cars, running their engines to keep the heaters going. I imagine them hunkered inside, muttering angrily about the boy who was welcomed into Hollywood's teen elite, and went into seclusion when he was caught selling secrets to the enemy. They probably think that I'm the most despicable traitor, even as they continue to milk the Sabrina revelations for all they're worth.

I can't control what they think. All I can control are the words on each page.

Dad brings me food. Gant reads everything I write, and corrects the errors. I don't sleep much, because I'm afraid of what I'll see. Awake, I can shut out the image of Sabrina seizing and Annaleigh changing before my eyes, and focus only on telling my story honestly. Ryder may bend the truth, but not me. If I lie, Sabrina will see right through it.

I start at the beginning, from the time Ryder discovered me after the performance of *Romeo and Juliet,* through my "audition," to the first time I met Sabrina. It's amazing how much I feel like a character, writing a book about myself. Or maybe not so amazing. That was Ryder's intention, after all—to play God with our lives and reduce us to pawns on a cinematic chessboard.

But we were never characters. Sabrina and I were people, real people, and our stories were never his to tell. So I plow on. Word after word, page after page, until hundreds of pieces of paper lie scattered across my desk, all with Gant's pencil markings. I write about dreams and madness, rising stars and a beautiful sunset. I write in first person, present tense so that Sabrina will understand that I never saw any of this coming.

Will she believe I could be so blind? Will she ever read this book at all?

Sometimes I overhear the TV. Gant keeps the volume low, but I catch snippets of conversation, chat show hosts hashing out more revelations, all strategically leaked by Brian to keep us front and center while Ryder edits his movie. With each new piece of footage Annaleigh appears increasingly innocent and the case against me builds.

Seth Crane, the social climber. The sociopath. The undisputed antagonist of *Whirlwind*.

One day I hear Ryder being interviewed. I join Dad and Gant in the living room and watch Ryder talking up his precious movie.

The interviewer asks, "Why would Seth Crane do these things, knowing that he's being filmed?"

It's the all-important question. Ryder shuffles in the black leather seat. "When I look at the footage," he begins, "I see a confused boy. It might be partly my fault. I wanted to make a movie that would generate headlines, but I never figured on how far he'd take that idea. Seth didn't just cross the boundary between reality and fiction, he acted like it didn't exist at all. Sabrina Layton confided in him, and he shared her secrets like it was nothing. Annaleigh Ware fell for him hard, and he betrayed her too."

Ryder throws up his hands as if he's out of answers. "Maybe I'm giving him too much credit. Even though Seth won a coveted role, it was obvious he never felt comfortable in the spotlight. I think he took his insecurity out on the people around him. You know, some kids are just bad seeds."

Dad and Gant look at me. They're worried, but they shouldn't be. This changes nothing.

After a few quiet seconds, Dad puts on another pot of coffee, and Gant continues to read over the latest page, and I keep writing.

The ending is hardest: Standing in Annaleigh's room, watching her change from girlfriend to stranger in the blink of an eye. Then sitting with Gant and Dad in our kitchen and drawing strength for one last fight.

And writing, writing, writing. Writing for Sabrina's forgiveness. Writing so that she'll know I'm not the bad guy.

Maybe it's my penance, to relive every moment in a desperate attempt to set the record straight. Well, so be it. I believe in the power of words.

What are actors without lines?

February 6. Dad prints out several hundred pages and tells me to sleep. He squeezes my shoulder and we hug, and I break down in tears, just realizing that he and Gant don't hate me, even though I hate myself.

I give Dad Kris Ellis's phone number. He calls and introduces himself, says they need to meet. He stammers, but his tone is defiant. He doesn't apologize for anything I've done. He doesn't sound like a victim. He sounds like Gant. A fighter.

They leave me. I hear the car engine rumble to life, the stop-and-start squeak of tires. I don't think they're afraid of what Kris will say or do.

Fighters can't be afraid of conflict.

February 10. Dad pulls up before austere wrought iron gates. A guard asks for his driver's license, verifies our names with someone on the other end of a walkie-talkie, and opens the gates.

There are no paparazzi to witness this. They've grown bored and moved on to more newsworthy subjects, I guess.

We follow the snaking driveway to an ivy-covered building. The bright white doors are flanked by bright white columns. They promise orderliness and a clean start.

A nurse is waiting for me, although I'm not sure they call them nurses here. I hug Dad and thank him, and he hugs me right back—tight, like we're unbreakable.

I follow the woman along the carpeted hallway, straight through the building to a large conservatory on the other side. Tropical plants spread tendrils over every surface. The air brims with lavender and lilac.

There's only one person in here. She's sitting on a cream sofa, hands folded neatly in her lap. Gray cardigan over a white T-shirt. Worn jeans with holes in each knee. She doesn't look sexy or sultry or even alluring. She looks like . . .

A girl.

Sabrina pats the seat beside her. I'm nervous as hell, just like the first night I saw her. But I join her now as I joined her then, and she rewards me with a large stack of paper.

My book.

There's a Post-it note on top with three handwritten words: *I forgive you.*

I swore to myself that I'd be strong, but I'm struggling to hold it together. Sabrina wraps her arm around me and rests my head against hers. Her fingernails are unpolished. Her hair hangs loose about her. She smells of cigarette smoke, but not as much as I remember.

"I didn't think Kris would give it to you," I say.

"I guess he hates Brian and Ryder even more than he hates you." She swallows. "He never knew I was pregnant. I still don't know how he feels about it. He says we'll talk when I'm feeling ready. But he told me to read this now. He wants to make them pay, Seth."

"What do you want to do?"

"I want you to publish this."

I sit up straight. "Why would I do that?"

She sighs. "I don't think you wrote several hundred pages just so I'd understand what really happened. You wrote it so that *everyone* could understand. Maybe so that you could make sense of it yourself. But it's my story too, and you don't want to hurt me any more. Which is why you'll never release it unless I give you permission." She taps the pages. "I'm giving you permission."

"But the things I've written . . . you don't come off looking good."

"Oh, please. There's nothing about me people don't already know. I just want people to know the truth about everything. And everyone."

"We signed nondisclosure agreements."

"Yeah, we did. And I almost hope Brian and Ryder try to sue us. Can you imagine how that would play out after the hell we've been through?" She gives a humorless smile. "I'm serious. Look around you. Off-white paint. Soft fabrics. Restful decor. This place is like a movie set for the pearly gates. Which is ironic, because last month the real ones were calling my name, and I'd decided to go."

"I'm sorry."

She rolls her eyes, and with that famous gesture, she transforms momentarily into Sabrina Layton, movie star. I don't want to look at her that way anymore, though. Nothing good comes of holding someone to an impossible ideal.

"Listen," she says. "My agent did a better job of looking after me than my parents, and I fired him because I didn't like what he was saying. Kris tried to warn me that something weird was going on, and I shut him out too. Both of them could've stopped this if I'd let them. Instead, I convinced myself that everything was fine." She bites back tears. "Maybe you were blind, Seth, but we were blind together. And if you hadn't found me on New Year's Day, I would've died. Alone. That's why this book needs to be read. So that other people will know the truth too."

I run a finger across the top page. *Imposter*—even now the title rings true. "We'll never get the book out in time," I say.

"Yeah, we will. I spoke to my reporter friend. If we give her the go-ahead, she'll have it out in e-book within a week."

"Who'll read it?"

"Are you serious? I've had more than twenty interview requests, just this week. Big money offers too. What if you and me go on together? Tell everyone there's a book that sets the record straight. Thousands of people will read this, Seth. Millions maybe."

"They'll still watch the movie, though."

"Will they?" Her question sounds genuine. "After they've read the truth, do you really think people will line Brian and Ryder's pockets? Anyway, I can't imagine many actors working with Machinus ever again—not when they realize how Ryder screwed us over." She shrugs. "Who knows? Maybe something else happens too. I know this young actor who has some pretty shady contacts. The kind of guys that'll stalk you in a Mazda. Harass you in a park. And sometimes, when he tells them to, they pirate movies and release them free online, just for the hell of it."

She flashes me a smile. Sabrina, who has been through so much, is *smiling,* as if what lies ahead might just balance what has passed. She has weathered the storm, and now she's ready to take flight.

"Why are you doing this?" I ask her. "Why do you want to help me?"

She pulls a pill bottle from her pocket. The sight of it sends me back to New Year's Day, to a drug overdose and an unresponsive girl in a Kermit nightgown. She uncaps it and taps the contents onto the page: a rolled-up check. Gant must have picked it up and given it to Kris along with the book.

"This is our story, Seth. It's *real*. Tell me you wouldn't give anything for people to know the truth. About everything, and everyone."

She hands me her cell phone. There's a number on the screen—the reporter friend, I figure—and I study it for a long time. When I turn to face her again, she looks vulnerable, like she's afraid I'll say no. But there's something else in her eyes too: hope, and a refusal to back down. She wants to start over. Wants us to fight this battle together, as the friends she always thought we should be.

"Let's do this," Sabrina implores me. "Let's steal their audience. Let's show everyone what really happened." She lowers her voice. "Let's fucking ruin them."

She holds my hand as I make the call.

ACKNOWLEDGMENTS

Navigating a thriller can be treacherous, not just for readers but for writers too. Fortunately, I had some extraordinary folks to keep me on track, and light the path whenever I was in danger of getting lost.

Kate Harrison, my wonderful and talented editor, knew just the right questions to ask, and worked tirelessly until I could answer them. Liz Waniewski got behind the project when it was still in its infancy, and gave early direction. My readers—Paula Stokes, Brian Katcher, Corey Ann Haydu, Audrey Odom, and Clare John—were equally generous with praise and criticism, and always available for brainstorming. Danielle Borsch, Children's Department Manager at the legendary Vroman's Bookstore, was my go-to source for L.A. insider information.

A big thanks to everyone at Dial for bringing the book to publication, including Ellen Cormier, Julia McCarthy, Regina Castillo, Jasmin Rubero, Lauri Hornik, and especially Lori Thorn, for the moody, atmospheric cover.

Last but by no means least, my phenomenal agent, Ted Malawer, who has been with me every step of the way.